Pasto

I'm blessed to have you as my

TRACTS IN TIME

 shepherd!

Steve Stranghoener

1

Steve Stranghoener

Keith Ellerbrook

This book is dedicated to dearest Bonnie, Steve, Eric, Chelsea, Jenny, Andrea, Sydney, Cooper, Ray, Lisa, Kay, Daria, Don, Chick and family, friends and acquaintances who have provided such rich treasures of memories. There is special gratitude for Vernon who taught me the value of work and Ginny who gave me her appreciation for the written craft. Finally, my reverence goes out to all of God's faithful servants who toil in relative obscurity with particular thanks to Alger Tormoehlen, the late William Bischoff and Keith Ellerbrock who taught me the value of broken tools.

PROLOGUE

Time passes so swiftly, especially when you are on the downhill slide of life. In our youth, it may seem like we're paddling upstream against a current of molasses. We struggle in slow motion anticipating the next mile marker leading to our potential, our bright and better futures, not realizing, as Carly Simon sang so well, these are the good ole days, right here and now. We spend a lifetime building memories only to lose track of so many before we can enjoy them. Are memories meant for our pleasure or edification; just the aftermath of lessons learned? Why are we so consumed with memories? Does our ego demand that we pass them along to preserve our legacy? Or are we more altruistic; seeking to spare others our misery by benefitting from our mistakes?

What is the substance of memories; are they manifestations of purely physiological functions? Some would believe that memories are simply electrochemical reactions occurring in the storage lockers we call our brains, destined to fade and crumble to dust like old photographs once our gray matter decays. Others are convinced that memories are our insights into life scripts that bridge a spiritual realm beyond the constraints of space and time; the object of recording angels. Wherever we fall along that spectrum, it's hard to argue against the value we place on memories even though some are delightful while others are excruciatingly painful and regrettable.

The older we get, the more we seem to cherish memories; hitting the play button much more than record. Our minds are like colanders that give us the strange ability to sift our memories, preserving only the good ones, where possible. For our remorseful retrospectives that refuse to stay buried, some people, unfortunately, try to drown them in alcohol or drugs while others seek to slay them through contrition. In a cruel twist of irony, we often lose our memories late in life when we desire them the most.

Old age has its benefits, though. We learn that our lives are not just albums or diaries filled with random photographs and arbitrary thoughts. Somewhere along the line, we are able to look beyond the cover and see a thread running through the pages or our lives. For some, this strand comes into focus early in life and serves as a guidepost. Others, like me, have much more difficulty connecting the dots. A sense of mission is lost on distractions; perhaps pain, misfortunes and afflictions or, in some cases, pleasure, indulgences and temptations. In my case, at least early on, it was more the former than the latter. Yes, sense of purpose was elusive for me.

Sometimes I seemed to be bumping and bouncing along aimlessly as I wrestled with life's big mysteries. I was willing to seek answers in the secular and theological worlds. More often than not, routine seemed to fill the void and devour the time. But there was nothing routine about the way I was finally able to discover the truth and come to grips with the meaning of my life. No, you might even say it was the stuff of fantasies and dreams that brought such revelation to me. I will leave it to you to decide if the intervening circumstances were temporal or emanated from a higher power.

This is my story; how I was able to turn back the hands of time. If it has any merit, it will be more than a collection of memories; a web connecting my life to the lives of those who have touched me along the way. When the particulars have long since faded from your memory, what will remain? Is there a moral to the story? Hopefully, you will be left with at least two things. When you look at another person, will you be better equipped to peer beyond the superficial and see what runs beneath the still waters? Also, will this help you find that scarlet ribbon of purpose in your own life; the kind that brings true peace? Let's take a stroll down memory lane and see.

INDEX

Prologue

BROKEN TOOLS

Book One: Granby

Book Two: Ike

DEAD MALL

Book Three: We're Not in Kansas Anymore

Book Seven: Redemption

Epilogue

BROKEN

TOOLS

"I will praise thee; for I am fearfully and wonderfully made: marvelous are thy works; and that my soul knoweth right well."

King David

Psalm 139:14

BOOK ONE

GRANBY

Chapter 1

Thorn in the Flesh

The human body is marvelous indeed. This has always been the case but it seems the more we learn, the sharper this truth comes into focus. Just think about all that has come to light since I made my entrance into the world in 1954. We've discovered this stuff called DNA which is a tiny, little blueprint containing all the information necessary to build a person. With a single skin cell or pinpoint drop of blood or saliva, they can clone a whole new, identical you or me. Of course, that's not recommended ... I know in my case that one is definitely enough. But look what it's done for crime fighting, not to mention police dramas. We've always known about the body's amazing recuperative healing powers. Is there any other *machine* on earth that can repair itself? How about those stem cells? Not only can we bind our own wounds from the inside out but now we can actually grow new body parts. Our immune systems are light years ahead of the fantastic advances we've seen in medicine. Our brains are immeasurably superior to and infinitely more versatile than the most powerful super computers in spite of the claims that we only use a fraction of the capacity. That includes me too, even though my wife says I often don't use mine at all.

Yep, my body is a regular miracle if I do say

so myself. Regular miracle ... hmmm, is that what they call an oxymoron? It's a miracle nonetheless. But it seems like the more we know the less we know. With every new discovery about the human body, it just leads to more questions. And that's just the physical aspect. Now, you take into account the soul and it's truly mind boggling. Speaking of the mind, does it reside in the body, the soul or somewhere in-between? In any case, there's just no disputing that we're engineering marvels, designed expressly for ... for what? There must be a reason for all of this, right? If you believe in a great creator or designer, God ... and I do ... he must have put us here for some purpose. And even if you're not sure about God, other than the most bitter of skeptics must admit that all of this didn't just happen by accident. How often have you heard this refrain from folks without a religious bone in their bodies, "everything happens for a reason"? So that leaves us with the $325,000 question, that is, the $64,000 question adjusted for inflation. Why am I here, WHAT IS MY PURPOSE IN LIFE??

Like all of you, I've pondered this question many times. It can't be avoided or ignored. It rattles down the corridors of time and clatters into our brains, as an unexpected, unwanted guest. We don't want to face this monolith because so often our lives seem so small, so petty in comparison to such an amorphous, cosmic calling. It makes me think of that ancient Peggy Lee song title, "Is That

All There Is". Now, the great ones among us may see their purpose clearly and be fooled into feeling fulfilled by their great *contributions* to mankind. But even they, in the context of the grander scheme of things and eternity, are left with doubts. Many of us avoid this discomfort through the haze of booze, pursuit of money, over stoked egos, blissful or stubborn ignorance or preoccupation with family, friends and the like. Nevertheless, in spite of our best efforts, this persistent question looms, sooner or later boring into our minds like a resolute, hungry worm.

I was baptized as an infant and raised a Christian from my youth, so I always had a sense of purpose being something much greater than myself. Religious instruction and family values are wonderful things in that they give you some kind of foundation for the trek of life, a rudder for your boat. With this, it's still a treacherous journey because the water will get choppy, the winds will blow and the currents will tug and pull in every direction. I can only imagine the difficulty of weathering the storms of life without any anchor whatsoever. Thankfully, I did have a kind of protective shelter set on firm footing all the way up until my misspent youth. Yet this did not prevent me from experiencing the same doubts and questions as others. How was I to serve, what was my gift? You know how it is when you're in your formative years. You want clear, simple, straightforward answers and your aspirations are the stuff of grandeur. Will my acting skills take me to the silver screen to thrill the throngs or will it be my voice or musical talent that will punch my ticket to stardom? Am I an athlete destined to be the hero of millions? Will I be a doctor saving lives and stamping out disease? Shall I become an astronaut and discover new worlds? And, oh yes, this is America ... every little boy or girl can be PRESIDENT! It's a simple equation really. My gifts, my blessings will be so manifest that my path to fame, fortune and the betterment of mankind will be as clear as a bell. This is how we think as children, that is, until reality sets in; cold, wet, clammy, tasteless, mundane, life sapping reality.

This whole process was short circuited for me. Before I discovered my gift, before I was even able to deduce that I had no great gift and must face the paralyzing prospect of mediocrity, something horrible and life altering befell me. My first seizure occurred in grade school. Initially, I didn't even realize I had a problem. I lost all awareness. But, oh, all of the other kids around me were definitely aware as I fell to the floor and jerked and shuddered uncontrollably. I must have scared the living daylights out of my classmates. No one had ever experienced anything like this before. Barring my teacher, no one had ever heard of the word epilepsy. Thank God for Mrs. Fletcher! You know those recurring nightmares where you wind up back in school naked? That's what it felt like when I came to, only it was, unfortunately, very real. I can't describe the level of my embarrassment when I woke up, laying on the floor, dazed, covered in sweat, foamy spittle drooling down my chin, pants soaked with urine, Mrs. Fletcher huddled over me with a dire look of concern and my classmates, yes my classmates circled around me at a safe distance with looks of utter horror on their faces. A real life alien space monster would not have evoked a stronger reaction. It would be several days before the shock and sympathy wore off enough for them to start teasing me unmercifully as only children can do. Mrs. Fletcher, bless her heart, tried to counter this by educating the class on the topic of epilepsy, at least the little bit that was known at the time. She tried to help by pointing out how some of the greatest people in history like Joan of Arc and Socrates were said to have suffered from epilepsy. Such attempts were futile against the beast that had been unleashed against me. The only abatement to the needling was a brief respite as my tormentors struggled to choose between the more appropriate of two nicknames, Pee Pants or Goldfish. Pee Pants was the inevitable winner since it was much easier for infantile minds to grasp toilet humor. Really, it's not much different for adults sometimes, right? It was a little tough for some kids to connect the dots on Goldfish ... my blond hair and me flopping about like a fish out of water … but I must admit some grudging admiration for the clever young mind that was able to conceive such an elaborate insult.

Thankfully, I was a little bigger than average and a pretty good athlete. That, the soothing salve of time and, frankly, the boredom of young minds that drives them to seek new prey, helped abate my torment. Oh would there have been hell to pay if I were small, ugly or, heaven forbid, a square; in today's parlance, a nerd or geek. It would have been a life sentence for sure. I was gradually accepted back into the fold and life went on with me happily being one of the gang again. Things would have been as normal as vanilla ice cream for me had it not been for one small thing … the seizures came again, periodically if not regularly. Regular seizures would have been a blessing. If I would have known when or why they occurred I could have at least avoided the ignominy of public occurrences. For a while I suffered about a half dozen episodes a year without any apparent rhyme or reason. Although most, thankfully, occurred outside of school, it was still enough to make others jittery around me or avoid me altogether. The worst possible fate for any child or adolescent is to be singled out, different, an odd ball, a square peg … a freak. It was torture, plain and simple and just so unfair. Here I was, a bright, good looking, athletic, funny kid and otherwise popular too, maybe even cool. But I had this one inescapable flaw that made me an outcast. Being religious and all, I prayed and prayed and prayed some more that God would remove my thorn in the flesh. I didn't understand why God would not listen to my pleas and became completely exasperated with his unresponsiveness, or so I thought. To say I was miserable would be an understatement but, over time, I learned to live with my plight.

My parents and doctors were ineffective yet a great comfort. Try as they might, they could not cure my epilepsy. It was not for a lack of effort. There were endless examinations, therapies and medications of every sort. No stone was left unturned but alternative treatments, primarily surgeries, were spurned as too experimental and risky. In a way, I came to resent all this attention and *help* because it just reinforced that I was different, a strange bird. I was alone, there was no support group, there were no other epileptics ... I hate that word ... at that time in my immediate community. Also, it really put a crimp in my style. Contact sports, in effect, all organized sports, were ruled out. I had to watch my diet closely. That's another great way to stand out among your peers as an odd duck. It's also a great, big pain in the butt. When we got into high school and the in-crowd invariably began experimenting with alcohol, I was sternly warned that even one beer might trigger a disaster when mixed with my loathsome medicines. No party animal here. And let me tell you, epilepsy didn't help me when it came to the ladies. Who wants to date a loser that can't party or compete in sports and may at any time go into convulsions? If only I had been smart enough at the time to play the sympathy card! I had some friends though, and good friends, not just a misery-loves-company thing. No, we weren't part of the in-crowd by any stretch but it was a godsend to have someone to confide in other than my own family. When my true friends affectionately referred to me by my new, high school nickname of Spaz, I didn't mind. But when someone else used that moniker in a malicious tone or hurled some other invective my way, I wanted to just pound them, to prove that I was not a big wussy. That too was off limits and my loving, or should I say overbearing, parents regularly cautioned me against the potentially catastrophic consequences of pugilism. Speaking of family, I must sound like an unappreciative jerk. However, in spite of my self-pity, I was eventually able to recognize the great sacrifices they made for me and the true love, care and concern behind all of their rules and restrictions. They truly had my best interests at heart and this was a comfort indeed.

As I learned to accept my lot in life, I settled into somewhat of a routine. Once I got past the sulking over all the things I was missing, I tried to take advantage of what was left. I had family, friends and was able to glean a good education from my unorthodox high school experience. I even got a job working in a bakery after school and on weekends and saved up a little dough ... yes, pun intended. This seemed quite appropriate, for a kid named Baker, Baker Paulson. Come to think of it, my last name was fitting too in that my namesake had his own, famous thorn in the flesh.

Chapter 2

Spaz's Escape

All things considered, I was a well-adjusted high school epileptic, no, make that spaz, I like spaz better. But one thing bothered me the most. Being a spaz did not shield me from that one, overriding, burning question. Why am I here, what's my purpose in life? It only complicated things for me. It wasn't enough that I was having trouble discovering my gift, developing a talent, honing a skill or even grabbing hold of an interest that would drive me to overcome this challenge. Before I could tackle purpose, I had to wrestle with another question, for me, an all-consuming distraction. Why me? Why me, God? What did I do to deserve this? Why are you punishing me in this way? Ugh! There I was, wallowing in the slough of despond again. Self-pity had me down for the count. I don't know how close I came to the breaking point but I can tell you that despair was looking pretty large in my side view mirror.

Then a funny thing happened. By no intent or particular effort on my part, I found a little bit of purpose, a respite if you will. The Bible says that when testing comes, God will give us the strength to deal with it or, before it becomes too great, he will provide a way of escape. That sure seemed true in my case. When I was at my wit's end, I found my escape, in of all places, a hot, dusty, sweaty *salt mine* called Dirk's Bakery.

Dirk was a wonderful, quirky old Dutchman who gleaned his skills from his immigrant father at a tender age. He had toiled for almost thirty years under other task masters, scrimping and saving, all along plying his trade, while learning and sacrificing to one day realize his dream. There was no lacking a sense of purpose in old Dirk. He had wanted to be his own boss and open up his shop for as long as he could remember. Bakers work weird, long hours and weekends too. It's hard, physical labor. It can be tedious at times. But Dirk loved it. He relished being the captain of his own destiny. He wasn't quite Fezzywig. No, he didn't look the part. Dirk was skinny as a rail but wiry and had thin curly hair that was only made more unruly by the sweat. He had a perpetual five o'clock shadow that was accentuated by a perky little moustache that curled up jauntily at the edges of his mouth. Dirk's eyebrows were a bit shaggy and arched too high above his eyes and could work independently to render some marvelous expressions. His long, thin nose separated his most telling feature ... his eyes had a twinkle, a mischievous glint that danced to and fro at will. He had a carefree bounce in his step and exuded confidence from the tilt in his short baker's cap and ever present cigar slung from the corner of his mouth. His white shirt and baggy pants sagging with sweat and caked with flour and corn meal, Dirk was a man in his element, at peace with his world.

Other than his physical attributes, Dirk had a lot

in common with young Ebeneezer's boss. Dirk's enthusiasm was infectious. He always addressed us at the start of a shift with a hearty, "hellooooooo bakers", at the top of his lungs in his unusual, almost comical accent reminiscent of Inspector Clouseau. It was almost impossible to be in a foul mood around him. Dirk's command of his craft was well earned and worked to his advantage but, surprisingly, he owed his success much more so to his managerial skills which came naturally or by osmosis rather than through education. It's not easy to find good people to work like dogs for baker's wages and even tougher to keep them happy and motivated. But Dirk had a real knack. At first, I though he hired me just because he got such a kick out of my name, Baker. Oh did he get a belly laugh out of that one. But, beyond that, he must have had a sixth sense to recognize something in me that I did not see myself ... and he didn't seem to give a second thought to the perils of hiring a spaz. He was kind of a spaz of sorts himself. In any case, he hired me and enthusiastically took on the hard task of teaching me the secret art of baking. I didn't have a clue but he was amazingly patient. I didn't mind the hours. Being largely a social outcast, my weekends and evenings were mostly free except for my studies. And the cast of characters at the bakery, topped off by Dirk himself, was more interesting than anything else I had encountered.

There was something therapeutic in baking. I was working with my hands and received immediate gratification seeing, smelling and occasionally tasting the fruits of our labors. Making the initial *sponge*, mixing the finished dough, operating equipment, dusting the boards with corn meal, shaping and preparing the bread, rolls and pastries, working the steam box and ovens and packaging the finished goods … everything had its own little purpose, everything was part of a plan … and I was part of a living, breathing crew, working together as a team to achieve our daily goal. It was simple and straightforward. It was rewarding in its own special way. While this was not my purpose in life, I had found purpose and meaning for the time being. It gave me a whole new outlook. I was a baker … I had stories to tell … I had a little money to burn and, most importantly, I had some optimism. I had made my escape. Despair faded from my rear view mirror and I was able to look at the road ahead with some confidence.

Yes, a funny, unexpected thing had happened to me. It hit me that, somewhere along the way on this baking odyssey, I wasn't consumed by the fear of seizures anymore. Oh, I still had occasional seizures but they were less frequent and, oddly enough, I never suffered a seizure at Dirk's Bakery. Was this a godsend; was this mind over matter or was there something physiological to it? Did my body chemistry change because of an altered state of mind that my new protective cocoon, my baking sanctuary induced? Part of me thought that this was God's hand guiding me somewhere yet unbeknownst ... a long awaited answer to my prayers. Another part of me thought there was a medical explanation, that somehow my flawed wiring was being untangled, maybe by God or just physical maturity ... or some of both. But, at the end of the day, I was not about to fret over this or let it take a negative turn. No sir, things were looking up for me now.

Some other good things happened that year. My body was benefitting from the hard work. I gained physical strength, endurance and toughness in spite of my exile from football, basketball and baseball. Also, I learned some valuable life lessons. Even though I still wasn't sure of what I wanted to do longer-term, this experience helped me with the process of elimination. Working at Dirk's was a magical, whimsical time that I still look back on fondly with great wonder. But something told me it wouldn't last. There was no future in this for me. I knew that, if I labored thusly, over the long haul, a twenty or thirty year stretch would be like a prison sentence. After the novelty wore off, when there was nothing new to be learned, as the challenges abated, drudgery could set in. No, I had to set my sights a bit higher. If nothing else, I knew I was destined to be a college man.

Chapter 3

L. M. O. C.

Life was good. I was doing well in school, steaming toward graduation my senior year. As a Tiger fan since birth, or as soon as possible thereafter, I was thrilled to be accepted at the University of Missouri. It might sound foolish but I didn't even apply at another school while getting the nod from Ol' Mizzou. This was one decision that came to me with complete ease, a no brainer. That being settled, I cruised through my final year of high school, dare I say, even enjoyed it along with my work at Dirk's and time spent within a close circle of friends. There's something about senior year. Perhaps it's the sense of accomplishment or the sweet relief that comes with completing a seemingly endless twelve year journey. Free at last, free at last! Most of all, I think there's a kind of naughty pleasure that comes from being top dog and gazing condescendingly upon the foibles of the silly, immature underclassmen. We are able to see in them all the mistakes we committed ourselves and realize the *vast experience* we've gained. Call it vanity, hypocrisy, inhumanity or any other vile label that might apply but it's all just part of the cycle of life in high school. It's the natural order of things. Seniors, at least those that survive the perils and pitfalls of the first three years, have earned the right and privilege to scorn the lowly, pitiful, hopeless mongrels known as underclassmen. That is, unless those

27

underclassmen are hot, young babes. That's another story altogether.

Even though I had been a complete spaz and still bore the marks, I must admit I fell into this trap too. If there's anyone who should have looked upon those awkward freshmen and clumsy sophomores with empathy and compassion, it's me. But it's so tempting to hoist oneself up on the maladies of others. We all want to feel important even if, unfortunately, it comes at the expense of someone else. I may not have overtly harassed them like some of my peers but I knew in my own heart that I took some twisted pleasure in watching the struggles of the newbies. If I have a defense, it is this … at least my conscience made me feel a little guilty at times. Yes, how soon we forget that we too were once similarly plagued. We forget how we were forlorn and desperately sought accommodation and acceptance. I had an advantage though, one that kept me from being consumed with false, damaging notions of superiority or true malice. My seizures were a blessing in that regard if you can count anything that abominable as advantageous. Thankfully, this monster only reared its ugly head occasionally at this point, hibernating for months on end. But when it came, it served as a good reminder of my own helplessness and knocked me off my high horse. Dirk, that vast repository of common sense and experience summed it up thusly, "baker" he said with a small b, "it's nice to be important but more important to be nice". The Dirk hath spoken.

Maybe I really was maturing. Altruism was taking root in a garden previously overrun by the weeds of self-centeredness. Instead of wallowing in self-pity, I was starting to recognize silver linings. I was starting to grow spiritually too. While I had been *into the word*, as they say, for a long time, I really only brushed the surface of the pages in my Bible. I had a lot of head knowledge. I knew right from wrong, guided by my catechism, but as much by rote as conviction. Now, it seemed, I was able to see a deeper meaning, to nibble on the pages and inwardly digest the pulp and ink. I even started to see that, perhaps, my prayers were being answered; just not in the way I wanted or expected. I still had my thorn in the flesh. But it was not as painful or irritating as it once had been. It was not an all-consuming force restricting and destroying my life. Although it was still very frightening at times, my condition had become more a hurdle than handicap. On my better, more optimistic days, I considered it just an inconvenience. Finally, at last, I was even able to see some benefit where before I only felt cursed. Wasn't I a better person because of my epilepsy? It had given me humility and empathy and probably kept me from going down some attractive but dangerous paths. It helped me to appreciate the small things, important things in life. It helped me to question things. And, eventually, in spite of my stubbornness and ignorance, it drew me closer to God. Yes, I may not have understood how but I finally realized that God really does know best.

Oh, before I forget, something else happened my senior year of high school. I met a girl. Not just any girl but a real, live, blond beauty of a girl. She was sweet, innocent, funny and gorgeous. I know, beauty is in the eye of the beholder, but I'm not just whistling Dixie. She may not have been your sophisticated, drop dead, runway model type. But, in her simple, pure, unassuming way, she flat out knocked my socks off. Sally had plenty of friends and everyone liked her but she was, thankfully, not A-list popular or in-crowd material. Maybe it was because she was only a sophomore but I think it was more just her nature. She was a Sally, not a Meredith, Courtney or Felicity. It's a good thing because I was not the sort to stalk more dangerous prey. Even though I was a senior, I lacked almost any useful experience in the female department. Looking back, Sally was perfect for me, pretty on the inside and out. And, miracle of miracles, she took a liking to me too. She saw me as Baker, not Spaz, and had a wonderful way of seeing the best in me and filtering out all the rest. The first time we went to the movies and she nuzzled up close to me during the scary part, sparks flew. I mean literally. I think she naturally sent a current of electricity through me that made the hairs on my neck stand up and sent cozy warmth flowing to my extremities. Our first kiss was not in July but there were fireworks nonetheless, big, bright, loud, amazing, spectacular sky busters. Who would have believed it? Spaz was a boyfriend!

Yes, it was a very good year indeed. That is, until it was time to embark on the move from St. Louis to Columbia. Going away to college should be exhilarating; the start of a whole, new life; emancipation. It's the total freedom to come and go as you please, wherever and whenever you want. Late to bed and late to rise, damn the torpedoes and my bloodshot eyes! Mom and dad would be over one hundred miles away, practically the other side of the world. I even had my own wheels, courtesy of dear old dad; a rusting, dilapidated, hulk of a 1961 Dodge station wagon but it was mine. What's not to like? There was just one minor, little monkey wrench screwing up the works. I was a boyfriend now. Sally gal and I had become quite attached to one another the past six months, sharing a close bond that was about to be severely tested. Whoever said absence makes the heart grow fonder was full of condensed weasel -poop. Just the thought of being apart made me feel, well, anything but fond. No more sneaking through the alley with Sally for me. And she didn't help matters. I guess I should have been flattered by the way she pined over me at the prospect of our separation but she was so sincere it crushed me. This was not some high school, puppy love drama playing out. We had become the best of friends.

But it was the hand we had been dealt and there was no way around it. It was a bright, beautiful, sun drenched August afternoon but this parting cast a pall over it. What should have been my bon voyage was more like the Bataan Death March as I departed for COMO.

The adventure of a lifetime was upon me as I cruised west on I-70 but my dauber was down as I thought about Sally and, especially, those grubby high school juniors and seniors that would be trying to invade my turf while I was away. To sooth my savage breast, I flipped on the radio but to my dismay the reception was terrible, like trying to reach Mars. However, I was prepared for this. I had wisely invested some of my hard earned cash in an under the dash 8 track tape player. There was only one problem; I couldn't afford tapes just yet so I popped in the only thing I had, an oldies greatest hits collection that was a gift from mom. That was a mistake because, in 1965-1966, every hit tune seemed to be about unrequited love. Elvis left crying in the chapel, the Righteous Brothers losing that loving feeling, Smokey and the Miracles tracing the tracks of their tears, the Beau Brummels trying to laugh, laugh to cover up feeling so lonely, oh so lonely … it was just so much burning salt in my gaping, wounded heart. The Count Five captured my mixed up emotions perfectly with Psychotic Reaction. Then, to make matters worse, Barry McGuire's Eve of Destruction followed to really add to the gloom and doom. Just outside of Kingdom City, the music and, with it, my fortunes took a turn for the better. Is there a better opening sequence than the Beach Boys' California Girls to break up a bad mood? Made me wish they could all be Sally girl. Then, hallelujah, The Stones were up next to declare their lack of satisfaction. I couldn't get no satisfaction either but it helped to get a little mad, rebellious and outspoken about it like Mick. I shouted right along, oblivious to passersby. The Sir Douglas Quintet really took my mind off of my troubles with She's About a Mover. I had no idea what that meant but it felt good to sing along, "Sally's about a moovah!" From all the way across The Pond, Petula Clark struck an upbeat tone with I Know a Place. Then the real breakthrough was achieved by one Roger Miller. Yes, I was King of the Road, clattering down I-70, suddenly without a care in the world. As I approached the Columbia Business Loop exit, Pet appropriately came back for an encore, Downtown. Yeah boy, look out Mizzou and watch out downtown COMO because here I come. I know a place or at least I had heard about a few … yee ha!

I'll never forget that day. My melancholy over Sally was relegated to the dark recesses of my mind for the time being by the carnival laid out before me. It was sunny and breezy with nary a cloud in the sky to interrupt the azure heavens. Celestial blue fell down to

33

engulf the emerald tree tops. Green grass was only interrupted by flowers and bushes, a kaleidoscope of colors that waved rhythmically with the gentle winds. The streets were paved with tradition and majestic buildings rose like spires. In the midst were monuments; Memorial Union looking like some gothic cathedral, Jesse Hall and its grand dome surely rivaled anything in our nation's capital and, most inspiring of all, the famed columns on the Francis Quadrangle. This, the only structure to survive the 1892 inferno that ravaged the original Academic Hall opened in 1843, symbolized the resiliency and indomitable spirit of the University. Soon I would take my turn at history along with the other incoming freshmen and march through those iconic columns signifying the start of my journey as a Tiger. Before I get too carried away, let me tell you about the dorms. No, they were not a sight to behold. Some were old enough to have character but the more modern housing resembled something out of East Germany. The stark accommodations didn't faze me though. I was too caught up in the wonderful hustle and bustle of students making their way back to campus or, like me, finding their way for the first time. I marveled at the inventive ways young people made use of the cramped quarters, two students stuffed into a 20' x 25' *cell*.

I was already blown away by exploring the campus proper but then gazing upon historic Memorial

Stadium/Faurot Field, Brewer Fieldhouse and the brand, spanking new Hearnes Center Auditorium, up close and personal, took my revelry to a whole new level. Nothing could top the experience of knowing that I was becoming a part of this fabric where so many past glories had been woven and new ones awaited. Now silent and practically deserted, I tilted my ear toward these havens to hear the faint echo of ghostly heroes that still inhabited these hallowed grounds and the muffled roars of the throngs, including me, that would soon return in a sea of black and gold regalia. I had reached the pinnacle, or so I thought. But I was not quite at the summit until I ventured to where campus melted into downtown Columbia. Then, I spied them off in the distance ... the holy grail of college life in COMO ... The Berg, Shakespeare's Pizza, The Shack and the new bar that would one day become legendary, Harpo's. I couldn't wait to start personally helping to erect that legend.

My guess is that most people have had similar experiences upon reaching college. There's just something enchanting about the ivy covered halls, loveable mascots, folklore and heritage that create a common bond and enduring fondness. It's a sojourn that usually results in a fierce loyalty to the old alma mater once it's completed. The first steps in that journey can be some of the most memorable ones, before the harsher realities of college life kick in. Ah, that first weekend before classes start when there's all party and zero responsibility! How did I cram so much into so little time? It seems I was on a mission to exorcise all my demons at once. I discovered the famous quarry and had my first drink and was delighted to find that the local cops would not roust you there as long as things were under reasonable control and you shared your beer with them. I played touch football with reckless abandon. So what if it was only co-ed, I was a risk taker! Another first; I was goaded into a fight by some obnoxious frat boys, was outnumbered and lost only to suffer the indignation of a beer dousing. Okay, maybe it was more of a scuffle but I still despise Sigma Nu to this day. Finally, somehow, within forty-eight hours of my arrival, I unearthed a gem of a campus bar where I could get served. It was a hoary dive, the Loading Zone, where, if faint memory serves me, it even had a dirt floor, or maybe it was just covered in sawdust to soak up the beer, blood and vomit. Even on my tight budget, I could afford twenty-five cent draughts. Normally, my meals were all inclusive, that is, I ate what was provided as part of my room and board courtesy of the dorm cafeteria's plenty. But just once in a while, I'd scrape together enough coins to enjoy the Loading Zone's fare. I can still smell the enticing aroma of the Zone's tantalizingly unhealthy bar food.

It's such a pity that all good things must come

to an end. Did I mention reality? At first it didn't seem so bad. Registration and book purchases were just minor nuisances but the first day of classes did a one eighty to my entire psyche. You mean there's some responsibility to college life? It's not all booze, parties, panty raids and football games? And money doesn't grow on trees? You mean I might actually have to flip burgers at Harpo's in my spare time to have a little pocket change? But I'm supposed to be eating and drinking there, not cooking and pouring. The injustice! Looking at my seemingly light, fifteen hour schedule, I thought, what am I going to do to occupy all my free time? You mean, unlike high school, you actually have to study outside of class, for hours and hours, sometimes late into the wee hours? This was looking a lot more like responsibility than liberty. My stress rose along with my indignation.

Worse yet, I soon discovered there was a pecking order ... and I was clinging to the dirty, smelly end of the stick. One of the cruelest tricks life plays on us is to struggle for years and years to drag ourselves out of the muck to finally ascend to that most lofty status of high school senior only to be cast down in a heartbeat to the nether region once again. Freshmen are just so many barnacles on this cruise ship. The bridge is occupied by administrators and faculty mans the guns. Accomplished sophomores and juniors are allowed to move up to the ship's vitals like the engine compartment. But the top deck, the party deck is reserved for seniors. At least that's how rigid and unfair it seemed to me, sloshing down there with the rest of the bilge. It would take time and a few prerequisites from the school of hard knocks for me to understand how the process works, how to master the system, how to strike that perfect balance between keeping one's nose to the grindstone and casting all care to the wind. At that stage, I was just too dazed and confused to see that the wildest, craziest, devil may care Animal House denizens usually had a whole different, serious side that afforded them the luxury of their laissez faire indulgences. No, someone who, at that point, couldn't recognize their posterior from a hole in the ground certainly couldn't discern such subtleties.

No small, cozy seminars here. Freshmen wallowed madly in the obscurity of lecture halls filled with three to five hundred frantic note takers. Dorm rats received nose bleed athletic passes while prime time was reserved for the Greeks. It seemed at every turn, the deck was stacked against me. And the magnitude of it all made things that much worse. Although I had attended a very large high school, this place was at least ten times larger. Four years seemed like an eternity away. I began to doubt whether I could cut the muster here. It's amazing how rapidly I fell back into old habits, unhealthy attitudes. I couldn't escape the reality that I had fallen from the mountain top all the way back down to the deepest trenches. My world had crashed and burned, I was L. M. O. C. Low man on campus!

Chapter 4

They're Baaaack!

I was suffering the kind of meltdown that sends freshmen packing for home. But I wasn't necessarily homesick. My old ghosts were coming back to haunt me; insecurities, anxieties, paranoia and despair. The good feelings and diversions that had helped me to put my separation from Sally somewhere other than constantly top of mind had evaporated like morning dew. I needed a friend, my best friend. That void in my gut had returned.

Thankfully, we didn't have PCs or cell phones back then. Communication was in person, by snail mail or land line phone. No, dorm rooms were not equipped with personalized, princess phones. Like in the military, you had to stand in line for a turn at the one pay phone hanging in the hallway. If I would have been bombarded by teary emails and text messages or sobbing cell phone calls, I would have gone bonkers in a New York minute. Just one call a week was plenty. Oh, they started cheery enough. Enjoyment comes from simple pleasures. Back then, long distance calls were expensive and hard to squeeze into a skinny budget so we learned to appreciate those short but sweet encounters. The phone company practiced the time-is-money theorem as well as anyone so we had to keep things brief. We were restricted not only by cost but, to me, the worse pressure was having the next guy in line breathing down my neck. There was no privacy. So, I cherished and dreaded these calls. They always ended the same way. Sally's initial verve would turn to soft whimpers as the seconds ticked by and then to weeping, sometimes hard gulping sobs. She didn't mean to make me uncomfortable but she didn't realize what it was like on my end, with my hand cupping my ear and the receiver to muffle the sound, straining the muscles in my face to appear stoic. I took to letter writing. Letters were better, much better.

Why do we do the exact opposite of what's best for us? When we're feeling pressure, why do we turn up our internal dial instead of tamping things down? If you're about to blow a gasket, wouldn't that be the time to open up the release valve? I guess that's why people idolize Joe Montana or are fascinated by James Bond. They are able to keep their cool under extreme conditions that would turn most of us into quivering jelly. I had been there before, in the dungeon of gloom, and was so exhilarated by my escape but was descending rapidly again while helpless to halt my slide. What was wrong with me? Faulty wiring, I assume.

That notion started to sink in with me and take root. The thought that my wires were crossed kind of made sense. Weren't we filled with electrical currents? Even way back then, we knew as much, even laymen like me. In biology class we learned about the nervous

41

system, muscle impulses, voluntary and involuntary reflexes ... and the brain with its synapses and compartmentalized control centers. And what did they resort to when someone's wiring was mixed up beyond some normal medical repair? Although it wouldn't be immortalized in film for a few years, I learned this lesson in reading Kesey's masterpiece: One Flew Over the Cuckoo's Nest. Yes, a good dose of electrical shock treatments would clear out the cob webs and get things running smoothly. When all else failed, you'd have to finally just cut off the current to the offending members with a lobotomy. I remember learning the hard way back in middle school how well the body can conduct electricity. I was trying to fix my parents' old high fidelity record player while it was still plugged in and unwittingly found the short with my left hand. I mean to tell you, we're good conductors. I think I also learned about alternating currents that day ... I could actually feel the pulsing as the shock coursed through me. Looking back, that current seized me much like an epileptic fit. The only thing that saved me was when, with herculean effort, I was able to grab the power cord with my jerking right hand and give it a good yank. My sanity was well intact for a good long time after that brush with science.

Understanding and fixing such a complex problem were two different matters. And I was not so sure that my troubles were solely the consequence of an electrical malfunction. There were still lingering doubts about psychological issues. I couldn't deny that my experiences with epilepsy and the accompanying scorn and isolation had left me with a lot of cracks and fissures even when my façade seemed strong and healthy. Then there was the spiritual side to contend with. I could not and did not want to escape the feeling, the belief that God would use odd, even painful measures to accomplish his purposes in our lives. If this sounds like I was rationally and methodically sorting through all the facts and possibilities to calmly resolve my issues, nothing could be further from the truth. It was more like sliding backwards down a slippery slope into a dark hole with some unknown, snarling demons waiting in the murky pit below. Unless you're Joe Montana, which I certainly wasn't, panic sets in.

My studies suffered and the pressure mounted. My feelings for Sally were confused and conflicted. I longed for her all the more but at the same time resented her constant, woeful reminders of our predicament. How could I console her when I needed my own consolation? My work was drudgery and my attitude reflected as much. Instead of bonding with new friends that might offer some release, I isolated myself from campus activities and the possibility of healthy, new relationships. Misery loves company but I had none. The sour grapes of my youth that had matured into a fine wine my senior year of high school was now just so much bitter vinegar that I wanted to spew it from my mouth.

That first semester which had started out so promisingly, went south on me. I had always prided myself on being an excellent student but now had lowered my standards, above average was okay. Since I felt I had nothing to lose, I obliterated all the healthy restrictions I had followed. COMO became my personal port of call for drinking, fighting and carousing. Maybe I got a late start but I was determined to make up lost ground on my misspent youth. And for the first time in my life, I stayed away from church and let dust collect on my Bible. Sally could sense the change in me too. Oh, I still called and wrote letters but they were hollow and shallow. It was a frigid winter that year, so cold that even Christmas break at home didn't thaw my Grinch's heart. When I left for the second semester, Sally sobbed again but not just because I was leaving but more so because I hadn't really come back home. I was numb to her tearful farewell.

Just when you think you've hit rock bottom, things get worse. My locomotive didn't have a wheel left on the track but I still had a conscience buried somewhere deep down there and it bothered me. Most troubling was the way I had treated my Sally. Jack Frost had nothing on me. I deeply regretted the lost Christmas but in my wretched state dissolved into self-pity instead of trying to make amends. I was pointed

44

toward the falls but instead of turning the boat I just stoked the engine more. That's when it happened. My seizures came back with a vengeance, more frequent and ferocious than ever. What had abated to an inconvenience or silver lining was back as a dark, ominous thunder cloud. It gave my roommate the willies ... me too. I was a jittery, trembling little rabbit living in the shadow of an overgrown, ravenous coyote.

Disaster finally struck when I fell into convulsions right there in the aisle of a quiet, packed lecture hall. Silence engulfed the room as the professor's lecture screeched to a halt and everyone's attention turned to the cacophony of manic grunts and growls emanating from my lurching carcass sprawled on the floor. Folks finally broke from their stupor to offer aid but largely stared at me dumbfounded having no clue as to how to help me, other than one fellow erudite enough to know to gently restrain me for those agonizingly long moments until the fit petered out. It was never the same for me after that. No it wasn't like grade school. There was no childish taunting or mocking; no nicknames or stinging labels applied, at least not overtly or in polite company. These were mature, well educated, compassionate college folks. They were well intentioned, helpful people. You know what they say about the road to hell being paved with good intentions. Their good intentions made my private hell that much more unbearable. And in spite of it all, they just couldn't help recoiling from me a bit from that point forward. It was almost imperceptible but I had developed very powerful antennae over the years. I didn't blame them really. It's natural to have some revulsion, while accompanied side by side with compassion, to deformity. It can't be helped.

What I dreaded the most was the formal support that necessarily had to follow now that my condition had been brought to the public's attention. The bureaucracy kicked in. My privacy was invaded by endless counselors and university officials. They were well intentioned for the most part but some were just in the CYA business seeking protection against any kind of liability or lawsuit. Where did all these people come from? Who was paying their salary? No wonder tuition was so high! I was forced to visit doctors and ensure proper treatments and precautions were in place. Of course, my parents were brought into the loop and, as you might expect, they were more than willing to help the university see that all the restrictions I had abandoned, and then some, were put back in place firmly. My roommate informed me that he had pledged a frat and would be leaving at the semester's end. I had plumbed the depths and found the bottom. My world had shrunk from the big, bright amusement park I entered on my first day of college down to a cramped cage in a freak show and I was the main attraction. What had been sprinkled with such promise was now drenched in bleak pessimism. My hope had bled out; it was DOA.

Chapter 5

All Things Work Together for Good

Where do you turn when you've lost all hope? I didn't have anyone to confide in. My college pals weren't much more than acquaintances. While I hadn't gone so far as to break up with Sally, I had let the distance between us grow in a figurative sense much further than the hundred miles that separated us. My pride wouldn't let me admit this folly and shame curtailed any earnest bridge building. With my self-imposed exile, the last place I would seek advice was from my ubiquitous campus counselors and I even spurned my parents who seemed to be in league with them. I was reminded of that black and white movie our teachers showed back in grade school on one of those old, whirring film projectors, The Man without a Country. It chronicled Philip Nolan, friend to traitorous Aaron Burr, who had foolishly declared "Damn the United States! I wish I could never hear of her again." He got his wish and was banished for life to an American warship with orders to the crew that no one would ever speak of the United States in his presence.

The last refuge of the nihilistically forlorn was thankfully, by the grace of God, not an option for me. My parents believed the words of Proverbs 22:6, "Train up a child in the way he should go: and when he is old, he will not depart from it". These words were so true. I may have avoided church and spurned the word of God lately with sins of omission as well as commission but that training still held sway over me in many respects. Suicide and its consequences were much too frightening to consider no matter what happened ... strictly verboten. No, there would be no easy way out for me. My desperation mounted. I began to coolly rationalize my situation like the fellow in Poe's Tell Tale Heart but worried more and more that I might descend into madness like him at the sound of some thumping, pounding heart, my heart. Was I at the breaking point, on the verge of losing my mind?

I thought, *perhaps I should quit college and get a job or join the army*. Lots of tarnished thoughts ran through my mind but I couldn't fool myself into believing that any of them offered good solutions for me. I was stuck on a roundabout with all the exits leading to dead ends. I had forgotten Paul's advice to the Philippians that we should rejoice in the Lord always; that meant even during tough times. Then, seemingly out of nowhere, I remembered back to when I was at another low point earlier in life and how God had made a way of escape. Sometimes we just have to be brought low to the very bottom, with absolutely no other options, before we'll turn to what should be our first place of refuge. I turned to God, dropped to my knees and prayed. This time, I didn't have to wait long for an answer. A short time later, like a bolt from the blue, one of our dorm dwellers who never seemed to sleep, Crazy Joe we called him, knocked on my door and curtly declared, "Paulson ... phone". It was Sally who informed me she was coming up to Columbia on a Greyhound to visit me on Saturday.

Just when I needed someone I could trust and open up to completely, there she was. Seeing her in the flesh was a much needed ray of sunshine. It raised my spirits and put me in the right frame of mind for what was to follow. All of the things I had projected onto her turned out to be nothing more than a grotesque mirage I had created. She wasn't aloof, uncaring, distant or out of touch at all. The wall between us had been of my construction and apparently a two-way mirror because, while I saw nothing but the cold stone of my own reflection, she had been able to peer at me through the glass and gain valuable insights that she graciously shared. In her own wonderful way, she laid out what was ailing me, not in any sort of judgmental manner but in a kind, gentle and generous way that showed she cared deeply about me. She had never stopped. She really did have a heart of gold and wisdom that belied her youth and innocence.

As she talked, I was able to see what had been troubling me so much, in the clear, unvarnished truth. Like Philip Nolan who went on to be a most loyal American, I had a complete change of heart. I could see my doubts and fears, my paranoia, my despair, self-pity and finger pointing, my lack of trust and, most importantly, lack of faith. My priorities had become terribly out of whack. My problem was me. Then Sally showed me a side I had not seen before, a depth and spiritual understanding that revealed the source of her surprisingly profound wisdom. She found my Bible under a stack of other books and papers and turned to Romans 8:28 and read aloud, "And we know that all things work together for good to them that love God, to them who are the called according to his purpose." Then she dropped down to verse 31, "What shall we say then to these things? If God be for us, who can be against us?" That opened the flood gates and we talked for hours. What seemed so perplexing before came into view easily. It seemed like a gauzy film had been lifted from my eyes. I, by my own actions, had steered way off course and was headed for big trouble. When I was riding high, my memories of lessons learned had vanished. In my euphoria, I had become like one of the nine miraculously healed lepers who didn't bother to turn back to God in thanks. I had been running ninety miles an hour in the wrong direction, away from my purpose. And I had taken Sally, a precious gift, for granted. You don't know what you've got 'til it's gone. I had paved paradise and put up a parking lot. But the dark thunder boomers were dissipating now and that silver lining was in focus again. Yes, my dreaded seizures were still a gift after all.

What a release, what relief, exhilaration and freedom … the endless possibilities and boundless optimism were back! But what's next? Was this a set-up for a vicious cycle of ups and downs, meteoric rises followed by precipitous plummets from grace? I took Sally around campus while we talked some more. We pondered this question as I showed her the sights, not realizing how my pride and fondness for College Town U. S. A. was showing through. She didn't say a word but she could tell how much it meant to me to be a part of it all in spite of the travails of my first year. Thus, she hesitated when I finally said, "so, what do you think I should do …where do I go from here?" Her pregnant pause elicited a stream of consciousness from me. I talked about how I didn't want to fall into the same, old snares again. I shared my desire to seek and pursue my true purpose in life. I even went so far as to open up and confess how I never wanted to put any wedges between us again. She waited patiently while I spilled my guts, until I finally asked her a second time but with a subtle change from singular to plural, "so, what do you think we should do?"

Again she declined and simply said, "I don't know, Baker, what do you think?" She was young but much more mature than me in some ways and sage enough to know that whatever happened now had to be my decision, had to come from my heart to have lasting effect. I was mere putty at that point and she could have used her wiles to coax me however she wanted but, being a Polly Purebread, she didn't play any games. She left me unencumbered to reach my own conclusion and was prepared to live with any outcome.

I didn't answer right away. Instead, we just enjoyed the rest of the day. We caught up on old times and took in every free pleasure 'Ol Mizzou had to offer. All free, that is, except one small budget buster. I sprang for dinner at the oldest joint in town, Booche's, where we shared a steamy hot, greasy delicacy, their famous cheeseburgers, offered up since 1884, most appropriately, atop a square of wax paper. It had been quite a while since I had felt this comfortable and care free. Eventually, we had to take the long walk to the bus station to get Sally back on her way to St. Louis. During this time we didn't say much to each other. She stayed true to her conviction not to press me and I was left deep in thought as we ambled along the tree lined streets. It's funny but silence was not awkward for us, even at our tender age. We just enjoyed being in one another's presence. As I ruminated, I was torn because, in spite of everything, I still felt a wistful connection to Columbia and the University. However, with all things carefully considered, it was pretty close to a no brainer. One of the toughest decisions of my life turned out to be one of the best. "Sally" I said breaking the silence, "I think I need to come home at the end of the semester." She didn't squeal with delight. She didn't take the ball and run with it. It didn't open the flood gates for endless suggestions on what should follow thereafter.

No, she just disarmed me with that amazing smile of hers and softly said, "That suits me just fine, Baker, just fine." Oh, and then to properly say goodbye, she softly, slowly placed her lips over mine ... and the rockets' red glare burst over Columbia, Missouri.

Chapter 6

Sweet Home St. Louis

Yours truly, a knight in the rusting armor of a '61 Dodge, arrived home in May of 1973 and my damsel, Maid Sally, was at my parents' cracker box castle to make it a warm and cheerful homecoming. It was good to be home and, being reunited with my gal pal Sal and eagerly staring summer smack dab in the face, I felt no remorse about my exodus from beloved COMO. No, I was much too busy for that kind of stuff. Besides the frivolousness of summer, I had to spare time for transferring schools and finding gainful employment. Things fell into place with amazing ease. The University of Missouri had a St. Louis campus so I was able to enroll and transfer all my credits without skipping a beat. To my delight, Dirk welcomed me back to the bakery with open arms. He arranged for me to work full time during the summer and log all the hours I could stand during the coming school year. I must admit it wasn't all peaches 'n cream. It was great to reconnect with my mom and dad but I couldn't help but chafe a bit being under their roof again after tasting such a big slice of freedom in Columbia. However, they did afford me the respect befitting a college man and we learned to co-exist. Any friction was more than offset by mom's hearty, heavenly home cooking.

It was an idyllic summer, one you might call a

time of our lives. There was no school work to worry about. I worked a lot of hours, as did Sally, but we had jobs we could leave at the door. There was no stress, pressure or deadlines. The evenings and some weekends were ours to do as we pleased, to our hearts' content. It wasn't pretty but we had wheels; we were mobile. We certainly weren't making big bucks but, with no other major obligations besides me helping out with my school costs, we had money to burn. There were movies and concerts, burgers and shakes, parks and picnics, and festivals, fairs and fishing. It didn't matter if we caught anything. Just lolling alongside each other by a lake or river was enough. As my dear old man liked to say, I had the world by the tail with a downhill pull.

As summer came to an end, a touch of reality set in. Sally still had to finish her senior year of high school. It was not the normal lark like I had experienced. Our relationship drew her away from that scene. Sally was naïve in the ways of the world but she was not your typical high school, teeny bopper. She was wise beyond her years in matters of the heart and her aspirations took a longer view than most. A homecoming date, finding just the right prom dress, the high school grape vine and the like were not her primary focus. She dutifully completed her senior year but in many ways had already moved on. Meanwhile, I found out that the University of Missouri-St. Louis, or UMSL, would be no picnic. It was an urban, commuter campus and lacked all the frills of Mizzou or any other typical college atmosphere; strictly business in the broad sense. They made up for their lack of collegiate panache by rigorously enforcing academic standards. Oddly enough, this Napoleonic complex benefitted the student body, as discipline has a way of doing. As for the bakery, the luster dimmed a bit over time and it became more like work than play as I matured. But Dirk and the crew still offered a welcome diversion to cares of the day. Unlike most of my peers there, I knew this was a temporary way station along a path stretching, I supposed, well beyond Dirk's. Thus, I could enjoy the camaraderie and that oddly liberating feeling that comes with physical labor.

Our new reality wasn't bad at all. After that summer ended, we settled into our roles like a favorite pair of old, worn jeans and that year passed in the blink of an eye. Sally tossed her mortar board and I said so long to my sophomore year. Summer magic returned and we grew even closer together, our root systems intertwined. I'm not sure when, why or how it happened but one morning I woke up pre-dawn, my brain clicked in, and I knew I couldn't fall back to sleep. I wasn't trying to think. It was more like my brain was off on its own and I was just reading the output. Then, the thought entered my head that I should marry Sally. Objections just didn't register. We're too young ... I'm not even out of school ... we can't afford it ... where will we live ... what will our parents say ... none of these things could hop a ride on the runaway train unleashed in my mind. It just made sense. She was the one. Everything would work out. Trust me.

When I proposed, Sally accepted without reservation or hesitation but she didn't go all gaga on me. It was almost like she had reached the same conclusion and knew this was coming. She wasn't a mind reader but she was awfully perceptive. Usually, there is a lot of joy and celebration that accompanies such an announcement but we faced somewhat of an onslaught of well-intentioned reason right out of the gate. Our parents pointed out the obvious; our youth, meager income, etc. They oozed worries ... how could I be married, work and finish my education ... what kind of bleak future were we sentencing ourselves to ... how could such a premature marriage stand the test of time? We were just kids! They enlisted friends, relatives and even our pastor to create an irresistible force to change our minds or at least slow us down. But this juggernaut of logic ran out of steam rapidly and plunged like Icarus with melted wings. There was just something about our faith, resolve and precociousness that convinced everyone we could not be swayed or deterred. Worries may have remained but were overwhelmed by the tide of good feelings we all shared that year as attention shifted to wedding preparations.

As for Sally and me, it was not as though we

didn't hear the concerns of others or sometimes entertain them ourselves. But we shared a much stronger feeling, based on faith, that this was meant to be … that it was all part of God's plan for us. I had not stopped searching for my exact purpose in life but learned how to take a much more measured approach. Maybe it was the maturation process or Sally's influence but I began to accept that we might not receive point-by-point Map Quest directions from God. We knew that we had a path to follow, one with milestones we'd recognize along the way, but would have to stay the course and trust God to lead us to our final destination in his due time. Exactly where the rails led beyond the horizon was not clear but we were definitely on the right track. This approach suited us to a T, yes to the very jot and tittle. Life was like a delicious, succulent, flavorful, crispy-skinned grilled sausage; it's best savored without knowing the exact ingredients.

Chapter 7

It's a Wonderful Life, Granby

Unlike George Bailey, it didn't take a cosmic interruption for me to realize what a wonderful life we enjoyed over the next thirty five years after our marriage. They said it wouldn't last. I guess we fooled them. Sometimes you just have a hunch. Ours was validated in a lot of ways not the least of which was the fact that I never experienced another seizure after our engagement. Some folks just grow out of epilepsy. Maybe Sally's super-charged kisses jolted my wires straight. Most likely, God decided I no longer needed my thorn in the flesh to keep me on the straight and narrow. In any case, things just had a way of working out for the best for us. Sally worked full time and I was able to manage about thirty hours a week at Dirk's. She didn't mind the sacrifice and, in some ways, preferred the real world to more formal schooling. Always thinking ahead, she had other plans in mind, such as a family. We didn't make much but we were able to afford our own tiny apartment just off campus and seemed to have everything we needed and then some. I graduated from college on time, with honors, no less. Years later, I even went back for a graduate degree at night.

Once out of school, I started lower than whale dung but was eager to climb the corporate ladder. As far as gifts go, I found out that I had a pretty good head for business. That along with youthful energy, natural competitiveness and a high revving internal drive motor led to success. In 1979, four years after our marriage, we bought a small house and had our first child, a boy, Baker Paulson II affectionately known as Twice Baked or TB for short. Family responsibility just added more fuel to the competitive fire in my belly. I had a voracious appetite for more responsibility and the perks that came with it. But it was not so much the money we were after but more so the peace and security and sense of accomplishment. If it were just about money, we would have been like most of our friends with dual careers being first priority. Or better yet, we would have been DINKs … double income, no kids. That didn't fit our mindset. I became the primary breadwinner and Sally *worked* as a stay at home mom. Note the emphasis on work. I know from experience that it takes a special gift in terms of patience, endless energy, dedication and plenty of smarts to run a household and raise children. Sally was a natural. For a number of years, Sally stayed at home exclusively but as the kids got older she went back to work part-time to maintain that connection with the outside, adult world. Part-time is not ideal for making money but it does wonders for the sanity. As for me, I used our chosen circumstances as motivation. I felt I had to achieve more, get a little further ahead than the next guy or gal to overcome the fiscal disadvantage of being a single income family.

61

I changed firms a couple of times along the way and we moved twice before settling down into our current neighborhood, our *final resting place*. Each decision was driven by that good feeling, by trust rather than some hard edged, highly analytical process. When you have life by the tail with a downhill pull, you just go with the flow. Or again, more accurately, if God's in your corner, how can you lose? I always felt we led a charmed life, not out of piety but grace. No, I certainly was no saint. You can fool others but you can't fool yourself. Sometimes I felt aptly named, Paul's-son, Chief of Sinners. I realized just how rotten I could be at times, how shameful my thoughts and the venom that could spew from my tongue. Yet, there I was with blessings more numerous than my countless sins. I was careful to never ask God for what I deserved for I knew better. Even the afflictions, troubles and tribulations we suffered seemed to work out for the best in the end, my epilepsy included. In spite of being unworthy, I never felt guilty about our good fortune. We may not have fully grasped God's grace, his undeserved love, but we were thankful nonetheless. The only thing I couldn't shake was a sense of obligation since, certainly, God had something in mind for these gifts other than my own pleasure. This always brought the parable of the unfaithful steward to mind.

Ours was a somewhat unspectacular existence which allowed us to enjoy the best things, simple things in life. Our family grew and we watched as babies grew to be young adults. We reveled in all the mundane yet fascinating things such a journey has to offer ... baptisms, pee wee football, Little League, dance & gymnastic lessons, school plays, birthday parties, family vacations, anniversaries, confirmations, high school sports, final exams, graduations and weddings. Outside the family circle there was work, functions, church activities, volunteering and relationships with friends, relatives and neighbors. Then there were the nuisances, detours, pains, disappointments, failures and downright tragedies that keep us grounded ... skinned knees, measles, temper tantrums, missed promotions, illnesses, accidents, conflicts, arguments, break ups, old age, hospitals and funerals. At the heart of it all was that rock solid, special bond that Sally and I shared.

I never made it to the top rung, no not even close. But I had a great run and marveled how far we had come from such humble beginnings. Besides a six figure salary, we enjoyed a generous 401k, what today would be called a Cadillac health care plan, performance based pay and something called a defined benefit pension which is pretty much extinct nowadays. We weren't filthy rich but these things, bundled together and then combined with a sensible if not quite frugal lifestyle; put us in solid financial shape, so much so that I was able to retire early at fifty five. It was a good thing too since I and many others fell victim to the

Great Recession of 2008-2010. Lots of folks were consumed with the thought of early retirement but it was just a pipe dream. For me, it was reality. I had made it to the Promised Land! Be careful what you wish for.

Unless you have hobbies, too much free time can be more of a curse than a blessing. With mercurial speed, I became stir crazy and actually missed the *salt mine* I had worked so hard to escape. Questions of purpose came bubbling to the surface again. For all those years, I had been content with chasing the next mile marker on the highways of family, career, church involvement and community service. I had always found deeper meaning in a common thread that ran through all these aspects of my life, a devotion to the truth. Long ago, in the throes of purposelessness, I had a Martin Luther moment. You may remember how the great reformer was often pictured in front of his Bible with Romans 1:17 illuminated, "The just shall live by faith." That one brief passage changed his life completely and helped him to shake the world's very foundation. My moment was not nearly as dramatic but just as personally meaningful to me. I could still see the words of John 8:31-32 jumping off the page of my Bible as though backlit by some kind of blinking LED display ... "If ye continue in my word, then are ye my disciples indeed; and ye shall know the truth, and the truth shall make you free." From that point forward, I always tried to tackle life's many conundrums with the truth by going to the source. If nothing else, it provided me with edification and guidance, a clearer sense of purpose. I also like to think that it brought something valuable to the other lives I was privileged to touch. Some people resented the truth and unfairly labeled me judgmental but others, truth seekers in their own right, sought me out occasionally.

Now I was at a crossroads again. Though troubled by my circumstances, I was in a much better position to deal with them at this stage of life. Growing old does have some benefits. Unlike in my youth, I didn't hesitate to turn to God in prayer as my first rather than last option. I poured my heart out proclaiming, certainly there had to be more than this. My life couldn't be about idling away the time while living off the fruit of the harvest. I turned everything over to God and asked for his guidance, "please light my path again and show me the way ... please keep me on the right track ... give me the privilege of serving you in whatever new way pleases you ... thy will be done." No, I wasn't about to ask for specifics. I knew better than that. It didn't take long to get an answer, and a very specific one. Soon thereafter, we received the good news that our first grandchild was on the way. What fun we had with TB and his wife Sara in suggesting names for him or her. Paul III was eliminated early on as too pretentious ... Thrice Baked just didn't strike a chord. Some proposed names were very thoughtful but others were just plain goofy, intended to get their goats. What comes around goes around. Eventually the tables were turned and it was time to pick a nickname for grandma and grandpa. At forty seven and forty nine, Sally and I thought we were much too young for this. They only rubbed it in harder. Of course, being a former Spaz, I was not too fond of nicknames anyway. It couldn't be avoided so I acquiesced. I thought the most sensible suggestion was "Grandpa B" to distinguish me from Sara's father. Over time, this would be abbreviated to Granby. I was amazed when I realized, all those years ago, that I had become a boyfriend. I was no less taken aback by this. I was a grandpa, imagine that … Granby. What a life!

BOOK TWO

IKE

Chapter 8

Granby's Great Commission

I remember the excitement when the ultrasound revealed it was a boy. Soon after, a name was locked in. He would be Isaac, nickname Ike. As the Granby, I approved. Isaac was a solid, biblical name and Ike was a perfect nickname. It sounded tough, something for a real boy's boy; a good name for a football player, maybe a QB, or perhaps a volleyball player, Ike the Spike. Once that little booger arrived, there would be plenty to keep me occupied. In some ways, it seemed like someone had just hit replay on my life's greatest hits. Would the cycle repeat itself with the same familiar milestones? In some respects, yes, but something told me being a grandparent would be a very different gig.

We had six months to prepare. For me, there was only so much to do so I couldn't help but delve further into that age old question, "Why am I here?" I had plenty of free time so why not try my hand at being an amateur philosopher for a while and finally nut down the meaning of life? I'd while away the hours studying and then sharing my pearls of wisdom with unsuspecting victims, anyone that would listen. The pay sucked but the fringe benefits were great. For example, I could go to work in my BVDs if I wanted. The hours were good and the work was easy on the back. I could even substitute a hot tub for a cubicle and drink a few beers to get the juices flowing. Lucky for me, I heard that pizza was a favorite food of philosophers too.

My philosophy was rooted in theology by necessity. I turned to my familiar Bible which is unique among all books. No matter how many times you read it, it never gets dull and you always gain some new insight. This happened again one night as I was finishing up the Gospel of St. Matthew for the umpteenth time. If I were a betting man, I might liken the experience to a sleepy, nearly comatose gambler who finally hits the jackpot after robotically dropping buckets of nickels into a slot machine into the wee hours of the morning. I wasn't comatose but my eyelids were getting a little heavy and the familiar words of this tome were not registering with full clarity. Then, in closing, I perused verses 28:19-20, "Go ye therefore, and teach all nations, baptizing them in the name of the Father, and of the Son, and of the Holy Ghost: Teaching them to observe all things whatsoever I have commanded you: and, lo, I am with you always, even unto the end of the world. Amen." Somewhere a switch clicked and it hit me. Yes, the Great Commission was meant for everyone. That included me.

Now, it's not like I hadn't evangelized before. I did my share of spreading the gospel or witnessing as it's known in Christian circles. In my own, low key, informal way, I had shared the Good News many times.

69

What did this new revelation mean? Did God give me financial security and oodles of free time so that I could take it to another level? Should I enroll in the seminary and study to become a pastor? No, I definitely knew I lacked the patience and temperament for such a calling and my past was not what you'd call chaste. No, the baptizing thing was out except for maybe special emergencies.

Perhaps I should get involved in a formal program, something like Dialogue Evangelism. With DE, you go with a group, knock on doors and conduct a somewhat structured conversation around two key questions: 1) If you died today would you go to heaven and 2) if you were face-to-face with God and he asked why he should let you into his heaven, what would you say? No, while DE was excellent, I worked better alone and liked to have a free flowing dialogue that could adapt to anyone's peculiar circumstances and questions. How about classroom teaching? No, that would also be too structured and I didn't want to follow someone else's curriculum or rules of engagement. What then, why was God flashing this neon light in front of me? I read the passage over and over and then it finally dawned on me. I had missed something very important in this oh so familiar Great Commission passage. Most Christians gloss over or simply omit "teaching them to observe all things whatsoever I have commanded you." As an amateur philosopher, I decided to partake in a bit of theological work and did a web search. As I mined deeper, I tip toed into something called exegesis and hermeneutics, fancy words that mean you interpret the Bible by getting into the ancient texts, autographs where possible, in the original languages. Not having a clue about Hebrew or Greek was no problem thanks to the modern wonders of the internet.

What I found was fascinating. These words were much stronger than they appeared in the King's English. To observe actually meant to jealously and carefully protect God's biblical teachings or doctrines by figuratively building a hedge of thorns around them. This made perfect sense to me in the context of John 8:31-32 and its advice to seek the truth in God's word. I could now see God's command to spread the Good News, baptize and make disciples in a whole new light. God was telling us that, in doing so, in witnessing, we also had a very serious obligation to keep his entire truth in mind, not to pick and choose what suited us. This was such an important element that he wanted us to guard and protect the truth against all false, soul destroying notions.

So what did this mean for me? I think it meant God wanted me to continue witnessing in my own way, reaching out to others informally as opportunities arose. But he wanted me to pay particular attention to speaking the truth, not being judgmental but with

71

humility, speaking the truth in love. I knew from experience that this could be a tough assignment. Sometimes the truth can be very unpopular. Sometimes they kill the messenger. But, I realized too that God had equipped me well for the task. Over the years, I had accumulated a good knowledge and understanding of biblical doctrine, not just a head knowledge but comprehension as well, at least in laymen's terms. Also, I had mellowed with age to the point where I could share and stand my ground without being an argumentative firebrand.

Having this sense of God's purpose for me, I felt reinvigorated but not sure where to start. I went back to what works, I prayed and asked God for opportunities to witness. Isn't it funny how quickly prayers are answered when they conform to God's will rather than our own? It was also amusing how directly he responded sometimes. For example, while packing for a flight to New York to visit our other son, DB (Notice a trend?), I prayed that God would use this trip to help me reach out to someone in need. He dropped this one in my lap before we even touched down at LaGuardia. I was killing time reading Genesis, which is a great way to get your bearings straight. Halfway through the flight, I was nearly finished, in chapter 49. I hadn't paid much attention to the fellow seated next to me, respecting his privacy and valuing mine. He too was reading, some odd looking, old book. He suddenly broke the silence, startling me a bit, "What is that you're reading" he said knowing very well it was the Bible.

I advised him politely and reciprocated with, "and you?" It turns out he was reading the Jewish Pentateuch, the first five books of Moses in the Old Testament, and, almost eerily was in chapter 49 of Genesis. We both marveled at the coincidence and he struck up a conversation.

It turns out he was a troubled soul, having certain doubts about his faith, searching for answers. He was most disillusioned by a fruitless, seemingly hopeless search for the coming Messiah. It was apparent from the discussion he was very intelligent, insightful and well read. The Old Testament prophecies just didn't add up, they pointed to so many dead ends for him. He poured out his frustrations to me, a total stranger. God surely equipped me for the task that day. All I did was point to verse 10 in my Bible and then turned the same digit to that identical verse on the open page in his Pentateuch, "The scepter shall not depart from Judah ... until Shiloh come." His education and instruction were apparent in the ensuing conversation. He accepted that the scepter represented Jewish rule and Shiloh the promised Messiah. He filled in the gaps of history to conclude that the Messiah had to have come long ago before Jewish self-determination was supplanted by Rome in 70 A. D. That led to a wonderful, enlightening discussion of the more than three hundred and sixty marks in the Old Testament pointing to the true Messiah, Jesus. I'm not sure what happened to that man and his personal search for the truth but it was an eye opening, very fulfilling experience for me. God blessed me with many others and the next six months passed quickly.

Chapter 9

Chip Off the Old Block

Isaac Baker Paulson was born on Good Friday in 2003. It was one of the best Good Fridays ever. I'm sure that the words, "It is finished" took on a whole, new meaning for Sara. By all appearances, Ike was a perfectly healthy, bouncing baby boy. It was a joyous time. He took center stage and gave me and Sally a whole new outlook on life. Of course, there were a few dandelions among the daffodils and posies. It had been so long, I had forgotten about how bad regurgitated formula smelled not to mention the explosive, volcanic bowel movements that sometimes diapers simply can't contain. But you take the good with the bad and the former outweighed the latter by a prohibitive margin. It's incredible how much impact one little life can have on so many others. Ike was a game-changer from the get-go, especially for me. I had already re-established my purpose, my general calling to provide a faithful and truthful witness, wherever possible. But this, for the first time, gave me something very specific and immediate to cling to.

From early on, I had a special bond with Ike. I had time to spare and was more than happy to share it with him. I enjoyed providing child care for him. It afforded me the opportunity to do more than feed him and change diapers. As he grew and developed, I was able to influence and guide him. There were boundaries, of course. I didn't want to be an overbearing, meddling grandfather. But I knew I could give him a firm foundation that no child care center could ever construct. The older he got, the more clear it became that Ike was a chip off the old block, one generation removed. It tickled me that he even looked like me. There was an amazing likeness when you compared him to my old baby pictures.

One thing had not changed from when we had raised our own children. I was anxious to get past the baby stage. As Ike got to the point of walking, then talking and finally conversing, it delighted me to no end. I was like the Skipper with his little buddy. But Ike was no bumbling dunce like Gilligan. He was smarter than a tack, more than the whole box. The apple may not fall far from the tree but this one had rolled quite a ways from the trunk. Even at three and four years old, I could tell that he possessed an unusual intellect unlike me or anyone else in our family. Sometimes I called him Ikestein in jest and wonder. He was so inquisitive with a curiosity that would put the cat to shame. Somehow his mind could grasp complex concepts that seemed impossible for someone so young. At the age of five he was already able to carry on a very meaningful conversation. When he was born, images danced in my head of Granby and Ike tossing the football or pitching and batting. I had fantasized about me grooming the next Stan the Man, Pistol Pete, Hammering Hank, Bullet

Bob Hayes or Dandy Don Meredith. Sure, we went to the park and played catch, hit the swings or climbed the jungle gym. We followed the Cardinals and went down to Busch Stadium together or caught the Rams on the tube. Our favorite player was Kurt Warner. I told Ike about my favorite player in the old days of the Big Red. I explained how the Wildcat, Larry Wilson, invented the safety blitz and one time even intercepted a pass against the Steelers with both of his broken hands in casts. But that was just a pleasant diversion for us. It helped to form a bond but I quickly gave up on any thoughts of glory on the diamond or grid iron grandeur. It's not that Ike was uncoordinated or lacked athletic skills. It was crystal clear that he had other gifts that were so compelling they overshadowed anything else.

He wasn't at all nerdy but Ike could be a real egg head. Sometimes he made me feel like a block head rather than the source of the chip. But there were enough other similarities that I certainly couldn't deny him. He was the apple of my eye and a chip off the old block. Unfortunately, tragically, in a way that rent my heart in two, we found out at the age of six that he was more of a chip off the old block than we preferred. Ike, you see, was an epileptic too.

Chapter 10

Sinking Sand

Life is an extremely fragile thing. How quickly circumstances can change completely. In the twinkling of an eye, my world was turned upside down. We were all consumed by it as if a precious page had been ripped from our family photo album. I couldn't contain a flash of anger against God, try as I might. Of all things, why Lord, why would you let this happen to Ike? Anything but this! Then I blamed myself too thinking I should have put an end to my wretched bloodline and fatally flawed gene pool long ago. I knew deep down this was irrational, flat out wrong, and I tried to stamp out these insidious brush fires but as soon as I snuffed one flame another sprang forth as if by spontaneous combustion. My will power failed so I tried leaning harder on my faith and a familiar hymn came to mind: My Hope is built on Nothing Less. Its powerful refrain echoed in my head, "On Christ the solid rock I stand, all other ground is sinking sand." But instead of comfort and assurance, all I could see was the sinking, claustrophobic sand.

Nearer My Lord to Thee was a more appropriate hymn. Recently, I had built my world around Ike but now felt useless, utterly powerless to help him or myself. God was not punishing me, of that I was certain. But why do this, why did it have to include Ike? Then it finally dawned on me that, perhaps, God

wanted to draw me closer to him. I turned to The Book
for answers. Job, faithful Job had suffered more, much
more, losing everything; wife, children, possessions and
even his health. Every biblical hero whose life I
recounted had some kind of malady or misfortune.
None had been spared. And my namesake, that great
evangelistic apostle, Paul, had suffered mightily, vastly
beyond any capacity of mine, but was undeterred.
Reading through Paul's letter to the church at Corinth,
these words hit home, "And he said unto me, my grace
is sufficient for thee: for my strength is made perfect in
weakness. Most gladly therefore will I rather glory in my
infirmities, that the power of Christ may rest upon me."
Those words kept the sinking sand from engulfing me
like they would have in years gone by. Those words and
something else kept me from being swamped. I couldn't
afford to wallow in self-pity, Ike needed me now.

Initially, Ike's situation seemed more tenuous
than mine had ever been. His seizures were unleashed
with a fury that frightened me. They seemed to possess
him with the strength of a legion of demons bent on his
destruction. If my wires had been crossed, his whole
system must have been infested with filthy gremlins. His
episodes were at least twice as frequent as mine at
their peak. Could his little body stand the wear and
tear? Panic nearly set in when I saw Ike wracked with
convulsions and just wanted to give in but couldn't.
Whenever it seemed I might lose control, I turned to

God in prayer and asked him to take up my burden. I prayed for understanding and guidance ... "Dear Lord, please show me the way out and please reveal the silver lining again."

God gave me a very practical escape route this time. First, I committed the bulk of my time to research and finding the best medical care possible. Simultaneously, I spent most of the remaining time leading a classroom of one. It's not that we objected to public education but it was better for Ike to stay at home and avoid being subjected to gawking and whispers. With my unique perspective, I was able to normalize Ike's situation as much as possible. Also, with the training I was receiving, I was able to provide safe care during his spells. I knew how to restrain him without harm, how to safely ensure a clear breathing passage and how to vigilantly maintain his pharmacological regimen. Most importantly of all, I had the personal experience and understanding necessary to welcome him back calmly from those violent hijackings in a way that would make him feel safe, secure, normal, accepted and loved.

As it turned out, there was a silver lining in this cloud. In all honesty, I had to admit that the special bond Ike and I shared had been imperceptibly squeezing God out of our own little world through my neglect and self-indulgence. But now, with the Gorilla Glue of his infirmity, our relationship grew even stronger but had plenty of room for Christ right there in the middle of us. Ike's home schooling with me, while unorthodox, was a blessing too. He received personalized attention and a depth of study the public school environment could never have provided. And speaking not just as a proud grandpa but a realist, Ike truly was gifted. The custom fitted education I tailored for him helped him to flourish in a way that wouldn't have happened with some off the rack outfit.

God truly does work in mysterious ways. Who would have guessed that this horrible affliction would result in an even better, richer relationship between Ike and me? This was the case not just for us but the whole family. The pressure on TB and Sara eased knowing that I was there for Ike rather than having to rely on detached outside professionals. They were able to concentrate appropriately on Ike, their careers and other responsibilities and sincerely appreciated the security and balance I was able to afford them. Sally was at peace too. Being the saint that she was, always thinking more about others than herself, she was happy because she saw that I was happy again. She stopped worrying about Ike and me so much and our relationship returned to its normal, wonderful self. Yes, we used that Gorilla Glue to put the torn page back into the family album, stronger than ever.

Let's be real though. That's not the end of the story; we didn't live happily ever after. We enjoyed good times mostly but they were punctuated by episodes, ugly, frightening episodes. Thankfully, most of the seizures occurred when Ike and I were alone. Although I couldn't hide the facts from Sally, TB and Sara for medical reasons as well as maintaining a clear conscience, I chronicled the attacks in an innocuous, almost laissez faire manner being careful not to let my own deep concerns show through. It wasn't healthy to keep this inside of myself but it couldn't be avoided. My own bouts with epilepsy were bad but not what I would call dangerous. I don't recall pain or really any sensation other than waking up from a deep sleep like coming out of anesthesia. My pain was more psychological than anything with embarrassment and isolation being my main tormentors. With Ike it was different. There was more awareness if not outright physical pain and his attacks were much more violent and frenzied. I feared for his well-being, with good reason.

Chapter 11

Where's Emmett?

The good times were very good and Ike and I enjoyed them immensely. But Damocles' sword was always overhead bringing with it a foreboding tension beneath the surface. Milton Bradley made a bundle off of this very emotion with the classic Time Bomb game. Sally, being a natural born hoarder, still had her family's Time Bomb from back in the '60s. I couldn't help but laugh out loud at the irony of her breaking out this ancient treasure for a recent night of family fun; each of us passing the ticking bomb frantically while trying to avoid being the one to absorb the pending blast. MB was a sadistic sick-o! Here's an example of just how brilliant Ike's little mind was at age six; the way he could piece things together. It was a few days after playing Time Bomb and, based on the pattern of past experience, probably getting close to the next epileptic fit. Ike turned to me and said, matter of fact, "Granby, I feel like we're playing Time Bomb but this time it's not fun. I know I'll be holding the bomb when it goes off." I couldn't have said it better.

When school was out, so to speak, I immersed myself in finding a cure. I didn't neglect God, no, I prayed constantly. But I knew that God worked through means and wouldn't want me to neglect all of the great advances that had been made in medicine. Epilepsy, much like autism, was still too much of a mystery to the medical profession. In a way, it was also like cancer in that there were so many variants it was next to impossible to nail down a single treatment, let alone a cure. Based on his age and symptoms, Ike's was somewhat of a rare case. That was good and bad with the good being that he was an attractive subject for advanced researchers. My job, I felt, with TB's and Sara's blessings, was to shepherd him through this maze of technology, leaving no safe avenue unexplored while avoiding dangerous alleys and dead ends. We met with a parade of specialists that year and sifted through every possible treatment to achieve the right balance between promising and risky ... pharmacological, surgical, diet, electrical stimulation, avoidance therapy, service dogs, devices, implantations, you name it. We even explored one of the latest technologies, gamma radiation, but, being of my generation, I couldn't help but think of David Banner; of turning Ike into some kind of little green hulk.

This was not easy for me. In spite of endless conversations with specialists and incessant, late night web crawls to educate myself, I was out of my league. Some of it was easy enough to understand and many of the doctors had a great knack for explaining the complex in simple terms. But much of it was so far out there that even the best medical minds were just speculating. There were just so many options to consider but everything was somehow intertwined. Some procedures might compliment others while some seemed diametrically opposed. We not only had to do constant risk-reward analyses but also had to ponder the linkage or disconnects between treatments. It was a real can of worms and made my head want to explode at times.

It was also tough on Ike; seeing the doctors, answering questions over and over, being pricked, poked and analyzed. It made matters worse knowing that, with his keen awareness and power of perception, Ike was not oblivious to the situation like most kids would have been. He knew this was risky business and picked up on my sense of frustration with the whole thing. Ike was amazing though; a real trooper. He didn't get frustrated or impatient. On one particularly difficult day when my patience was as thin as flies' wings, Ike astounded me by quoting one of his favorite scripture passages, "Granby, you know, with God all things are possible." Wow, teacher became pupil. This was a great reminder not to put too much trust in ourselves or anyone else, including physicians, or even that *almighty god*, technology.

There was a common theme among all the doctors. To a person, they were in agreement that we were in uncharted territory. There were no quick fixes or sure things. Our best allies would be time and alchemy. That is to say, they felt there could be a benefit of a cumulative effect of the treatments over time. As for alchemy, call it hocus pocus or wishful thinking as it struck me but they all held out hope, however slim, that, by chance, just the right combination of medical marvels might fall into place to achieve the right effect for Ike. That didn't do much to slake my thirst for a cure. I realized they were only human and we were dealing with an experimental realm here but my exasperation mounted nevertheless. "Where's Emmett when you need him?" I said to myself, sarcastically. You remember Emmett Clark from the Andy Griffith Show, don't you? He was Mr. Fix-it of Mayberry. He could fix anything, from a kitchen clock to a toaster to a tea kettle. If I could only find Emmett's shop, everything would be okay.

As the year wore on and this seemingly endless saga continued, I remembered Ike's good example and constantly turned back to God for guidance and strength. It made me think of that poem about Footprints in the Sand where there were two sets of tracks in the sand during good times, one for the traveler and the other for his companion, Jesus. He looked back to see only one set of tracks during the trying times only to think he'd been abandoned by God but finally learned that it was at those most difficult times the single set of tracks represented Christ carrying him. This kept me going, confident and full of faith in spite of our depressing circumstances. There's another thing you learn when you hang around doctor's offices, clinics and hospitals enough; you don't have it so bad after all. Our travails paled in comparison to the agony of many others. I felt down-right ashamed of my ungrateful self when I witnessed the startling plights of other children we encountered. But I was also uplifted by the dignity, courage and faith some of them exhibited in the face of such abject suffering. My heart would have vacated my chest to go out to them had it been possible. That aside, I included them and their parents in my prayers along with Ike. For us and them, it was a time to be carried; I was learning more and more to turn things over to God when I reached my limits, I was learning to listen to God's word from Peter, "Casting all your care upon him; for he cares for you." I whispered under my breath, "I forgive you Emmett." "Who's Emmett?" Ike wondered.

Chapter 12

Pop's Monkey Wrench

Heirlooms are usually the stuff of gold watches, ancestral crests, photo albums, old family Bibles or such. Mine was an anachronistic, greasy, crud caked crescent wrench handed down from my grandfather, Pop. We didn't call it a crescent or adjustable wrench though, no, that was too elegant; it was just a plain, old monkey wrench. Sure, I had accumulated all the modern accoutrements in my basement workshop; cordless drills, a hundred piece socket set, an all-in-one reciprocating screw driver, just about everything a hack like me might need, including a ratchet-style adjustable wrench that I never used. Why not, you ask? Yes, it was the perfect wrench combining all the ease of a crescent wrench with the utility of a socket wrench. But it just didn't suit me; I could never get the hang of it. No, I preferred my Pop's monkey wrench.

One time, with a metal bar through the hole in the lower end for extra leverage, the excessive torque caused it to crack mid-way across the center of the handle grip. Being determined not to allow this cherished treasure to be cast onto the scrap heap, I spent three times the worth of a new wrench to have a welder repair it. That brush with near disaster did not deter me. This was a working heirloom. It wasn't my tool of choice because of sentimental value alone.

Although it bore the scars of mending and was behind the times, grimy and somewhat limited, it was still useful to me. It fit me like a glove and was an extension of my arm; in my hand it could work wonders I could never achieve with state of the art implements. TB would give it to Ike one day.

Me and my star pupil were getting ready to start one of his favorite exercises one day, Heroes of the Bible we termed it. Once a week or so, we would pick out a biblical character, study their life and accomplishments and try to relate it to contemporary times. As the source of truth, the Bible cannot concoct fanciful super heroes. Oh, with God's help, they often see their way to miraculous, supernatural achievements. But the truth bares all, like HDTV, revealing the unvarnished blemishes of the reality and humanity of these historical figures. One of the most gripping aspects of these ancient accounts is how God so often used such ordinary people to accomplish such extraordinary outcomes. Just as I was ready to launch into the next section, Ike threw me for a loop, "Granby, why did God make epileptics like you and me?" Talk about getting off course! What could I say? I resisted getting into some kind of too-deep theological dialogue of how God created a good, perfect world but our sin corrupted it all and left us with an imperfect, devolving earth destined for destruction and rebirth.

I didn't want to get into matters of justice,

death and redemption just then. Satan, sin, consequences, atonement and salvation were topics for another time. As bright as he was, the doctrine of election would have been way over Ike's head, mine too. I didn't even want to get side tracked by explaining that God didn't intend for us to be epileptics or suffer any of the other terrible things that regularly happen in our world. No, I wanted to answer Ike as simply and directly as possible, "Ike, sometimes God delights in using broken tools, just like me with my monkey wrench." Smart as a whip, Ike latched onto the idea in a flash, "Do you mean like Moses?"

We traveled back to about 1350 B. C. and discussed Moses, the great law giver, immortalized by Cecil B. DeMille and Charlton Heston, mightily parting the Red Sea. Ike knew all about his super human feats so I took pains to focus on his failings and weaknesses, his humble beginnings and how it was God who charted his unlikely course away from infant death at Pharaoh's hand in a basket down the Nile all the way to great power in Egypt. We didn't shy away from the sinfulness of the murderous rage he succumbed to that necessitated fleeing to Midian and adopting the simple life of tending to Jethro's flocks. When it came time for God's great calling to Moses from the burning bush, he didn't don a cape and nobly go up, up and away to confront the Egyptian slave masters. He was so scared he wouldn't even look toward God. In so many words he said "Why me, Lord, I've got terrible communication skills, I think it would be best if you just sent someone else." God was not swayed, of course, but sent Aaron along for moral support, knowing how frail Moses was then. Buoyed by the Lord, he defied Pharaoh and led his people out of captivity and beat all the odds with that magnificent assist from the Lord at the Red Sea.

God blessed this once timid servant with such a faith that he was able to lead his people through forty years in the wilderness to the brink of the Promised Land. Along the way, Moses' imperfections were revealed time and again. After receiving the Ten Commandments from God on Mount Sinai, Moses once again gave into anger and dashed the stone tables to pieces upon seeing the idolatrous golden calf. God covered for Moses and provided them with the law a second time. Moses did not display a righteous, sinless anger like Christ did in the Temple with the money changers. No, he sometimes gave into blind outbursts of fury. For the most part though, Moses displayed incredible faith and patience with the fickle people of Israel and their repeated declines into idolatry and sinfulness. The Israelites unfaithfulness would be their undoing and eventually a whole generation was lost, exiled by God in the wilderness, never to see the Promised Land. Near the end, Moses had a lapse of faith when he failed to follow God's specific instructions to command the rock to bring forth water for the

Israelites. He offered up a question rather than a command and smote the rock with his staff to release the water. It seemed like such a minor infraction, to Ike too, but I explained that, at one hundred twenty years of age and after all the faith building he had been through, God expected more from his servant, Moses. This cost him dearly as he was allowed to see but not enter into Canaan with the children of Israel. Yes, Moses, the great prophet, deliverer and law giver was human, just like us.

From there, Ike and I spent nearly the entire day on this special lesson. This was one of the beauties of home schooling. When great, very pertinent learning opportunities arose, we could just go with the flow. We talked about mighty Samson and the legendary strength he used to kill lions with his bare hands or the leagues of Philistines he defeated single handedly. Ike knew all about treacherous Delilah and the shorn mane that brought Samson's downfall. It was important that Ike learn there was nothing magical about Samson's long hair. It was a testimony to his faithfulness but God was the real source of his strength. His downfall was not the loss of his hair but rather his unfaithfulness to God, moral weakness and lust for devilish Delilah. I made it a key point to stress how Samson's subsequent afflictions and trials, the gouging of his eyes and slavish hard labor in the grinding mill turned out to be great spiritual blessings because they drew him back to God and regenerated his faith. I tried my best to explain that the re-growth of his flowing locks possessed no magic but was a visible sign of his faith's restoration. Ike, I think in his own way, was able to comprehend that it was Samson's reconciliation with God, his reconnection to his true power source, that helped him to regain such strength that he could move the immense columns and bring Dagon's Temple crashing down upon the evil Philistines.

Onto King David we galloped, that inspired writer of so many of God's beautiful psalms. This was a bearer of the promise, the great king from whom Jesus himself later descended, who won battle upon battle and forged Israel into a formidable and prosperous nation, who begat Solomon the king of the golden age. Forget about Rocky Balboa. Here was the original underdog. The son of Jesse, a mere shepherd boy, young David went to supply Israel's troops, including his older brothers, as they assembled for battle against the hated Philistines. There, a literal giant, Goliath of Gath, standing nine feet and eight inches tall with a coat of armor weighing one hundred fifty pounds and an enormous spear with its head alone at nearly twenty pounds, taunted the Israelites to send forth one man for a winner take all battle to the death, as was sometimes the custom of the day. Needless to say, there were no takers, no suicidal fools among the ranks. David, rankled by the blasphemous ranting of the gargantuan heathen, stepped into the breach that Israel's battle tested veterans shunned. With one miraculous shot from his trusty leather sling, guided ever so meticulously by God to just the right vulnerable spot on his forehead, David felled Goliath and cut off his massive head, launching a legend in Israel and sending shock waves through Philistia. David was anointed by God to be the next king and, by God's providence, avoided evil King Saul's murderous intentions. What a life he led, oh how blessed by God was he.

But wait, he was also a miserable sinner like the rest of us. His most famous failing was brought on by his covetousness for beautiful Bathsheba, the wife of one of David's most loyal, trustworthy soldiers, Uriah. It started innocently enough when David spied from his rooftop the captivating Bathsheba bathing and then what a tangled web was woven. When David impregnated Bathsheba, he arranged for Uriah to come home from the battle front to create a ruse that the child was legitimate but, much to David's dismay, Uriah honored the military code of the time and did not take advantage of the situation. Not to be thwarted, the careful way that David cunningly plotted Uriah's death in battle against the Ammonites truly shows the evil depths that every one of us can descend to, even the very best of us. After the prophet Nathan brought David's sin to light, God was merciful in the sense that he let his sullied servant live to carry out the rest of his calling. But there were still consequences and the cost to David was great, in some ways much worse than his own death. His family life, which he cherished, was thenceforth often the source of great pain. David and Bathsheba lost that child to death after only seven days. Later, Absalom would die in revolt against his father and still later Adonijah earned a similar fate, thus making way for Solomon to reign. David's humanity, his

94

sinfulness, is best summed up by his own confession in Psalm 51; "For I acknowledge my transgressions: and my sin is ever before me. Against thee; thee only, have I sinned, and done this evil in thy sight: that thou might be justified when thou speaks, and be clear when thou judges. Behold, I was shaped in iniquity; and in sin did my mother conceive me." The best lesson from David, in that same Psalm, is repentance; "Create in me a clean heart, O God; and renew a right spirit within me. Cast me not away from thy presence; and take not thy holy spirit from me. Restore unto me the joy of thy salvation; and uphold me with thy free spirit. Then will I teach transgressors thy ways; and sinners shall be converted unto thee." God is faithful to forgive us.

How could we forget Isaac's dad, Abraham, the bearer of the promise and father of many nations? Now, you can't question his faith, right? I mean, he was even willing to sacrifice his beloved son, Isaac, if that's what the Lord required. Sorry, but he too was just a lowly sinner like the rest of us who accomplished great deeds by God's power rather than his own. Don't you remember when he failed to trust God that he could bless Abraham and Sarah with a son at ages one hundred and ninety respectively? Yes, Sarah even laughed disrespectfully at the notion. And thirteen years earlier, their lack of faith was so great that Sarah gave her Egyptian maid, Hagar, to her husband to bear them a child, Ishmael. Ike didn't like to hear how even Abraham was sinful but was delighted when I told him that Isaac probably showed even more faith than Abraham just before God's stay of execution at his sacrifice. I explained that, unlike most accounts, it was possible that Isaac was not a little boy after all but a

95

young man who could have easily resisted old Abraham if he had wanted.

Now Ike began to pepper me with challenges, "How about bold Peter?"

"Nope, he denied knowing Jesus three times. When the going got tough, the tough guy cursed and slunk away in bitter sobs of repentance."

"What about Jonah," he proposed "wasn't he faithful for three days in the belly of the whale?"

I retorted "Sorry buddy but God had to put him in that great fish because he was stubbornly refusing to embark on what he wanted Jonah to do." I explained Jonah's great hatred for the Assyrians, so much so that he didn't want to bring them the Good News about the coming Messiah and God's plan of salvation. At least that showed Jonah's faith in God's power to save even the vile, bloodthirsty Assyrians. Finally, Ike played his trump card and called upon our namesake to save our honor.

Has anyone ever served the Lord more faithfully than Paul? Is there another who can claim as many victories for God in the building of his kingdom of grace? Can anyone this side of the Son of Man claim to have suffered more in doing the Lord's bidding? Paul journeyed far and wide under incredibly harsh conditions to spread the word. There were no planes, trains and automobiles or Holiday Inns. He was tormented, mocked, threatened and persecuted, beaten, imprisoned, shipwrecked, violently lashed and eventually suffered a martyr's death. Yet Paul counted it all for joy and steadfastly declared "The sufferings of this present time are not worthy to be compared with the glory which shall be revealed in us." Paul spoke before commoners and kings alike. He possessed great gifts; a monstrous intellect, oratorical splendor like no other and a knowledge of the Old Testament laws and scriptures that was unrivaled. His inspired epistles brought countless thousands to faith over the ages. As he revealed in Romans 1:16, God's word contains real power, dynamite power in the original Greek (There goes that Herman Neutic fellow again!). And, I had to admit, I had personally felt the benefit of that power, many times, as I read Paul's letters. But, as beholden as I was to Paul, as much as I looked forward to chatting with him someday in heaven, I had to break the news to Ike that Paul was not just expressing false humility when he labeled himself the chief of sinners.

Paul, the erstwhile Saul, was perhaps the greatest example of God's use of broken tools. For all his great gifts, Saul had been a most despicable miscreant even though, in his own eyes, he thought he was doing God's work. He went far out of his way to persecute Christians and tirelessly attempted to squash the fledgling church. It was he who held the robes of the perpetrators at Stephen's martyrdom so they could get more velocity on their stone fastballs. When Saul met the risen Christ, he was on the road to Damascus in an attempt to spread his terror against the church further. I guess he was running out of innocent victims in Jerusalem. What a hard, stone cold, dark, black heart Saul possessed. His miraculous conversion, more than any other, shows that it is by God's power and not the will of man that faith is created in a human heart. This final lesson sunk in and deflated Ike a bit. Even Paul could not stand before God and claim any righteousness of his own. But, to put a little air under his wings, I talked about how God afflicted Paul with a thorn in the flesh, how that turned out to be a blessing to the great man even as unpleasant and unwanted as it was. It made for a great segue to parallel the epilepsy I had suffered and Ike was now battling. This really hit home with Ike and he began to realize that this was not a punishment but somehow would lead to blessings from God. He was greatly encouraged to see that there were no limitations on him or me; God truly does delight in using broken tools. Yes, we were broken tools. But nobody's perfect.

To wrap things up, we hit the fast forward button and talked about contemporary heroes. It was easy pickings. Ike didn't need a lot of help for this part. He watched the news too. You name it; baseball stars, football legends, movie icons, singers, doctors, educators, police, soldiers and even religious leaders. In every category, it was easy to find broken tools, some repentant, some not so much, just lots of crocodile tears. Then we turned to politicians and I gave up. It was much tougher to name a good one than the opposite. I hesitated to use the term broken tools on them. Somehow it seemed too good for their sort. It provided a great parallel though between ancients and us. We talked about the hypocrisy and utter injustice of having modern day tax cheats crafting the laws that squeeze tribute out of the rest of us ordinary citizens. With that as the back drop, Ike was able to see for the first time why Jesus was vilified for hanging out with a tax collector like Matthew. We surmised with a hearty laugh that even IRS employees could be saved. This had been a great day and the lessons learned would stick with us forever. Yes, I said us. I benefitted at least as much as Ike did that day.

Dead Mall

"You can't judge a book by its cover."

Bo Diddley

1962

BOOK THREE

WE'RE NOT IN KANSAS ANYMORE

Chapter 13

Funeral for an Old Friend

Outside the cozy confines of my home and other than COMO and just about any beach you can name, I think Northwest Plaza is probably my favorite place on earth. It's a mall in St. Louis County that, to put it mildly, has seen better days. It is so far gone that it's what they call a dead mall. That's retail parlance for malls with so few customers that store revenues cannot cover the lease fees required to sustain basic services like mall maintenance and security. NWP is a classic case with vacancy rates well above ninety percent and the lone anchor, "old faithful" Sears, attracting its business primarily from the street side rather than the mall entrance. You could demolish the whole complex and leave Sears standing alone and somehow it would still survive, I thought. The multiplex and free standing restaurants were distant memories and, more recently, the last of the food court purveyors had vacated the premises. Even the ubiquitous gold chain and jewelry kiosks were gone. I can't say that I miss them since I felt they were endemic to what had sapped the life from NWP. With the closing of the last true anchor, Macy's with its majestic, once futuristic rotunda, I could count the functioning stores on one hand and a finger; a plus size women's shop, an urban style shoe store, a kid's sport shoe & apparel store, a thrift store, a fitness center and a fix-it shop for shoes and clothing. I'm guessing that their leases were so onerous that it was better for them to remain open even though customers were as rare as humming birds in winter. Other than Mr. Fix-it who seemed to be the one proprietor benefitting from the lousy economy, we pitied the poor souls who manned these shops that were so many dying leaves waiting to finally drop to the ground. We hoped that most of these doomed clerks were college students who could at least kill the time with homework.

Each time another store closed, it was like losing a loved one. A slice of life, our lives, was being discarded like so much garbage. Who would preserve the memories? This always left me with mixed emotions. On the one hand, it brought a rush of good feelings as recollections popped up; something unusual that happened there, another time of life, a gift purchased for someone special at Christmas or for a birthday, or just hanging out with friends. Then there was always regret; the realization that those times were gone, never to be recaptured; our own mortality. This was certainly true when Dillard's, the once proud anchor first known as Stix, Baer & Fuller was reduced to a discount flea market before shuttering. But, I think I was hardest hit when Macy's, formerly Famous Barr, called it quits. For weeks, every time we passed by there I felt like I was attending a funeral for an old, dear friend.

There were a few other marginal signs of life. Somehow there was just enough traffic, parents with kids tagging along, to support three batteries of coin operated candy dispensers, one in each of the mall's three main wings. These glass globes must have been hermetically sealed to keep their treasures at least edible; sour cherry balls, gummy bears, jaw breakers and off-brand M&M's. The attraction of a twenty five cent respite from the kids still had a strong allure. During tax season, an accounting service would set up temporarily to take advantage of cheap space. Ironically, NWP seemed an appropriate place for this annual, cruel pilgrimage; death and taxes go together like a horse and carriage. The office tower still enjoyed a fair occupancy. Across the hallway from there, Senior Towne still plodded along although there never seemed to be many Townies out and about. Why would any self-respecting old codger want to spend time in such a dreary, depressing, uninhabited old place? It reminded me of the desolate elephant's grave yard from the old Tarzan movies, except that there was no redeeming feature like a mother lode of ivory treasure. I mean, what's there to do if you can't at least talk or people watch? No, if you weren't too old to move about, even at a snail's pace, you came to the mall for one primary reason, to walk. Later, I would come to find that there was some very special, buried treasure in Senior Towne. For now, my eyesight was clouded by my own bias. As is usually the case, my prejudice was based on fear; my fear of growing old and decrepit. Don't rush to judgment until you've walked a mile in someone else's shoes. I thought, *as Tarzan might say, "Ungawa!"*

That, and the memories, brought Sally and me there regularly, especially when the weather didn't permit the lakeside, river trail or neighborhood strolls we enjoyed so much. If nothing else, a dead mall was custom made for walking; never wet, muddy, too hot or too cold. Goldilocks would have approved. Even in winter when they turned the heat way down to conserve energy costs, it was just right with a light jacket once you worked up a good head of steam. It's a massive place with 1,700,000 square feet so there's plenty of room and you never have to worry about tripping over the crowds. But the deserted surroundings never made us feel unsafe. There was a semblance of order provided by the lonely, wandering security guard and small but ever present janitorial staff. I don't know what there was to clean up but we had to admire the pride, dedication and devotion of the tireless few porters that kept the place spic and span. I guess there wasn't much to attract the criminal element; just a few oldsters walking around, usually without any money on their persons and a few deserted stores with little cash in the registers. The topper was the PA system which constantly piped in nostalgia from NWP's salad days. The tapes with '60s and '70s music must have been held over from those days because occasionally the tunes would be interrupted by a shopper's alert that was obviously grossly outdated. As such, these tapes were not reproductions containing just the songs now deemed to be hits but rather featured some of the more obscure ditties that only an experienced ear could really appreciate. It lent the perfect ambience.

Chapter 14

The Great Outdoors

Sally and I, we can still remember NWP's heyday like it was yesterday. When we walk there now, it takes me back to bygone days like Peabody and Sherman in the WABAC machine. Now I'm really dating myself. Does anyone else still remember this strange cartoon with the pooch professor and his sidekick, Sherman, traveling through time in the "way back" machine? Hey, if not, just Google it and it might blow your mind. In any case, with my keen sense of such irrelevant history, I can recall that Northwest Plaza was not the first mall in our area. That distinction went to either Northland or River Roads, as far as I know, way back in the '50s or early '60s. Northland was a great place to watch Fourth of July fireworks from the parking lot. It also had a wonderful Christmas display with towering candles affixed to the main roof. Later on, it even added a free standing cinema nearby; two theaters in one building if you can imagine that! As an aspiring musician, I once took drum lessons at the Northland Music Shop from St. Louis legend, Bob Kuban, he of the one-hit wonder fame for The Cheater; "look out for the Cheater, make way for the fool –hearted clown ... he's gonna build you up just to let you down." That was before I realized I had no musical talent at all. Anyway, could you imagine the staccato, Gene Krupa-like rat-a-tat-tats that might emanate from an epileptic drummer during a seizure?

Today, like my musical aspirations, Northland is gone, replaced by what I'd call a glorified strip mall. At least it's some comfort to know that this hallowed ground is still used for retail and a new generation is able to enjoy the vagaries of commerce there.

The same cannot be said for River Roads. Ah, River Roads; I can still remember riding my bike there with my playmates. I think I was in third or fourth grade at the time. I can still smell the aroma of the piping hot gravy atop the open-face turkey sandwich at the counter of the Woolworth's Steamboat room. I loved to spin around on those stools. If you wanted to live high on the hog, there was the Harvest House cafeteria or the Pavilion Restaurant inside of Stix. A malt or ice cream soda with a cheeseburger at Walgreen's was par excellence, pre-dating most fast food joints. There was even a bowling alley, Spencer Lanes. Kids, as young as me, could wander freely at River Roads. We weren't worried about child abductions and we were generally well behaved enough, much more so than some of today's rapscallions, that store keepers didn't mind, especially since we were likely to spend our allowances there.

It could be that I'm forgetful or being a little too easy on my generation. I do recall one incident, early on, where some trouble makers really cut loose. Back then, such toughs were referred to as hoods, short for hoodlums, not gang bangers. They infiltrated the large crowds that gathered for a grand opening type of promotion where little rhinestones were inserted inside of balloons and then interspersed with hundreds of other empties. The idea was to drop them from the ceilings above some of the store fronts and the lucky winners would be treated to free merchandise. To this day, I still find it hard to believe what happened, so you can imagine how astounded I felt as an eight or nine year old kid witnessing such a melee. The hoods didn't have the patience to get there hours in advance to secure prime spots up front. Instead, they came late and pushed their way from the back toward the falling balloons causing a surge that catapulted hapless victims through the display windows. Back then we didn't have safety or plexi-glass, so when those huge panes splintered and shards came crashing down, many people were badly cut; it was a bloody mess. The cops showed up and everything. I felt like I was in a movie, completely stupefied.

That incident did not stop River Roads from enjoying its halcyon days for many years. It was strategically located near the borderline between the outskirts of the city and the populous north county suburbs. Just two blocks east was the Riverview circle that, in terms of mass confusion, rivaled the British roundabout that bedeviled Chevy Chase on his European Vacation. If you dared to traverse it, the Circle could spit you out in any of six directions with one that could quickly jettison you into St. Louis proper if you so desired. River Roads was just a stone's throw from Northland so great minds must have been thinking alike. But you know what they say about the best laid plans. Over time, this geographical strength became a death knell.

While Northland, just a bit further from the cityscape, was able to reincarnate as a lower life form, River Roads did not enjoy such a felicitous fate. North St. Louis City starkly deteriorated within crime's iron grip and the nearby county was not immune. Urban blight led to flight and the money left for farther flung parts of St. Louis County and then beyond to St. Charles and westward ho. It's sad but today the spot where River Roads once stood is a vacant, gaping hole in the ground. It could be ground zero in Manhattan or some bombed out rubble in war ravaged Iraq. In either case, it's awfully hard to take a stroll down memory lane there. Driving back from there, through what were once solid, middle-class neighborhoods, a regular Pleasant Valley Sunday, now reminded me of Bedford Falls morphing into Pottersville. I guess that's why they say you can't go back.

Ironically, Northwest Plaza which opened in 1963, helped to hasten the demise of Northland and River Roads. It's located in St. Ann, a quaint, blue collar neighborhood, but is adjacent to the more affluent middle class domains of Bridgeton and Maryland

Heights. It also sits astride a major thoroughfare, Lindbergh Boulevard, and is within shouting distance of I-270 which nearly circles the suburbs and I-70 which has a straight shot to the airport and then downtown St. Louis about twenty miles further away. It was ideally situated to draw shoppers from all across the area. It started as an outdoor mall and according to some sources, perhaps urban legend, was purportedly the largest open air mall in the U. S. until being eclipsed by others such as Minneapolis' Mall of America. That mystery aside, it's safe to say that NWP was the largest mall in Missouri.

I don't remember much about the early days but was front and center when NWP hit its stride in the early '70s. During my senior year of high school when I was finally coming out of my shell, I was drawn there like a salmon returning to its spawning grounds. Being a couple of years younger, Sally missed out on some of this but, for me, it was the only place to be. If variety is the spice of life, NWP was cayenne pepper back then. With close to two hundred stores at its apex, there was something for everyone. There was an incredible assortment of just about everything; if NWP didn't have it, it didn't exist or you didn't need it. It was THE gathering place; kind of a combination between a lush, manicured park and a raucous carnival. In the language of the day, it was happening. There was a perpetual buzz about the place with crowded walk ways, jammed court yards, wait-listed eateries and vibrant stores. Just stake a claim, kick back and observe and you'd be entertained for hours. If you were lucky enough to have a girl like Sally, you could spend the better part of a day just walking, holding hands, looking around and grabbing a snack.

We felt privileged that NWP was in our neck of the woods. It was a show place of the Show-Me State and garnered some national attention. Although I was not yet much of a student of business and had my head in the clouds in many ways, there was an innate sense that NWP's booming business was good for our area; the tax base, schools, infrastructure, real estate and reputation in general. It was a source of community pride. Everyone was flocking to the great outdoors, that spectacular open air mall, the Great Northwest.

Chapter 15

Tumbleweed Connections

Have you ever noticed how many times the Bible warns against complacency? It seems to be a constant theme. I suspect it's because God knows how disobedient we can be and prone to back sliding. He has good reason too. Look at how the great flood caught almost everyone unawares, in spite of Noah preaching repentance for up to as much as one hundred years beforehand. Look at Israel in the Old Testament, repeat offenders if there ever were any. Look at you and me. But I don't see God as a stern judge in doing so but rather a doting father. I think of the stabbing pain we feel in our guts when some tragedy, even a small one, is suffered by our children. We want to guard and protect them at all costs. Don't go near that hot stove!

When kids are born, we undergo some kind of invisible transformation where self-preservation disappears and we become like Secret Service Agents, willing to take a bullet for them. As far as God's love-motivated warnings go, the biggie is when Jesus cautions us in Luke 21:28 "And when these things begin to come to pass, then look up, and lift up your heads; for your redemption draws nigh." End time prognostication can be alarming and down-right frightening to many but it's very reassuring when you think of it in the context of a caring, compassionate father.

I was by no means complacent, I thought. My life seemed purposeful and I tried to stay in the word to be equipped for every opportunity to witness, which God was always faithful to provide when I sought him out. But I had to admit that I had fallen into a pretty comfy routine what with retirement and home schooling. Ike was pretty much at the center of my world. Even dealing with Ike's epilepsy and searching for some kind of silver bullet cure with the doctors had become part of the routine in an odd way, although still disconcerting, no doubt. Sometimes we need a good crisis to keep us on point, right?

I was Fred Astaire and Sally was my Ginger Rogers when we walked, completely in sync with one another. But she might have been getting a little burned out on our mall walks preferring to bundle up and go outside or hit the treadmill more often. Maybe it was hearing me say for the millionth time how much I missed Dick Clark's American Bandstand Grill or the Pasta House Company whenever we glided past those locations with the latter being worse with not one but two former locales within NWP. Everything was purely a recollection since all the signage was down and store front windows were shrouded in black plastic sheets as if a Good Friday service were about to commence.

Sally was probably a little tired of my worn out

trivia questions, "What preceded the Pasta House in the old location near the office tower before they moved across from the cinema?" Of course she remembered by now that it was John Henry's. "What was that dish we always ordered at Spinnaker's?"

"Why, I think it was called Golden Gate Pasta, dear."

"Oh yeah, it was sprinkled with real apple wood bacon bits and the pasta was green." Perhaps Sally didn't enjoy these strolls down memory lane as much as me because she didn't have the same connection, the same collection of memories. It's kind of hard to get caught up in the moment when it's someone else's moment. You had to be there. Why did I have to pull keepsakes out of my own personal locker instead of the treasure chest we shared? It could have been that this didn't bother Sally at all. Maybe, unclouded by so many memories, she more clearly saw NWP for what it really was; a cavernous, abandoned relic of a mall; a desert drear; a spooky old cemetery.

With my new routine and everything I had to keep me busy, I wasn't wrestling with that purpose thing anymore. But something was still bugging me. Like a junkie, I needed my regular NWP fixes. It was almost as if my epileptic seizures had been replaced with fits of nostalgia. There was something hollow inside me that these trips to the mall filled but it seemed like a bottomless pit in need of constant replenishment. Was this my mid-life or should I say late-life crisis? Maybe I needed to relive those times because I felt short changed by everything I missed as a young spaz. Or maybe I was just a stubborn old man who couldn't accept the ugly truth that time marches on and things change; they were changing in ways that I couldn't stomach. I recalled my father's fond recollections of the idyllic North St. Louis of his youth and how it had become some type of Dresden aftermath. Now on the rare occasions when I drove through there trying to rediscover some old landmark or summon up some childhood retrospection, I kept my doors locked and prayed for no flat tires, aghast at the level of deterioration.

My own childhood haunts were not faring much better. Occasionally, I'd drive by conjuring up my past but it just wasn't the same. Was this happening right before my eyes to our current neighborhood where our own children came of age? Why do we try to hang on, why do we resist the inevitable? Do we fear our legacies will be meaningless as memories of our lives and deeds fade? Are we worried that we didn't make one bit of difference? Would my children or grandchildren experience the same type of shock and awe when visiting here in years to come? The signs were becoming increasingly noticeable and were nowhere more evident than at Northwest Plaza. I even heard a rumor that old reliable, Sears, might call it quits.

I just couldn't give up and accept that as reality. Say it isn't so, oh Ghost of Christmases to come! No, I had to hold out hope for a white knight. NWP was up to at least its fourth owner by my count and I reasoned that they wouldn't let their investment go down the tubes although it was purchased for a song compared to its original value. While I was hoping for a retro transformation that would take us back to the good old days, I would settle for any kind of makeover that would save the place. Maybe NWP could be the subject of a new reality show, Extreme Mall Makeover, yeah, that's the ticket.

In spite of my optimism or self-delusion, clearer heads would say the odds of a comeback were very long. Northwest County shoppers were flooding to the new St. Louis Mills which was only five minutes away or taking a longer course to flock to one of the newer or renovated malls in West County, St. Charles Mid-Rivers or Chesterfield or the Galleria even though the latter was starting to experience some of the same telltale throes that usually precede dead malls. Some people avoided malls altogether preferring big box stores, discount clubs or specialty shops in local strip malls. Not me though, I was holding out for the Comeback Mall of the Year award. And in the meantime, I'd cling to the memories of by gone days with a white knuckled grip.

For a while, I took to walking NWP's vacuous hallways alone. I couldn't help thinking of Roy Rogers atop his trusty palomino steed, Trigger, warbling about the Tumbling Tumbleweeds. Oh, lots of other country-western artists had covered this tune, from Marty Robbins to Eddy Arnold to the Sons of the Pioneers and more but, for me, it was Roy's voice I heard when I recalled those solitary lyrics ...

> *I'm a roaming cowboy riding all day long*
> *Tumbleweeds around me sing their lonely song.*
> *Nights underneath the prairie moon*
> *I ride along and sing this tune.*
>
> *See them tumbling down*
> *Pledging their love to the ground*
> *Lonely but free I'll be found*
> *Drifting along with the tumbling tumbleweeds.*

That was me, a lonely cowpoke drifting through stark aisles. If I squinted, I could almost see the tumbleweeds silently rolling down the corridors ahead of me. Walking alone was not for me. No, I needed a sidekick just like Roy had with jolly, old Jingles. I knew just where to find one, Ike, of course. It was easy to justify bringing Ike up to the mall. Field trips I called these regular excursions to NWP. And it was so educational too, combining history lessons with a little PE. Ike was the perfect little tag along; he was eager, inquisitive, energetic and, best of all, had a voracious appetite for my tales since all my stories were new to him.

My troubled psyche received a catharsis when I reminisced with Ike along. I desperately needed to connect him, the future, to my past. If he could see my tumbleweeds, if we could share this tumbleweed connection, my legacy would live on. Ha, that play on words made a vision of my first Elton John album jump into my consciousness. The cover was made to look like an Old West scene. One haunting Bernie Taupin lyric that Elton John brought to life with his own, unique style came to mind ...

> So where to now St. Peter
> If it's true I'm in your hands
> I may not be a Christian
> But I've done all one man can
> I understand I'm on the road
> Where all that was is gone
> So where to now St. Peter
> Show me which road I'm on
> Which road I'm on

These were odd lyrics. Did they reflect a search for the truth or a conscience troubled by the perception of a vengeful God of wrath? I don't claim to know what they had in mind with those lyrics but from my perspective, it reminded me of my search for God and purpose. I hoped their questions were answered affirmatively like mine, that their path had been lit, that they found peace. Ike and I walked the same path at

119

NWP, literally and figuratively. We were simpatico.

Chapter 16

Dr. Howard, Dr. Fine, Dr. Howard

We had suffered through over a year's worth of seizures with Ike. While, over this time, our determined search for the magic elixir had taken on a routine vibe, it was no less exasperating for me. How long, oh Lord, how long? I hoped and prayed that Ike's affliction would not span years like mine had. I thought, Ike is seven now, maybe this will be lucky number seven. How did seven become a lucky number anyway? Maybe there was some theological explanation long ago that was lost on popular culture. Wasn't seven God's number, the number for perfection? God's Word, like silver tried in the fire seven times, right? I whispered to myself "Is Ike being refined through this ordeal, Lord, or is it really me you're working on?" If it was me, I prayed that I would get the intended lesson through my thick skull promptly, for Ike's sake.

Ike's seizures still seemed quite menacing to me, much worse than what I had suffered. It troubled me immensely because it was not just my imagination. Try as they might, the doctors could not completely hide their sense of foreboding over Ike's condition and rare, somewhat unique manifestations. At least it gave them a real sense of urgency and, me, an ulcer, figuratively speaking. It kept me going and gave me more patience with the doctors than I thought possible.

All of this angst pushed me, Sally, TB and Sara beyond our safe, normal limits in seeking a cure. We agreed to medicines and procedures that were contrary to our conservative nature. At the same time, we were pulled in the opposite direction by fear, concern and a longing for some normalcy in Ike's life. This internal conflict wore on me. Sometimes solar flares erupted that singed the nearest doctor's eyebrows. "What kind of voodoo are we practicing here, witch doctor?" I bellowed.

"That's uncalled for, Mr. Paulson. Please calm down."

"You want me to calm down, do you? I'll show you calm, you lousy quack." Doctors have huge egos and normally would never stand for such an undressing from a mere mortal like me but I had been through so much for so long that he sheepishly accepted my rant with chin bowed and eyes toward his clip board. On I vented "I'm sick and tired of all this mumbo jumbo." I openly mocked him in my best girly man voice "These things take time ... it's impossible to know when just the right combination might kick in when you're sailing in such uncharted waters." After a long, dumbfounded pause, in a resigned, apologetic tone, he offered his best advice; a vain, fleeting prescription for hope, as I saw it.

These experimental medicines and treatments always came with a heavy, ominous downside risk.

122

Anyone who's ever read the warnings on normal prescriptions has to wonder if the cure isn't worse than the illness. On this far edge of medicine, the stakes were much higher and the downside more grim. I had nothing against this one doctor, personally. It was more a cumulative thing. I was just sick and tired of the constant runaround. It reminded me of the classic Three Stooges episode, Men in Black, where you hear over the hospital intercom "Paging Doctor Howard, Doctor Fine, Doctor Howard". Only this wasn't funny. I wished there was a magic pill that would make it all better but everything our doctors prescribed seemed like very expensive snake oil; like Moe, Larry and Curly selling Brighto in Dizzy Doctors, "Brighto makes old bodies new … woo, woo!" If only it was that easy. I gathered myself and said "I'm sorry Doc, I didn't mean that. I'm just a tired, frustrated old man." Now in a calm but deadly serious tone I posed "Think about it Doc. Think about someone you love, the person you cherish more than any other; perhaps your wife or a child. Would you recommend this for them, would you?"

He raised his head and looked me sadly, straight in the eye and confessed "I just don't know. I really can't answer that question. I'm very sorry."

That was the day I really put things in God's hands. Oh, we still went through the perfunctory motions with modern medicine and all; me, Sally, TB and Sara; but never ventured onto thin, highly experimental ice again. Yes, sometimes it takes a good crisis and we had all reached that point. When you lose all hope, in a temporal, earthly sense, that's when you're best able to let go and give the reins to God. We left it to God to work through medicine or any other means he chose. Depending on his power and wisdom rather than our own, we prayed, "thy will be done."

Chapter 17

Somewhere Over the Rainbow

God answered our prayers swiftly and in the most unusual way. Skeptics might say it was just coincidence; that the right combination of meds finally kicked in. That might be part of it but I knew that God's hand was on the helm. Regardless of that, there was no doubt that the change snuck up on me. It started a watershed of events that would change our lives forever. It happened one day soon thereafter as Ike and I were enjoying one of our field trips. I'm not sure what he liked more; my history lessons or the people watching. I do know that the sparse offerings fascinated him because Ike would always quietly quiz me after other walkers were a safe distance away. "What happened to that man, Granby?"

"Nothing unusual, Ike, he just got old, really old."

On dark, cloudy days, Ike was a little spooked by the other mall rats. Once he said they reminded him of the ghostly spirits floating by Scrooge's window when Jacob Marley made his mournful exit. Ike marveled that old people liked to walk even though it seemed like such a struggle for some. Others defied gravity as they sped by, putting us to shame. There were so few people at NWP, mostly just walkers, that we usually had plenty of time to observe and size each one of them up. It was a challenging game to surmise much of anything since these old books were covered with such leathery skins and so many wrinkles and age spots. Sometimes if they were in pairs, you could pick up a hint from snippets of their conversations while passing by. Occasionally, I'd recognize something familiar that might offer a clue. "Hey Ike, I think I remember that fellow. I used to see him in the stands when your dad played high school football. He was there a lot. Must have been a big fan or had a son on the team or maybe his daughter was a cheerleader. Maybe he was a teacher." That got me off on a happy tangent, chronicling TB's grid iron exploits for an amused Ike.

Unfortunately, we didn't get to talk to folks too much other than passing pleasantries. No, grizzled old mall walkers were typically on a mission and did not like to be interrupted. Not to worry, there was plenty to cover by ourselves. Each blank store front or abandoned shop led to a labyrinth of life gone by. "What's that down there Granby and why is it roped off?"

"You would have loved that place Ike. It was a super arcade called Tilt; a paradise made special for kids, although the parents had fun too. I remember the time when your dad was nine or ten and we had a birthday party for him with a bunch of his friends and school mates. They played games, won prizes, had pizza, cake and punch and even played miniature golf. I was the king of Skee Ball and topped everyone in the Big Shot basketball game. I think I contributed at least two hundred tickets to the cause that day." I laughed, lost in thought, bringing a curious smile to Ike's face, "I'll never forget the clown Grandma Sally hired to entertain the gang. That was one weird dude; scared the pee out of your dad; freaked me out a little too." I offered a mock shudder. Ike was dying to go down there and check it out but bright red caution signs barred the way.

Another day, I couldn't help but bend the rules a tad. We ducked under a rope, climbed the motionless escalator and pried open a loose plywood panel to venture into the old multiplex cinema. The once grand lobby area that hovered above the mall's main level was strewn with the remains left behind by a demolition crew and only a few glass concession cases left a trace of its past purpose. "They had the best popcorn here, Ike. It wafted down into the mall, grabbed you by your nostrils and lifted you upward with its buttery hydraulics. It was heaven scent; pun intended, get it, SCENT, oh never mind" I chuckled. Then we tip toed quietly up the steps to the dark corridor leading to the theaters; our heart beats racing from our own mischievousness and the prospect of being apprehended by a hapless security guard. The lack of lighting restricted us from going too far so we just poked our heads into one of the theaters, the screen blank and most of the seating removed.

"This is where we saw The Burbs; one of your dad's favorites to this day. You know that DVD you like; Who's Harry Crumb? This is where we saw it, long before we had the DVD. I miss John Candy."

Ike chimed in "I think The Great Outdoors is my favorite, Granby; you know when they're trying to catch that bat, and especially when he shoots that bear in the butt."

My reel kept turning, "This is where we saw Cyborg with Jean-Claude Van Damme. That boy could fight. Look down there Ike, right up in the front row on the right. That's where we saw the first Batman movie, the good one with Jack Nicholson as the Joker. We had to sit there because it was sold out. I didn't mind getting dizzy with a crick in my neck. It was one of the first big comic book movies and Batman was my favorite as a kid. I was so excited, I bought Batman t-shirts for everyone; your dad, aunt, uncle, Grandma, me and even two of the neighbor kids who tagged along. We looked like a bunch of tourists. It was an event, it was." Finally, we left and scurried back down the escalator undetected by Barney Fife with our secret and clean records intact. Grandma Sally admonished us roundly when she heard about our caper.

I had become fairly well attuned to some of

Ike's warning signs. With my own personal theory that epilepsy was basically the result of faulty wiring, of human electronics run amok, I was convinced that I could tell when a seizure was coming by watching the hairs on Ike's neck stand on end or even pick up on any unusual display of static cling. Maybe it was something imperceptible in his mood or body language that I was able to sense. Whatever it was, perceived or real, I had been able to sometimes take quick, minor precautions such as getting Ike out of the public eye and placing him in a safe position on a soft couch or bed. However, my guard was completely down that day as we cruised along our normal NWP path.

I had adopted a habit of bringing a few quarters along just in case the sour cherry balls or gummy bears tempted Ike. They had him in their sugary clutches that afternoon and I couldn't resist after our second pass. As we approached the next treasure trove, I handed Ike two quarters and told him to "Go crazy." He kicked it into overdrive, leaving me in his dust as he sped toward the prize. An invisible toe seemed to stretch out and trip him as he galloped and giggled toward the colorful confections. Maybe it was a crack in the tile or a slick spot but nevertheless he took quite a spill, tumbling head over heels. He slid to a stop, face down, almost at the feet of a couple of fellow mall walkers as I hurried frantically to catch up. My mind seemed to capture the scene in slow motion, although it was somewhat jumpy from my running, like one of those headache inducing Blair Witch movies. Later, I would be able to play this clip back over and over in my head but to no avail. There seemed to be no real harm done and Ike showed none of the telltale signs of a pending attack as he rolled over and accepted a hand up from his unknown benefactor. That's when it hit him. No, he didn't have one of his horrible, violent seizures; nothing of the sort. It was completely different, as if he had fallen into some kind of trance. From that very moment forward, Ike would never suffer another epileptic seizure. No, this was a different animal altogether. Another beast, a whole new species was stalking Ike now. We had crossed over the rainbow; we weren't in Kansas anymore, Dorothy Gale. I just hoped the Wicked Witch wasn't lurking nearby.

BOOK FOUR

Where's the Beef?

Chapter 18

Oh God, Part IV

George Burns was an unlikely god. His wisdom, as concocted by Hollywood for this part, was, of course, terribly flawed for an omniscient deity. The movie, while charming in a sense, was pretty ridiculous. If there was a redeeming quality beyond the clever gags and some good laughs, it was the steadfastness John Denver displayed once he was convinced god had actually been revealed in the form of the cuddly, cigar puffing curmudgeon with the dark rimmed, coke bottle glasses. Once he had been won over, by an indoor rainstorm no less, Denver's character suffered some hilarious slings and arrows for old George. Burns reprised this role twice in Oh God Book II and Oh God You Devil; regrettable and forgettable follow-ups. Now I felt like I had the lead in a new sequel. No, I wasn't seeking the wise counsel of Mr. Burns and I didn't need any convincing about God's existent. I had a solid line on the one, true God and was well past any kind of skepticism or rebelliousness. To the contrary, I was clay putty, ready and willing to be molded, to do whatever God wished to rescue Ike. But I was consumed by a very similar burning question; Oh God, what now?

The innocent bystander and his walking companion, though complete strangers, stood by patiently as Ike lay peacefully on the cold tile floor. They could have gone harmlessly on their way with nary an eyebrow being raised by me but they stayed close to see if Ike was okay and lend a hand, if possible. These two gents were of a more courteous generation, I guessed they were maybe five years older than me. Beyond just curiosity, they seemed to share a genuine concern for Ike's condition. I was puzzled, as were they, because Ike appeared fine, fully in charge of his faculties right up until the one fellow, Tim was his name, clasped hands with Ike to pull him up. Just at that moment, Ike's whole body went limp like a sack of nickels. If not for Tim, he would have crumpled to the ground in a heap. As we hovered above, Tim's pal, Stan ... he preferred Stash ... took off his jacket and wrapped it around Ike to keep him warm. Tim offered to call for help. I asked him to hold off for a moment. "I'm kind of an amateur paramedic when it comes to Ike" I explained. "Ike is an epileptic so I'm used to providing critical care. But this isn't like anything I've seen before." I began my simple, methodical diagnostics as they carefully observed. "His airway is clear, he's breathing fine, heart rate is normal and he has no signs of convulsions of any sort."

Stash offered "Should I contact security, just to be safe?"

"That's probably a good idea" I said "thanks." It took a good twenty minutes to track down the lone guard on duty and another ten for an ambulance to arrive. In the interim, Tim and I played junior physicians displaying our lack of knowledge regarding concussions and medicine in general. It helped to pass the time and keep us calm. We were mainly focused on keeping a close eye on Ike. No warning signs arose, no cause for alarm. To the contrary, Ike had every appearance of sleeping like a baby. He even displayed some subconscious emotions with frowns and goofy smiles that would have been hilarious under other conditions. Then oddest of all, his eyeballs began flitting to and fro beneath his eyelids, reminding me of what dream researchers call the REM stage of sleep. Then, as if on cue, right as the real paramedics were readying the gurney and I was preparing to call TB and Sara, Ike snapped out of it like someone threw a light switch. Ike protested, said he was fine and asked to go home but we took him to the hospital as a precautionary measure. As we parted ways, I thanked Tim and Stash and said "I hope we cross paths again, guys."

Stash promised, "We'll keep you in our prayers."

On the ride to the hospital, I hit Ike with the third degree. I was dying to figure out what had happened to cause his fall and subsequent collapse. "I'm not sure, Granby. I think I just tripped."

"Are you hurt?" I prodded.

"No, I don't think so." I pursued,

"Do you remember what happened when that man helped you up?"

"No, I don't remember that part, Granby." I was fumbling along down a dead end. Ike simply had no recollection; a total blank.

I was just about ready to give up when Ike volunteered "I had the funniest dream, Granby. But it wasn't like other dreams. It was so real, like I was really there. But I wasn't in the dream. I was just kind of watching." Ike was really anxious to share his oh so cool dream but, by that time, we were at the hospital and got caught up in the prodding, poking and questioning routine. Afterwards, TB, Sara and I got the post mortem from the attending physician. There had been no head trauma and the EEG came back normal. There was nothing to indicate that a concussion or epileptic seizure had occurred, no reason to order a more expensive CAT scan or MRI. I described Ike's condition during the ordeal and the doctor concurred that it sounded like Ike had fallen into the kind of deep sleep that might occur after resting for hours in bed.

"Strange" he said "just when you think you've seen it all in the ER, some new wrinkle comes along to keep you guessing." He assured us Ike was fit as a fiddle but advised us to get a checkup from his regular pediatrician soon.

135

Ike was still intent on telling me all about his special dream but it was late and everyone but Ike was exhausted from all the commotion. I put him off by saying that perhaps he'd have another, similar dream after going to bed. As tired as I was, I didn't sleep well that night. My mind was restless, trying to get a grip on what had transpired. While I was thankful that Ike had not been hurt and especially grateful for not suffering through another frightful seizure, I was fit to be tied. I needed some kind of explanation, a simple cause and effect. The refrain echoed in my mind, *oh God, what now?* I wrestled the enigma until my body finally capitulated.

When I awoke, my face sagged revealing the sluggishness of a fitful night's sleep. Although I normally shied away from caffeine, I choked down a bitter cup of instant coffee from an ancient jar of crusty crystals I kept for unwanted guests or moments like this one. I needed to be hitting on all cylinders to start the school day with Ike. He didn't miss a beat, picking up right where we left off. With most dreams, you tend to forget them if you don't go over the details right away. There was no such luck here. Ike was raring to go and so revved up that I agreed to put this on the top of our agenda so as to, hopefully, clear the way for our other studies. I really didn't have any choice since it was clear this little tea pot would explode if I didn't allow him to let off the steam.

As Ike lit into the task, I was reminded of Dorothy, with Auntie Em and the others at her bedside, relating her Oz adventures, fully convinced of the reality. However, there was one critical difference here; Ike was not in the story, he was only an observer; cub reporter. But he still had a firm conviction that what he saw had really happened. I tried to help him, "Ike, was it like watching a movie?"

"Yes it was Granby, but different."

"Tell me Ike, how so?"

Ike furrowed his little brow and looked heavenward for assistance, "Well, you know how you see movies on a screen or a TV?" I nodded, sliding toward the edge of my seat. "It wasn't like that."

"What was it like?" I tried to feign patience.

"I don't know how to say. I wasn't in it but I was there. I was able to see it all around me, not on a screen."

Fearing another dead end, I moved on, "Okay Ike, that sounds pretty cool. Go ahead and tell me what you saw."

This is where it gets tough. Imagine a movie, any movie with a complicated, mature, theme, for example, The Godfather, Apocalypse Now or Saving

Private Ryan. Now, assign the screening to a seven year old boy and ask him to give you an oral report; kid critic's corner. If you had never seen the film yourself, would you be able to gain a full appreciation for the picture? Granted, Ike was not your typical seven-year-old. He reminded me a bit, intellectually, of wunderkind Haley Joel Osment. He was only six when he played little Forrest Gump. Shoot, he was only the ripe old age of eleven when he was nominated for Best Supporting Actor for his role in The Sixth Sense. Ike displayed some of the same precocity but, of course, didn't have near that level of sophistication. He was more akin to little Ronnie Howard, a genius in his own right but completely unassuming as innocent Opie Taylor. Ike was a blank slate, reflecting what he saw; "Just the facts, ma'am" as Detective Joe Friday was wont to say. I was able to glean the gist but received very little analysis or commentary. What surprised me were the adult themes that cropped up, certainly not out of Ike's mind, not some regurgitation of TV or movie dramas. He was just playing back what he saw without a full understanding of the meaning behind it. Oh, he understood enough. Like Haley Joel when he said, "I see dead people" Ike caught my attention when he said "They did some bad things Granby."

This took me back to my Oh God moment. What was going on here? Would I now have to contend with this on top of the epilepsy? I didn't know if I could handle a puzzlement wrapped inside a conundrum within a riddle. I searched the scriptures for some kind of answer. Dreams were mentioned in various places but these passages didn't seem to apply or at least I couldn't figure out the connection. For example, there was Joel's prophesy, " And it will come to pass afterward, that I will pour out my spirit upon all flesh; and your sons and daughters shall prophesy, your old men shall dream dreams, your young men shall see visions." This had already been fulfilled on Pentecost. Was I to receive the power to interpret dreams like Daniel did with King Nebuchadnezzar? No, these things didn't apply anymore. Since the death of the last apostle, gifts of the Holy Spirit like miraculous healing powers and speaking in tongues had ceased, regardless of what TV evangelist charlatans and snake handling zealots might say. God made it clear that he chose to work through his means, word and sacrament. That's the whole point of the Bible, why God revealed his plan to us in writing, right? It had taken a lot of years and many fires but God had refined my faith and I would put it to good use. I knew there was a purpose behind all of this and answers would come in time. In the meantime, I'd stay in the word and pray. I was reminded of a recent dinner at my favorite oriental restaurant where we enjoyed the corny tradition of closing the meal with fortune cookies. Now, I pulled out the little slip of paper I had saved with the words, "Focus on your long-term goal." Yes, be patient, Grasshopper.

Back to Ike's dream or vision or whatever you want to call it. I listened carefully and tried to avoid interrupting him with too many questions. Other than seeking clarifications, there was no point really. There was no deeper meaning to plumb; he was just doing play-by-play mostly and not much color commentary. I found myself getting caught up in the fabric of the patchwork quilt he was weaving; forgetting about the implications for Ike's health and well-being for the moment. I was in the grip of a rather fascinating tale, made all the more so by the certainty that this was not the type of yarn that could possibly come out of Ike's naïve imagination, with one exception. Somehow, through that brief encounter, our two mall buddies, Tim and Stash, showed up. Ike didn't even know their names but somehow in the matter of a millisecond, his brain was able to absorb and incorporate them into his dream. Perhaps this was an Oz experience like where the farmhands, Hunk, Zeke and Hickory morphed into the Scarecrow, Lion and Tin Man. I was further intrigued by the time period which was set way back in my prime and long before Ike's time. Where did Ike come up with all these '70s references? God only knows. Ike offered one very perceptive insight on the dream that really piqued my interest, "They were just like the prodigal son."

Chapter 19

Thursday Night Fever

I'm not going to replay Ike's account for you. That would leave too much up to my own interpretation. It would also be like watching a French film with English subtitles. Everyone knows that subtitles suck; that is, everyone but the artsy types who go to bohemian flick fests to puff up their own egos rather than for pure entertainment. "Hey, look at me, I'm intellectual!" No, I'm going to let you see this one for yourself; the uncut version with my own editorial comments tossed in for good measure. How can I do that, you say? Well, I'll let you in on a little secret, sort of a preview of coming attractions. Later on, well after Ike's first *screening* at NWP, I was granted my own private viewing. But that's all I can say for now; I don't want to get ahead of myself. Ready, lights, cameras, action ... roll 'em! Here's Ike's dream as seen through my eyes.

Mr. E's Boogie Man Club was borne out of the disco craze that swept the nation in the '70s. This former North St. Louis County neighborhood watering hole, Edward's, was transformed almost overnight with a little paint, black lights, strobe lights, glittery, mirrored disco ball and, the piece de resistance, a fully functional DJ booth and sub-lit dance floor. Later, Mr. E even came up with his own logo to suit the time; a ghoulish, green boogie man happily decked out in platform shoes, white suit and long-collared, silk shirt appropriately flared over the lapels. His right index finger was thrust skyward. Although it was just another Studio 54 wannabe, it was the place to be in this neck of the woods and even attracted disco disciples from as far away as South County near the Illinois border. It was the spawn of Travolta.

I don't know if any other movie has had quite the same sweeping impact on pop culture as Saturday Night Fever and the accompanying album by the Bee Gees. It boosted disco into the mainstream with a meteoric rise whose sudden ascendance was matched only by its abrupt, thudding demise. It was a short, strange but glorious run. Disco swept the land like a plague of locusts devouring every cultural underpinning in its path; from the faux chic night clubs to outlandish polyester cloths, garish shoes and longish, plastered coifs, everything seemed to change in the blink of an eye. Somewhere in the '70s, we took the black Chevy sedan that was America and slapped a coat of metal flake, day-glow orange paint over everything including the tires and hub caps and replaced the headlamps with purple neon lights. I still can't figure out what possessed us to do this. What were we thinking?? Were we looking for some kind of escape? Was it a case of temporary insanity? Was it a popular uprising against Rock 'n Roll's long dominance? Was it the me generation trying to hang onto some part of the psychedelic '60s while blazing its own, new trail?

You could make a case that disco had a hand in further eroding our morals, loosening our sexual mores and increasing our collective appetite for designer drugs. But the greatest impact from the disco era was undoubtedly in the music and accompanying dance styles. Music was turned on its ear and not just by architects like the Bee Gees, Donna Summer, Yvonne Elliman and KC and the Sunshine Band. No, well established musicians from other genres, bona fide stars in their own rights such as Rod Stewart, Diana Ross and the Jacksons jumped on the bandwagon. It was a tidal wave; even Paul McCartney, for heaven's sake, got swept up in its wake. You have to give credit where credit is due though. Disco made dancing fun and cool again. Everyone wanted to be like John "Tony Manero" Travolta and believed they could. Dance studios cropped up everywhere, even at community college night classes. If you couldn't afford that, all you had to do was tune the TV into Denny Terrio's Dance Fever to catch a few of the latest moves. Dancing became a national past-time again, along with booze, drugs, sex and other assorted immoralities.

Mr. E's was the backdrop for Ike's *movie* and where our two foils, Tim and Stash, burst onto the scene. The only thing was, they went by their nicknames or you might say aliases to cover their tracks. No, not Scarecrow and Tin Man. They were Ace and Nature Boy, better known as the Faces. When Ike first relayed his vision to me, he threw me off with talk of the Faces. I thought he meant he saw faces and I kept asking, as if parroting Abbott & Costello, "Whose faces do you mean, Ike?"

He insisted, "No, the Faces" and even talked about t-shirts with "Faces" on the front.

Looking back, I had to laugh about me quizzing poor Ike, "Whose faces were on the t-shirts?" It all made sense now, if anything of the sort can be deemed sensible. You see, Ace and Nature adopted the name of Travolta's, I mean Tony's, gang in Saturday Night Fever; Bobby C, Joey, Double J and Tony were the original Faces. Tim and Stash formed their own ultra-exclusive club, a gang of two. They adopted the name on a lark thinking it was funny, irreverent and cool but never thought it would stick and had no idea of the parallels. It was actually very appropriate in that both sets of Faces were good guys with solid upbringings. No, they weren't bad guys. They were only out for a good time ... they were just out of control sometimes, not thinking beyond the moment. Somewhere along the line they had jumped the tracks but didn't seem to care; they were tearing it up and having a blast. The Faces were always the life of the party; let the good times roll!

As if on cue, the Faces entered Mr. E's as the DJ was cranking up A Fifth of Beethoven. Their animated struts were in sync with the beat and didn't seem out of place. They weren't trying to be cool. They exaggerated their walk for effect; everything was a big joke to them, anything for a laugh. Joey, the 5'9", 312 pound bouncer gave them each five and smiled broadly, "Hey, it's the Faces ... what's going down boys?"

Ace replied, "Jo my man, we're here to drink a fistful, kiss a few girls and help you keep any bad boys in line, brother."

"Now you're talking! First one's on the house." Ace and Nature were a little old for this game at thirty and twenty eight respectively but looked younger and were more than athletic enough to fit in. Nature was tall and angular with kind of a surfer dude look and Ace was shorter but powerfully built, taking pride in the bulging biceps he called his pythons. Reconciling these two images with Tim and Stash was nearly impossible. I wouldn't have put two and two together if it hadn't been for Ike's keen perception. Age and time and apparently some heavy, destructive drinking, what they might call recreational, had taken its toll. But, back in the day, they had it going on, except perhaps for their clothing. The Faces were macho guys who didn't buy into the sissified silk and polyester look. They preferred knock-around duds, typically athletic wear that made it look like they were always on the way to some game. Their somewhat out-of-touch style was considered nonconformist trendy by some during this anything

145

goes, do your own thing era, but most didn't notice since everything else was overshadowed by their charmingly obnoxious, larger-than-life personas. Betty the bartender, Betty Boop to the Faces, asked, "What will you have guys?"

Ace volunteered, "How about two pitchers of the King and four Long Island Teas?" Betty Boop didn't bat an eyelash at this super-sized order, knowing how the Faces liked to pound them down.

A call came out of the crowd, lights, smoke and pounding music, "Hey there boys, Faces, over here!" The sea of bodies parted and two pretty, dolled up gals approached.

"Hey Nature Boy" Ace whispered "what's her name?"

"The brunette looks familiar but I don't have a clue about names." Naturally gregarious and now fueled by several beers and a Long Island Tea, this was not a problem for the Faces.

"Hey, remember me?"

"You know I do, doll face." Thereafter, she was Dolly to the Faces even though her real name was Julie. The Faces gave everyone nicknames.

Dolly was a brick house brunette, "Let me

introduce you to my friend Laurie. Laurie, this is Ace and Nature Boy." While the particulars escaped them, the Faces had apparently crossed paths with Dolly before and she was back for more. Laurie was a slinky blond who reminded the Faces of Jackie the space queen in Thank God It's Friday. From the look in her eyes, you could tell she was doing something other than Jack Daniels.

"Those sure are funny names. How'd you get the name Ace ... and what's a Nature Boy, anyway?"

"My dad called me Ace before I was born. I was the last of six kids and the other five were girls. As his last shot, the old man guaranteed a boy ... he said I was his Ace in the hole. It just stuck after that." It was very unusual for the Faces but Ace was actually telling the truth without any embellishment.

"Laurie, my dear, they call me the Nature Boy because I'm friend to all animals," he dead panned. Actually, his namesake was the flamboyant wrestler, Ric Flair, but this explanation sounded as good as any.

Then Ace started laying it on thick, "I must warn you girls that we are not just two big, blond sex machines ... we have feelings and emotions too." The Faces were light on their feet, so to speak. Laurie was gullible when sober and just plain ditzy when not, so she was dubbed Lunar Laurie.

Dolly took charge, "You guys want to dance?"

Ace extended his hand with mock chivalry, "Before we do, let us take you on a little ride in our helicopter." With that, the Faces lifted Dolly above their heads and proceeded to spin her around swiftly. Dolly just laughed; this didn't seem strange at all at Mr. E's when the Faces were around.

During the course of the night, the Faces made all the rounds, renewing old acquaintances, making new connections, tearing up the dance floor and even did fill-in stints behind the bar and the DJ's desk. The Faces were multi-talented and, take my word for it, not shy. Like most nights, they closed the place down. It didn't matter that this was a work night. To the Faces, Thursday was the start of the weekend. Mid-week was no different either; every night there was some occasion for the Faces to celebrate. That Thursday night, it didn't end when Mr. E's shut down. They invited Dolly and Lunar Laurie back to their bachelor pad for drinks, as if they had not already consumed enough alcohol to drown a tuna. Any reservations by the ladies were cast aside when Nature Boy offered to show them the Faces' pet piranha, Mr. P. That ensured the gals that the Faces' intentions were strictly honorable. "I'm Ace the Face, welcome to our place."

To cover some insecurity or perhaps just out of sheer bravado, Ace had a habit of openly advertising his

148

prowess with the ladies. Lunar Laurie seemed up to the challenge and offered one of her own. She kept daring Ace to prove his courage by dangling his *bait* in the piranha tank. There was quite a hooch filled romp that night at the Faces' crib. To make matters worse, Laurie produced a small glass bottle of amyl nitrate which was sold legally under the name Popper; Ace came to call it Popper Juice. The Faces were not into drugs but were already three sheets to the wind and readily accepted a whiff and a sniff which sent everyone over the edge. In her near stupor, Lunar Laurie did not believe the piranha was real. She egged on Ace to violate Mr. P's quarters. With the last of his slim inhibitions demolished by the Popper Juice, Ace gleefully complied and unzipped. The last thing Nature Boy remembered was doubling over in uncontrollable laughter that drew tears as Ace went *angling*, calling out "Here fishy, fishy." The next morning, in the aftermath of another night's insane debauchery, they found Mr. P floating belly up. Ace always claimed proudly that Mr. P had been frightened to death.

I paused from the dreamscape for a moment to gather my thoughts. I needed a break since my face was flushed with the embarrassment that might come from telling your son about the birds and the bees. Only, this was worse because these were nefarious fowl and depraved drones. I couldn't imagine what purpose God had in mind in exposing Ike to such outrageousness.

Thankfully, it seemed that many of the profligate subtleties I was able to pick up on went over Ike's head. In his view of the dream, he seemed to have a G-rated filter that spared him from some of the baser implications. In his version, some of the things I would have cringed at explaining were, to Ike, cast as almost harmless tomfoolery. For example, he compared their dangerous binge drinking to the amusing antics of Mayberry's lovable lush, Otis Campbell. This didn't mean Ike couldn't recognize bad behavior when he saw it. I remember him relaying with childish disgust, "Granby, that man was being nasty."

Still a bit perplexed, I went back and reread the story of the prodigal son. It reminded me how God doesn't pull punches or varnish the truth to get his point across. The lost son had rebelled against his father and took his full inheritance, a very large sum, and blew it all on "riotous living" (Luke 15:13) and sank so low in his debauchery that he went from being the privileged son of a wealthy lord to a hired hand working in a stinking pig sty. He hit rock bottom when he found himself coveting the swine's disgusting food. I thought, *okay Lord, I get it*. Sometimes we have to clearly see how low we've sunk before we can ask for your help in picking us up out of the mud. With my second wind, I forged ahead to see what else these riotous Faces had in store for me.

In spite of their previous late night, it was just

another day in the neighborhood for the fabulous Faces. Unbelievably, incredibly, Tim and Stash actually held down very responsible jobs during the daylight. They were always a little far out there in any setting but at work they tried their best to put on the glasses and maintain a more mild mannered, Clark Kent posture. You had to pull down some heavy coinage to maintain the Faces lifestyle, right? They exhibited super human endurance, functioning quite well after so much booze and so little sleep; it was something to behold. There's no telling what they could have accomplished if they had channeled all their energy and efforts into something constructive. As it was, they did pretty darn good, all things considered. Tonight was Friday night and they had something even bigger planned. It was time to sneak out a little early and head down to Busch Stadium to catch a Cardinals' game.

They had been fans since childhood like most people in St. Louis but were not really interested in baseball this Friday night. To the Faces, it was just another venue for their traveling act. To them, it didn't matter where they went. They were going to do their thing and just needed an event, a gathering, an audience. As weather goes, it was a spring masterpiece and they were in a jovial mood, ready to bust loose. They didn't know who but were sure they would come across people they knew down at the old ball yard; ready to be entertained, and they wouldn't disappoint.

As part of their preparation, they stopped Nature's red Camaro at a grocery store along the way to buy an aperitif. Even a super market provided a stage for their act and the Faces had people rolling in the aisles with maybe a few in disgust. They saved the best for last with a closing monologue that left the checker in stitches. The Faces were allowed to skate by with what normal folks would call rude behavior because they entertained; they offered a little comic relief and somewhat harmlessly stirred up otherwise humdrum lives. That was their mission in life; how they justified their otherwise aimless existences. In any case, this particular mission was nearly accomplished with the purchase of a gallon jug of artificial lemonade, a quart of the cheapest vodka they could find, Popov, and a bottle of Vess Tiki Punch soda. Right there in the parking lot for all to see, they merrily poured out half of the lemonade onto the pavement and emptied the entire contents of the Popov bottle into the jug. Then to top things off, they added a healthy splash of the Tiki Punch as the finishing touch; cap on, shaken, not stirred, Mr. Bond. They called this VooTiki Punch or Voot for short. The entire gallon jug was empty before they parked the Camaro in the stadium garage. Being the responsible citizens that they were, they properly disposed of the jug and bottles in the appropriate receptacle.

Since they knew no limits, the Faces also

quaffed numerous beers while making themselves happy spectacles at Busch Stadium. They had no idea of the score and didn't really care who was winning as they took their leave in the fifth inning to head to Mr. E's for more liquid refreshment. Ace was a happy drunk but Nature tended to become aggressive if not just plain mean when intoxicated well over the edge. He had no business being behind the wheel but indignantly spurned Ace's offer to drive. Ace was well over the legal limit too but knew he would have been much safer since he had a habit of driving as cautious as your grandmother, whether sober or crocked. Nevertheless, he carelessly consented, "Off then to see the Boogie Man, Jeeves!"

Nature said "Watch this" as he turned the Camaro from Clark onto Ninth, gunned the engine and headed north. "What now?" Ace implored somewhat shaken from his lethargy.

"I'm going to set a record" Nature proclaimed confidently as he crossed Walnut heading toward Market.

Now on full alert, Ace noticed the crazed, blank look in Nature's eyes as he demanded, "What's wrong with you, you crazy sum bitch?" Nature's eyes reminded Ace of that crocked turtle on speed in Bye, Bye Birdie.

"Let's see how many stop lights we can make it

through" was the determined reply. In true Face fashion, seeking thrills and glory over the safety of life and limb, Ace curiously hunkered down and acquiesced, then laughed deliriously while hurling expletives in every direction. They seemed to have a death wish. The lights were synchronized and started turning yellow as they passed Chestnut and Pine so Nature floored it and the speedometer climbed to sixty five. Lucky for everyone, St. Louis rolls up the sidewalks at 7:00 except on game nights but, since it was in the middle of the game, the downtown streets were nearly deserted. The only thing that diverted them from a true disaster was the St. Louis police officer that caught their act as they sped through a red light at Olive. Ace was thinking quickly, aided by the siren induced rush of adrenalin, when he forced Nature to pull over and turn right onto Locust. Before the cops caught up, he had yanked Nature across the console into the passenger seat and did a Chinese fire drill to plunk himself down into the driver's seat.

Things were a lot different in the '70s. Today, the Faces would be hit with the book and maybe even see some jail time. Besides their red light rampage, they were more than twice over the legal limit. And the St. Louis City Police are not to be trifled with; they mean business. But enforcement of drunken driving laws was lax at best back then. Even underage drinking and driving was a minor infraction that might get you a slap on the wrist and confiscation of your beer; a phone call to mom and dad at worst. The Faces had two things working in their favor. First, Ace was a veteran of this sort of thing; he knew the drill. Thankfully, they didn't have ready access to breathalyzers back then but normally employed field sobriety tests when necessary. Drunk as a skunk, Ace passed with flying colors demonstrating the agility of a lynx and the soberness of a nun. As for being appropriately respectful and deferential; Eddie Haskel had nothing on him. It was not just adrenalin, for Ace it was a gift. This would become just another chapter in his legend. There was still the matter of the speeding and red lights. Mr. Smooth dropped names tactfully, almost subliminally, and hit the jackpot. It turned out that this cop was a pal of Officer Stankowski who patrolled the area near the dairy company where Ace was a manager and regularly enjoyed the free samples of milk, orange drink and cheese that he was given to take home to his family. One call to Stan the Man and the Faces were free to go. Hallelujah, onward to Mr. E's for more cruis'n and booz'n!

Chapter 20

Bad Movie

The Faces might be considered losers by the hoi polloi but they actually excelled at anything they put their minds to, whether at work or play. Unfortunately, they were usually up to no good. But something they took semi-seriously was sports and fitness. They actually worked like dogs when it came to these things. After binge drinking all night and suffering through a sobering day at work, they would religiously drag themselves outside to run four or five miles regardless of the weather. They had awesome recuperative powers. It could be ninety eight degrees and you'd still see the Faces hitting the pavement to sweat it out. Then it would be off to a park or school to practice softball or football. Touch football was their first love. The late '70s was the golden age of touch football in St. Louis. Budweiser sponsored an apartment league that drew real talent; lots of ex-college and even NFL players participated. The big boys typically lived in the large, more affluent, West County complexes but there was an unusual concentration of talent in North County where Ace and Nature lived.

Football eclipsed all the other sports to where the Faces would practice year-round; just the two of them running endless patterns and throwing in the heat of summer while everyone else took to the ball diamonds. Though it was an apartment team, the boys were able to coax Mr. E to sponsor them. With his backing and money, The Boogie Men were arrayed in the sharpest uniforms around. They chose black and silver just like the bad boy Oakland Raiders. Of course, they had to put their apartment complex name across the backs of the jerseys to meet regulations but "Boogie Men" was proudly emblazoned on the fronts. The trophies they won were displayed behind the bar at Mr. E's rather than the manager's office at the complex.

It wasn't a large squad but deep in talent; quality over quantity so everyone had to be in top condition. It was a tight knit bunch, a real band of brothers. Although they were a pack of incorrigible party animals, the team shared a great work ethic. Most everyone had at least some high school football experience so the team was able to digest an imaginative, fairly expansive playbook. As soon as early autumn rolled around, the Boogie Men would practice at least three, maybe four times a week until they were able to execute plays in their sleep. In spite of all this preparation, with Ace at quarterback and Nature at wide receiver, they would improvise at the drop of a hat. They liked to give pet names to these gadget plays; like white boy go long or the bump on the head. Ace was the glue that held the team together, providing rock solid leadership and a swagger that other teams lacked. There was a rite of passage during the first full practice of the year where Ace ingeniously established his leadership credentials. There was always some wannabe guy who had no real business trying out for the team. Ace would line him up at right wide receiver where a chain link fence loomed just yards out of bounds and call his number for a ten yard square out. Ace called it the *screen play*. After the victim made his cut, Ace would loft the ball perfectly over the mark's inside shoulder so he would have to look up to make the catch, only to crash face first into the fence just as the ball arrived to his outstretched hands. Another one bites the dust. It may sound cruel but it was effective in weeding out the weak links. Life can be tough on the grid iron ... you do what you've got to do to be a winner.

Win the Boogie Men did. They regularly won their division and relished being cast as the underdogs against the West County winners. They didn't always beat them but they won their share and always gave them a good fight. One place the Boogie Men never finished second was at the parties after the games. With the beer and testosterone flowing freely, the players from all the teams would gather together at one of the sponsor's bars to let their hair down and recall, or better said, embellish the day's highlights. Of course, this type of assemblage of manhood attracted plenty of babes. The Boogie Men were small in number but were usually the center of attention, not least of all because of the Faces' antics. There were plenty of other characters on the team too and everybody had an appropriate nickname that was assigned by the team. Much like Native American names, these monikers usually pointed to some personal characteristic or memorable past event. For example, Wrong Way was renowned for his uncanny ability to wreck motor vehicles. Bad Knuckles was a linebacker with a propensity to drop potential interceptions like they were bad habits.

For all their hard work and accomplishments, the Boogie Men were best known for their off-field exploits. They were the undisputed champions of alcohol consumption and the accompanying bad behavior. They were a reflection of their leader, Ace. It's ironic when you think of how the league was formed to promote camaraderie among apartment dwellers while reaping the benefits of healthy physical activities. There was physical activity all right. That is, if you include gorging on hot dogs and nachos, guzzling gallons of beer, lewd dancing, bad language, shoving matches, fist-fights, occasional barroom brawls and projectile vomiting. This was right up the Faces' alley. It provided them with endless opportunities to do their thing and add to their already impressive resumes. I'll spare you further details regarding the Faces' escapades. I think you get the picture. It reminded me of how, when one of the young Turks at work offered up a horribly flawed business plan, one of my wizened old former colleagues used to try to rescue them from themselves by saying, "I've seen this bad movie before."

The Faces, however, were in syndication, never tiring of their own reruns. Every day was the same; outrageous behavior and wanton disregard for anything resembling decorum. The setting made no difference to the Faces. If nothing else, you had to give them points for consistency ... and stamina. What they did would have killed mortal men. However tedious their behavior, it was hard to dislike these lovable louts. They meant no harm really and there's no denying their entertainment value. Their ability to captivate and charm onlookers was their saving grace; that along with the genuine, good hearts that were still beating, buried somewhere in all the muck and mire. But anyone with half a brain could tell that this couldn't last forever. The Faces were human after all and were in a downward spiral even though they didn't realize it yet. In time, even they would see the signs ... wasted money, brushes with the law, deteriorating health and, most of all, an inescapable hollow feeling.

Chapter 21

What's it all About, Rick Dees?

The Faces were living in Never Land suffering from Peter Pan disease. "I'll never grow up" was their silent mantra. While most people their age were settled down and busy building their careers and families, Ace and Nature were still burning the candle at both ends and in the middle. They didn't want to acknowledge it but the demise of the Faces was as inevitable as the death of disco. With all due respect to Rick Dees, I think his parody, Disco Duck, heralded the pending doom … the bell tolls for thee, disco era. According to Newton's Third Law of Motion, for every action there is an equal and opposite reaction. Perhaps punk rock, Johnny Rotten, Sid Vicious and the Sex Pistols were part of that equation in the '70s; more of an overreaction I'd say. The renewed popularity of golden oldies in the '80s may have been reflexive too. People didn't like the King being banished to the sidelines by the likes of the Village People. No matter, the signs became undeniable with the popularity of mottos like Disco Sucks or Death to Disco. The backlash had been building and the end was swift with disco being swept out with the lost decade.

To me, it's still an unexplained phenomenon, both the coming and going of disco. I can live with it though; it's not one of life's great unsolved mysteries; a cold case to be reopened. There's no need to bother Rick Dees for an explanation. Disco is dead and we've moved on; that is, other than watching Saturday Night Fever occasionally and spiriting the Bee Gees from the archives to my car's CD player. Not much has survived that era but I must admit that I still feel the need to shake my booty when KC comes on the radio. No, I haven't lost any sleep over the disco dilemma. But I am troubled by this whole flashback to the Faces. I couldn't conceive of a good reason for any of this to happen to me or Ike. I mean, what is the point of exposing Ike to something like this with no apparent redeeming value? It would be like ending the story of the prodigal son with him lying in the filthy pig sty and no repentant homecoming or joyful celebration with the fatted calf. It reminded me of that old Michael Cain movie, Alfie. Alfie lived a promiscuous life much like the prodigal Faces but eventually came to his senses and tried to settle down and make something of his life. In the depressing end, Alfie's long awaited good intentions are thwarted by the object of his affection, Ruby, who hedonistically dumps Alfie for a younger fellow. I was feeling like Alfie at the end of that movie, recalling the tune it birthed: What's it all About Alfie? Is it just for the moment we live, like disco had its moment in the sun?

I was perplexed on two levels. First, I still had no clue about what Ike's dream meant from a physiological standpoint. Was it even a dream or something else? If it was a dream, how could Ike have conjured these outdated images and incorporated so many historical references unknown to him? If it was not a dream, then what was it?? Regardless of what it was or how it happened, I still firmly believed that God had some hand, some purpose in it all. But what was it? Try as I might, I couldn't find the moral to the story. It was an interesting but inevitably sad, depressing tale. What a letdown. Where's the beef? Turning to the Bible for edification didn't seem to help me. I read in the first chapter of James, "Blessed is the man that endures temptation: for when he is tried, he shall receive the crown of life, which the Lord hath promised to them that love him." That's a wonderful lesson of hope but it didn't appear to apply to the Faces' moribund story. No, Philippians 3:19 seemed more appropriate for these unrepentant prodigals, "Whose end is destruction, whose God is their belly, and whose glory is in their shame, who mind earthly things."

Was this dream meant to serve as some kind of warning? Did God see some horrible detour in Ike's path or mine that this vision would serve to help us avoid? Surely that was not the case. Being completely flummoxed, I turned to my one tried and true remedy and found simple, assured comfort and peace in these words ... "Therefore I say unto you, What things so ever ye desire, when ye pray, believe that ye receive them, and ye shall have them" (Mark 11:24). I believed these words, kept my trust in God and thanked him. This brought joy back to my troubled heart. With God, there's always cause for some joy, no matter what ... "rejoice evermore" (I Thessalonians 5:16).

Chapter 22

What Say You, Old Pro?

There was something about these two characters that endeared them to me in spite of the apparent lack of any redeeming qualities. It reminded me of the sympathetic treatment we often give to criminals regardless of their despicable deeds, at least in the movies. We actually cheered on Don Corleone and his murderous clan as though they were somehow more worthy than the Tattaglias, Don Barzini, Virgil Sollozzo or the corrupt Captain McCluskey. This was not driven by some kind of misplaced, populist ideology that gave Robin Hood hero-worship status to the likes of Bonnie Parker & Clyde Barrow or John Dillinger.

No, in spite of the axiom to the contrary, there was a warped code of honor held by many mobsters, in stark contrast to their otherwise malignant morals; that we respected in an odd way. Omerta, the code of silence; you never rat on anyone, not even to save your own skin. It's okay to deal drugs as long as you keep it away from the kids. You must never betray the family. Bludgeoning, blasting, slashing and strangling your enemies was praise worthy but don't dare drag their wives or children into the fray; that would be an infamia. We admired these qualities of honor, loyalty, discipline and trust that somehow bubbled up from the cesspool of their depraved existences. Now, I don't mean to compare the capricious misdeeds of Ace and Nature Boy to the thuggish exploits of bloodthirsty gangsters. But there is a parallel to be had.

Some traces of their solid, Christian upbringings remained intact in spite of their indulgent rebelliousness. Down deep, there was still a flickering flame of goodness in their hearts. And, like the Corleones, they had their own admirable code of conduct. Although everything was tongue-in-cheek with them and it was hard to separate satirical from serious, this attitude of common decency and virtue could be summed up in one of their favorite catch phrases, "You don't talk mean to your momma, and you don't mess with the Faces." Buried within the self-deprecating false bravado was a hint that, in spite of appearances, the Faces still held to certain, traditional values that were not up for debate; simply non-negotiable ... for example, honor thy mother and thy father. In the midst of all the bawdy behavior, the dream offered a few small glimpses past their rowdy facades. Underneath all the banter and bombast, the flippant and sometimes irascible attitudes, was a compassion that coaxed them to always help a friend in need. It was always secretive though, done on the down low so as to not damage their carefully cultivated, devil may care image.

They were especially loyal to one another,

reflecting again the early nurturing they had received. Don't get me wrong, they didn't grow up in Mayfield and weren't raised by Ward or June Cleaver. But it was a solid, old school rearing they received. Speaking of Leave It to Beaver, their friendship, on a private level out of the public glare, reminded me a bit of Damon and Pythias, at least as interpreted by Beaver and his pal, Larry Mondello. In one episode, Ward tried to impart his fatherly wisdom to Beaver after a fight with Larry. He told the story where Damon asked for a brief leave to settle his affairs before his death sentence was to be carried out by the tyrant, Dionysius. Fearing he would never return, Dionysius denied this plea until Damon's faithful friend, Pythias, offered to stand in his stead and suffer death if need be. Dionysius was so impressed by their trust and loyalty when Damon returned, that he commuted the sentence and let them both go free. Larry, that lazy little fink, took advantage of Damon Beaver and convinced him to give him the homework assignment Larry had failed to complete. Beaver felt betrayed when he incurred the wrath of Miss Landers but, true to Pythian form, Larry finally admitted guilt and Miss Landers, of course, demonstrated the wisdom of Dionysius and let them both off the hook. Yes, this was old and corny but it's really the way Ace and Nature came to each other's aid in a pinch. I thought, maybe these guys aren't so bad after all and felt a little bad about comparing them to Michael and Sonny Corleone.

But wait, the dream still had no moral and left me clueless as to what lesson we might glean. However, there were a few snippets that at least helped explain how the Faces arrived at this sorry point. This is just background, mind you, and is not intended to excuse their unruly habits or raucous lifestyle. The Faces, you see, were brought together by a common misfortune, divorce. This was revealed in an isolated scene in the dream during a private conversation while their guards were down. It was hard to tell how much of this went over Ike's head. As they were jogging several miles one day, things took on a rare serious tone when Nature asked Ace "So, how is Billie boy doing?" Apparently, Ace had a young son.

"He's okay, I guess. I got a cute letter from him the other day. I wish I could have kept her from moving him to Arizona."

"Yeah, that's pretty rough. At least we didn't have any kids before our break-up." This was deep stuff coming from the happy go lucky Faces. Nature submitted "Isn't it funny how married guys think they'd be so much happier if they were divorced and free again? I never wanted it. It was the last thing I wanted to happen."

"Me too," Ace concurred "it really rocked my world. I've never told this to anyone before but I actually had a nervous breakdown. Yeah, I was in the loony bin for a couple of days and they even zapped me to get my head on straight."

"There's no way!"

"Yes, it's true. But just keep that to yourself, eh Nature Boy?"

"No problem, Acer."

Both had been caught off guard by their unfaithful spouses and were seriously wounded, emotionally and psychologically. In one fell swoop, everything crumbled around them. It's tough to handle, when you're in your twenties and on the receiving end. Your closest companions become loneliness, anger, doubt and aimlessness. What's the point of work, much less a career? How long must you heal before you can even begin to try to pick up the pieces? Then there's the spiritual dilemma. Why God; I was following your plan of action, wasn't I; so why did you pull the rug out from under me? You can't get over the injustice of it all. Church, the best refuge of the weary, is just a painful reminder, so you stay away. You have no rudder and no compass. This was their frame of mind when fate brought Tim and Stash together in the same apartment complex.

As they settled into their new existence, they gravitated toward one another. Misery loves company. But macho guys can't show any vulnerability. Instead

169

they found ways to act out their anger and frustration. They took out their bitterness on the female persuasion in general, treating them like objects, not objects of affection. They would show them. This helped them channel their aggressions for a while but sooner or later bitterness eats away at you. So, eventually, malice gave way to rambunctiousness and riotous living. They quickly found out they were very good at it and received plenty of reinforcement for their rollicking ways ... the fabulous Faces were born.

They didn't talk about the dark times that gave rise to the Faces much. It would only cramp their style and get in the way of their mission, fun at all costs. When it did creep into their consciousness, they tried to deal with it philosophically and, of course, with a laugh, perhaps tinged with a bit of scorn. The Faces borrowed some of their most cherished principles from the metaphysical mind of the Old Pro; a crazy, grizzled uncle who had a knack for reducing the wisdom of the ages to the bare essentials. What do you think about material possessions, Old Pro? "A fine cage does not feed the bird." Old Pro, I just don't think this job is right for me; should I hold out for something better? "You can't race a Maserati on a dirt track." Ah, how the pearls of wisdom flowed from his loquacious lips. Once when they were feeling dejected about their break-ups, they sought out the Old Pro for sage advice. He summed it up for them so succinctly, with words they would never forget. These words would allow them to write off their ex-wives and be similarly dismissive towards women in general. "Boys," croaked the Old Pro "when the money's low, love will blow."

The Faces thought, *"How true, so true"* and had a good laugh every time they recalled this particular proverb from the Old Pro.

Chapter 23

Gumshoe Granby

I felt better having some understanding of the cause behind the effect but felt no closer to putting two and two together. So the Faces weren't total ne'er-do-wells; did this help explain the meaning of this figment of Ike's imagination any better? I still wasn't getting the greater message behind it all. Did I look past something; was there a reason to bust out the fatted calf that I had missed? Nothing in the picture Ike had painted seemed to impart any particular wisdom or give cause for celebration.

Maybe I was driving myself crazy for no reason. After all, wasn't this just some quirk resulting from Ike's untimely spill in the mall? So what if Ike had somehow transposed our two mall walking comrades into his chimera within a nanosecond? I'll admit it still freaked me out a bit but did that make this any less fanciful, less hallucinatory? With the passing of time, I was ready to write this off and get back to normal. But as days turned to weeks, it dawned on me that something very real had changed that fateful day at the mall. We were long overdue for one of Ike's seizures. Now, I wasn't complaining by any stretch but needed some certainty, some closure that perhaps our prayers had been answered and Ike was free of his monster. I couldn't be sure but the more that time passed uneventfully, the more optimistic I became since Ike's attacks had been so frequent and regular. Ike noticed the absence of his usual episodes too and even asked one day, "Granby, do you think I'm cured?"

Cautiously, I replied "Let's hope so."

I didn't want to look a gift horse in the mouth but felt compelled to seek some kind of explanation. I didn't doubt God's providence but perhaps he had used some earthly means to accomplish his ends. Curiosity nudged me back toward medical science. If EEG's and CAT scans were no help, how about MEG or magneto-encephalography? This newer technology sounded very powerful and perhaps could provide us with a break-through but it was much too expensive. In sifting through the latest literature, I heard about fMRI which, to my limited understanding, meant they had equipment with the potential to read minds. They had even conducted experiments where subjects were allowed to view three videos then were asked to recall one of them. With fMRI and some fancy algorithm they had concocted, they could tell which memory was being recalled by scanning their brains. With access to something like this, perhaps we could figure out just what was happening in Ike's brain. Maybe we'd be able to conclude that the whole thing was just some weird, hopefully harmless, physiological phenomenon. If they could isolate the activity to a particular area like the hippocampus region, we'd have a clue as to whether

173

this was something contrived or the product of an actual, episodic memory. I had to curb my enthusiasm because this was not only expensive technology but was also in a very early, experimental stage. My best shot was to convince some researcher with a lot of grant money to take Ike on as a subject.

I shifted into full-fledged gumshoe mode, figuratively donning trench coat and dark glasses. That was me, a gumshoe or old school private eye living in a CSI world. My motivation far exceeded my capabilities. I couldn't pronounce half of the medical jargon I had encountered on the web, much less understand it. But I hoped my enthusiasm could compensate for my technical incompetence. Effort has a way of making up for a lot of other ills. But it was not meant to be. It wasn't my ignorance that threw me off the case, no, it was a chance encounter. One night, Sally and I were at a local bar & grill, enjoying a burger and a beer. Sally noticed a guy, about our age, at the bar who seemed to be staring over at me. With my eyesight not being what it used to be, I didn't recognize the fellow but feigned a bathroom break to get a closer look. It took a little bit for it to register but finally came to me that this was an old high school classmate, Simon, who later was a colleague for a while at my first place of employment after college. I asked Simon to join us for a frosty, cold one and we exchanged pleasantries and a few war stories from the glory days. As if on cue, somebody in the joint decided to drop some coin into the juke box and take us all on a trip back to the '70s. I tipped my imaginary cap to no one in particular and thought, how apropos.

In the mood and the spur of the moment, a beer turned into pitchers. I asked Louie, I mean Simon, to tell me my favorite joke, if he could remember it. Rather than Simon, I used to call him Louie in reverence to the main character of a joke he once told me. It wasn't all that special except for the way Simon told it. He was a natural funny man with the timing, facial expressions and everything else required. It cracked me up as he told it again using that whacky, exaggerated accent; it went something like this. Louie went to the doctor with a mysterious condition that, as it turned out, could only be cured by ingesting human milk. As Louie fretted, the doctor assured him that, with his note, he could see Mrs. Booblinski who was nursing a child and receive the necessary care. Following doctor's orders to the letter, Louie visited Mrs. Booblinski who dutifully supplied the magic elixir, straight from her large, perfectly rounded sources. Louie was not too bright or experienced in the ways of the world. He was just happy to be receiving special medical attention. However, Mrs. Booblinski couldn't keep her passions bottled up during the process and developed amorous intentions. She suggested, very demurely at first "Hey, Louie, maybe I give you something else?"

"No, this is fine" he politely replied.

As this continued, Mrs. Booblinski became more insistent "Hey, Louie, how about I give you something else, eh?" Oblivious of her true intentions, Louie continued to decline. Finally, desperate with flaming desire, Mrs. Booblinski grabbed him in her clutches and demanded, with a lecherous look in her eyes "Louie, let me give you something else with your milk, okay Louie?"

Finally seeing the light and not wanting to disappoint, Louie sheepishly consented "Um, maybe you got some cookies?" It still killed me; I almost shot beer through my nostrils. I guess you had to be there.

Just about then, the Ohio Players came on with Love Rollercoaster. Louie and I did a wild-eyed double take, looked at each other and simultaneously declared "Say what?" The opening guitar riff followed by the horns' funky blare got us moving. Even Sally couldn't contain a rhythmic wiggle right there in her chair. When Hot Chocolate came on with: Everyone's a Winner; it brought our house down so to speak. Louie jumped out of his seat and starting doing his old parody of the lead singer, Errol Brown; he of the clean shaven pate, glittery striped pants and syncopated dance moves. Louie gyrated in a tight circle with hips moving but his upper body seemingly detached and almost motionless and that perfect, uh-huh-I'm-hip smile, flashing as he

176

turned. This took our minds off all our cares as we relived the past.

We finally gave into fatigue and returned to our seats to share more '70s sagas. From out of nowhere, Simon said "I haven't danced like that since the old days back at Mr. E's."

I paused, "I didn't know you hung out there."

"Oh yeah, for a year or so, that was the place to be." My mood snapped and I was back in gumshoe mode in a heartbeat, adopting my best Sherlock Holmes persona as though now regaled in a deerstalker hat with pipe and magnifying glass. I hesitated with my next question fearing it could backfire leaving me to look like some kind of idiot.

But I could not hold back, "Did you ever come across a couple of really wild and crazy guys there?"

I winced anticipating a sharp retort but was floored when Simon quickly countered "You mean the Faces, Ace and Nature Boy?" I had to gather myself and do my best to wipe the incredulous look from my face so as not to raise eyebrows.

"Yeah, you knew those guys?"

"Well, I knew them but I didn't *know* them. Everybody knew who the Faces were. I know this much, they were the two craziest sons of guns I ever met."

"Have you seen them recently?"

"No, as far as I know they dropped off the face of the earth back in 1979 or 1980 when that whole scene kind of disappeared."

Sally knew something was wrong and Simon could tell the air had been let out of the balloon. I said something about one too many beers getting to me, offered a good bye and left with Sally. As soon as we got to the car, Sally exclaimed, "What came over you Baker? I've never seen such an about face. We were having so much fun. Are you okay, honey?"

I took a deep breath and exhaled "I'm sorry dear but I was just punched in the gut." She tilted her head ever so slightly and looked at me quizzically. I had told Sally all about Ike's dream but I didn't get into the gory details and had not revealed how troubled I was by all the loose ends. For her sake, I had put on a happy face and played up the promising circumstances of Ike's longer than usual stretch without a seizure. I had to say something so I nonchalantly rendered "Simon just said something that caught me off guard." I could tell from her pregnant pause and tight lipped, skeptical expression that she would not let me off that easy. But if I told her that Simon's comments spoke volumes about the nature of Ike's dream and cast my understanding or lack thereof in a whole new light it would have frightened her to no end. There was no good reason to do that, not on something so speculative. I didn't really know what I was surmising anyway and needed time to collect my thoughts. I tried to play it down "I never realized Simon hung around with those two guys from way back when; a couple of real maniacs, major league goof balls. It just caught me off guard and brought back a lot of memories; not particularly fond ones." Before she could pursue it any further, I decided to play possum "Here, you drive. I'm feeling a little light headed."

Once at home and alone with my thoughts, my mind raced. This was no dream … these guys were real! There was no connection to me or Ike. How did they worm their way into his head? Did the Faces have anything to do with Tim and Stash? That had to be it. It just had to be. There was no other explanation. My only chance was to track them down and give them the third degree. But how could I find them? We had seen them at NWP once and never again, there or anyplace else. I guess I could ask around about Tim and Stash but I'd need a good excuse so as to not come across as some kind of stalker. The odds were not good but I had no other choice. Ike and I would have to keep our eyes peeled at NWP and elsewhere. What would I say if by chance I found these two wraiths? What could I say that wouldn't sound absurd? I figured I would just have to cross that bridge when I came to it. Things had gone from bad to worse, Instead of looking at some far out, medical quackery for a solution, where was I now? Was I venturing into the paranormal here? Or worse, could kindly Tim and Stash be secretly dabbling in the occult? Would I find them down by the river with a coven of black caped loony tunes chanting around a pentagram? C'mon, Baker, get a grip. Were my nerves that jangled, or was it just the beer getting the better of me?

BOOK FIVE

Whatever Happened to Baby Claire?

Chapter 24

A House Divided

Things returned to normal, or as much as they could, as I proceeded with Ike's schooling. One day, he showed me a free pamphlet he had picked up while killing time at the hospital. The title was: Strength Through Diversity and it was aimed at indoctrinating our youngsters about the marvelous advantages of our pluralistic society. It was replete with praises for every religion, including atheism, culture and ethnic group. There was also a recommended dose of tolerance for alternative sexual orientations and a call for objectivity toward various types of governments and economic systems. Being the old school adherent that I am, I had to work hard to resist the urge to regurgitate and demonstrate my objectivity to Ike as I perused the profane document. I wondered why this type of subject matter was aimed at kids and why it was being distributed in a public place like a hospital waiting room. Instead of letting this get under my skin, I decided to look at it as a good learning opportunity.

It was time for our history lesson anyway so I decided to talk about the great American melting pot. I told Ike how we became a great nation by taking advantage of all the different types of people who came to our shores. "So diversity is good, right Granby?"

"Well Ike, yes and no. It depends on how you define it and how you use it. A lot of good things came from our diversity … everything from different art forms, music, clothing, holidays and food to special skills, educational backgrounds, knowledge, methods and especially ideas. By having people eagerly come to America from all over the world with such a variety of talents gave us a big advantage. But to realize all this potential we had to form a strong team. If you have too much diversity, the wrong kind of diversity, it can work against you."

Ikestein caught on quick, "Do you mean like when the Rams start yelling at each other when they're losing badly?"

I chuckled, "Exactly. You see, what really turned the United States into a great team was when all these types of people were able to give up some of their differences and come together with one language, one form of government and a set of laws and values we could all share. They called it a melting pot because, in some ways, we all got heated up and stirred until we were all blended together in this wonderful recipe called America."

"But what about the advantages you said we got from our differences; did we lose them when we melted?"

He never ceased to amaze me in being spot on, "No Ike, that's the real beauty of our melting pot. It takes away differences that could pull us apart but lets us keep others. Everyone learned to speak English but it was okay to also keep their native languages. It's why we can enjoy tacos, pizza and gyros as much as hot dogs and hamburgers."

"So, Granby, why don't you like my book?" Perceptive little booger, I thought.

"Ike, it's just that I think your booklet gets some things backwards."

"Like what, Granby?"

I rubbed my chin, "Well, let me put it this way. If you have a team with members that only think about themselves and have nothing in common to hold them together, they'll never win. Or they could just get torn apart completely like when the Cardinals all split up to play for their home countries in the World Baseball Classic. Sometimes you have to put the team ahead of your own interests."

Ike surmised, "I think I know what you mean. When Jim Edmonds became a Cub, we couldn't cheer for him the same way and I had to stop wearing his t-shirt."

"That's right, Ike. We became a great nation

because, in spite of our differences, we all loved America and were willing to sacrifice everything for her if need be."

"Granby, if we're a melting pot, why is there so much trouble and fighting in America?"

This was getting deep, "Ike, people aren't perfect and neither are countries, not even the United States. Our melting pot didn't always work so well. Do you remember when we studied the Civil War earlier?"

"Sure Granby, the North versus the South."

"That's right. That terrible war with all its bloody destruction was all the result of a melting pot problem some eighty years beforehand. When we declared our independence and formed the nation and our constitution, we left some people out, the slaves. The biggest mistake is that this went against God's plan. How could we have a Constitution and Bill of Rights based on the principle that all people are created equal with rights granted by God and then deny those rights to a few? It just didn't make sense. Oh, politicians were no different back then than they are now. You can justify anything if you put your grubby, little mind to it, especially when money is involved. They simply declared that some people weren't people at all, just property. You remember the Dred Scott case at the Old Courthouse; it was right here in St. Louis of all places.

Treating some people like property was a bad idea from the start and God didn't like it."

Ike was listening intently. I caught my breath and continued, "It wound up dividing us into two camps, the North and the South. Abraham Lincoln, before he was president, when he was running for the Senate in Illinois, gave a speech on slavery called A House Divided where he warned against the North and South being split over slavery. He got the idea for that speech from Jesus in Matthew 12:25, 'And Jesus knew their thoughts, and said unto them, every kingdom divided against its self is brought to desolation; and every city or house divided against its self shall not stand.' He was certainly right and our nation almost didn't survive the Civil War. Lucky for us, Honest Abe knew the score and got us back on track with God's plan. But there was a heavy price to pay. Even after the war ended, lots of people didn't agree, we didn't really pull together as a team and some of those differences have haunted us ever since. So, do you see what I mean Ike when I say the melting pot wasn't perfect and America has had a lot of problems even though we still are the best team in the world?"

"Yes, I do, Granby." I breathed a sigh of relief thinking, mission accomplished.

"Granby, I'm still not sure about why you don't like the booklet." Oh, oh ... time to regroup.

"Well Ike, it's like this. We live in a country, thank God, where we have a right to think and say what we want. People have the right to have different ideas as long as they don't go up against what we've all agreed to abide by in the law. When we can't agree on some of these different ideas about how to do things, which is a lot of the time these days, we have a system of settling our differences peacefully. We get to vote and elect people to represent us and our ideas. These folks can even change the laws if necessary as long as we don't violate the basic principles that were laid down in the Constitution. You can even make adjustments to the Constitution but it's really, really hard."

"The founders were so protective of the Constitution that they set up our government in such a way as to avoid any power hungry sorts from taking our rights away. The President keeps an eye on the Congress and vice versa. And if those two get together and make a bad law, the Supreme Court can strike it down if they think it goes against the Constitution. Nowadays there are a lot of people who don't think much of the Constitution. In fact, most people don't know what's in it; seems they've stopped teaching about it in a lot of the schools. A good many of these folks are more interested in what they want versus what's good for the country and everyone else. They form what they call special interest groups to push for their own agendas. They're down right selfish is what they are. Pop used to say, 'doe, ray, me and the heck with everybody else.' Anyway, are you following me?"

Ike nodded; he was tracking all right ... "It makes me think of those greedy agents who are always messing things up for the Cardinals." I smirked and wondered if the Cards would still have DeRosa if Holliday wasn't teamed up with Scott Boras. In that fleeting moment, I shuddered to think, *would we be able to re-sign Albert*? Shaking that dreadful thought from my mind, I got back down to business.

"Ike, that's right but it's not just them; we're all greedy including you and me. That's why we need what they call checks and balances to keep us and especially our politicians in line. Everyone has the heart of a dictator deep down and we'd turn into tyrants if we thought we could get away with it. But our government was designed to prevent anything of the sort. So, what some people have figured out is that if they can't get what they want on their own, they'll team up with a bunch of other like-minded, selfish people to push their ideas on the rest of us through greedy, cowardly politicians. Yep, these types of politicians are a lot like some of the greedy sports agents. So let me see if I can tie all this together for you. These people, being not very honest, will take something good like diversity and twist it around to mean something entirely different. The trick is figuring out when they are using it as

188

intended, meaning they want to find the advantages in our differences that make the whole team stronger. Unfortunately, some of what you see in that booklet is just people using the term diversity to justify their own selfish desires at the expense of everyone else."

We were in the home stretch now. "I see what you mean, Granby, but I'm not sure how to tell which kind of diversity it is.

Okay, I thought, I've got this; time to wrap it up with a tight little ribbon. "Ike, it isn't easy for any of us. But there are two things we can always use. First, there's the Constitution. What you'll see most of the time with the false diversity crowd is that they don't have much respect for the Constitution. They will refer to it as a living document. That's a clever way of saying that it loses meaning over the years and should be constantly reshaped to match up with the times. That's a very dangerous notion because without a rock solid Constitution we would be subject to the whims of people rather than a nation of laws. We'd be right back where we started with tyrants like King George or more likely the next Hitler or Stalin. There's one thing even more important than the Constitution and it's the Bible. Honest Abe knew it. The founders knew it. When you go against God's plan, you're surely headed for trouble." Ike didn't say anything but he had that I've-got-it look on his face. "Ike, I know some of this is confusing but just think about it in baseball terms. There's a lot of

189

diversity on the Cardinals and it gives us a lot of advantages but that's not our real strength. Diversity is an advantage but it depends what we do with it; our strength is in our unity. A house divided shall not stand regardless of how much 'diversity' there is."

Speaking of a house divided, I needed to pay attention to my own lesson. Sally hadn't forgotten the way I left her hanging after our blast from the past with Simon. She knew there was more to the story and wouldn't let it rest. I saw it doing a lot more harm than good for Sally to bring her into the loop so I kept dodging her peppering. But I could tell she wasn't about to relent and the law of diminishing returns kicked in; I finally determined that keeping this wedge between us was worse than opening the kimono. I tried to downplay the whole thing by prefacing how I was a crazy old man with too much time on his hands; a worry wart that was letting his imagination get away from him. Then finally, "Sally, there's something that's been troubling me about Ike's dream when he took that spill at the mall. I don't think it was a dream at all but I'm not sure what it was."

"What makes you say that, Baker?"

I hesitated, "Well, I didn't want to bore you with the details but there's a lot of stuff in Ike's dream that just doesn't make sense."

That opened the flood gates and I began to gush. I went over the whole thing leaving no stone or pebble unturned, emphasizing along the way how unlikely it was that Ike could have picked up so much precise, historical minutia from TV or the movies or anyplace else. I finally got around to Simon's comment about the Faces and Sally then understood the ramifications; that since the Faces were not imaginary characters, Ike could not have been dreaming in the normal sense. There was no way he could have so definitively incorporated two such distinct individuals that we had never heard of or even knew existed. Of course, I didn't say anything to Sally to raise concern about Ike's condition and what this might mean for his health. I didn't need to. She could add one plus one and was floored just as I had been when Simon dropped the bomb on me. "What should we do, Baker?"

I tried to disguise my desperation, "We first need to stay calm and not panic. This may be nothing. We could be making a mountain out of a mole hill."

Sally proposed, "You're right dear. But, if nothing else, we need to satisfy our curiosity or this will drive us crazy."

She had read my mind, "The only thing I can think of to solve this mystery is to track down Tim and Stash. The first thing we need is more information. I don't know where to start except to walk the mall and hope they show up again." Sally looked at me with her hands firmly planted on her hips as though preparing to admonish a child.

"That will take forever, you old coot; look at all the time you've wasted already. I could have cracked this case by now."

All I could muster was a weak, "What?"

To my surprise, Sally was not consumed by worry or grief. To the contrary, she was focused and full of the Energy Bunny's verve. "Where's the place to turn if you need the scoop on anybody about anything?" I nodded and smiled. Ah yes, not the local news team, not the police, not Homeland Security, not the FBI, not even the CIA; this was a job for marvelous Martha. Martha, Sally's BFF she liked to say, was Dear Abby, Rona Barrett and Joan Rivers rolled into one.

"You're so right; if anyone can break this case open, it's Martha." It would be difficult to explain the situation to most people and incredibly awkward to ask for such a favor. But not Martha; she saw this as manna from heaven and seized the opportunity with the fervor of a happy bloodhound. I didn't worry about bringing Martha into our inner circle and the toll it might take on our own privacy. At this stage of the game any help was welcome. Magnum PI was ready to team up with Cagney and Lacy if that's what it took.

Chapter 25

Getting Down at Senior Towne

It was mainly the Cagney and Lacy show at that point. Magnum Granby had other fish to fry; namely the day-to-day responsibilities of Ike's schooling. While there was a lot of flexibility and freedom, there were still official state requirements we had to adhere to, even in a stubbornly independent place like the Show-Me State. One day, TB dispatched Sara to deliver a letter they had received from the State Board of Education. TB had misgivings about what kind of reaction he might get from me, the old reactionary. I guess I had railed one too many times about the public schools pushing the unscientific myth of evolution on the kids at the expense of the true story of God's creation. Perhaps it was my ranting about the disrespect shown to Christian holidays. To appease a few litigious atheists our local public school system took to calling the Christmas break the Winter Solstice. I really became unhinged when they did the same thing to Good Friday. They didn't want to sacrifice their day off so instead of eliminating it altogether, they kept the date on the calendar but referred to it as the Spring Holiday instead of Good Friday.

I can still remember how mortified TB and Sally were when I threatened to give the School Board a tongue lashing. My coarse old school exterior must have been more threatening than I realized. Actually, I was an old softie in many respects and much more level headed than most people imagined from my bluster. At least that's how I saw things. As a case in point, I didn't see this letter as intrusive but welcomed it. Although I definitely have a libertarian streak, when you get to where the rubber meets the road, you welcome any help you can get. In my experience, Missouri treated home school practitioners fairly and offered a lot of valuable support and resources. This letter offered guidelines for incorporating community service into home school curriculums. I read it more as a suggestion than a requirement but thought it was a good idea in either case. And I had the perfect idea in mind.

I decided to assign Ike the task of creating a journal from someone else's memories. Wouldn't it be a great learning experience for Ike to go straight to the source and learn some history first hand? I pictured a scene from Little Big Man where a bright eyed, young reporter interviewed an ancient Dustin Hoffmann to get the scoop on the Old West: real cowboys & Indians stuff, from an eye witness account. I figured this would be a community service of sorts since it benefitted both the story teller and the journalist. It did old Dustin good to get it off his chest, didn't it? The worst thing about getting old was being irrelevant, isolated and ignored. Sometimes the best thing you can do for the elderly is just to give them an audience and a little respect; just listen to them.

As I mentioned before, there was a very under-utilized community center at NWP called Senior Towne. It's not that it didn't offer something meaningful and worthwhile. It provided the chance for some togetherness with your aging peeps while maintaining the type of independence foreign to a retirement home. You could come and go as you pleased and take advantage of some useful resources that were available free of charge along with the help of a friendly staffer or two. Still, most people, at least the more mobile ones, used it mostly as a base of operations while taking advantage of the mall walking experience as much as possible.

One of the not so lucky ones in terms of mobility was a sweet, old lady I'll call Claire out of respect for her privacy. She had a couple of other stage names a few of you might still recognize. A portion of her life had been in the limelight but she preferred the anonymity she had enjoyed for nearly forty years. Most people who were lucky enough to be alive at ninety two like Claire, were either home bound or sentenced to death row in one of those prisons known as assisted living communities. As for me, I planned on dying of a heart attack, God willing, long before that happened to me. Claire was fiercely independent and still just spry enough to get around with the aid of her walker and some assistance. Her razor sharp, mental acuity, charm,

195

wit and sense of humor more than made up for her physical limitations. She was very inquisitive and still loved learning new things; particularly in talking to young people. When I approached Senior Towne about Ike's community service project, Claire jumped at the chance.

She and Ike hit it off right away. They shared an intuitiveness and penetrating wisdom that belied their respective ages. I could have walked while Ike worked on his assignment but was so fascinated and delighted by their exchanges that I hung back, the proverbial fly on the wall. Claire personified the adage: you can't judge a book by its cover. To look at her was like seeing an indistinguishable, rusted out piece of equipment resting in an abandoned farm's overgrown pasture. I don't mean to say she was unkempt. She was always well groomed, presentable, prim and proper. But Claire was just so frail and etched with time. However, as soon as she spoke, she came to life and brought everyone around her along for the ride. Her age disappeared as her eyes lit up like fire flies.

Claire's life was a rich tapestry, woven in many layers. She was born in 1918 at the end of the War to End all Wars; she laughed at the irony of the phrase. She started life with a bang, born into a family that was more a vaudevillian troupe than anything else. "I was born back East but didn't really have a home town. I guess I was from Everywhere, U. S. A. We traveled the circuit like nomads and gypsies, crisscrossing the country. My daddy danced mostly and mother sang and must have played six or seven different instruments. All the other kids were blessed with some variety of acquired talents, even juggling and plate spinning. Everyone was obliged to act in some form or another, mostly skits, and pull off any manner of stunts, gags and acrobatics. Those were tough times. You learned to do anything the audience wanted if it meant a paying job.

My daddy used to brag about how there wasn't a dance invented he couldn't master. Maybe *master* was misapplied; he was more a jack-of-all-trades and a master of none. He was even able to buck dance but admitted he was no Ray Wollbrinck."

"Miss Claire, what's buck dancing?"

"Oh, I'm sorry honey, maybe you've heard of clogging."

Ike interjected quickly, wanting Claire to get right back to her story, "Yes, we saw that in the Ozarks once." He didn't even ask about Ray Wollbrinck, a non-essential detail to him.

She went on "I was nothing more than baggage for the first few years until I was able to start training. By the time I was six, I was ready to carry my share of the load. They dubbed me Baby Claire since I was so small and looked even younger than I really was. I don't mean to brag but I was more than just a novelty, with a natural talent for hoofing and singing. Before long, I was a featured player of sorts rather than just an amusing after-thought." She paused, closed her eyes and offered a wrinkled, satisfied smile as though watching a home movie.

"We never really made it to the big time but we had our moments. For a while we traveled the prestigious Orpheum Circuit. Once, we were even booked as an opening routine at the Palace in New York City. Mostly, we bounced around the smaller houses but it was a living. And an experience I'll never forget. The family that works and plays together, stays together, my daddy used to say." Then Claire's countenance drooped and Ike, watching and listening with rapt attention, immediately had a look of consternation sweep across his face.

Claire forged ahead, "Things took a turn for the worse in the late '20s." Ike was dying to ask Claire if she knew Al Capone but didn't want to interrupt. "Movies started coming into vogue. Nothing can beat live entertainment but movies just made more sense economically. They were a lot cheaper than paying real, live people and didn't require meals or health benefits. For a good while, most houses mixed live acts along with the movies. But things really bottomed out in 1932, mid-November I think it was, when The Palace switched exclusively to cinema. By that time, things

198

were not looking so good for me personally anyway. I mean, it's tough to pull off Baby Claire when you're starting to sprout, well you know, develop a lady's figure."

It amused Ike to think of Claire as a young woman, "What did you look like back then?" A woman of lesser understanding with thinner skin might have been offended by such a question.

"Oh, you'd be surprised Ike. I was quite a looker."

Ike confessed, "I figured you were really pretty." *Nice recovery little buddy*, I thought.

"The boys took a real shine to me back then. My daddy didn't like it too much. I'm not sure what bothered him more, the boys coming around or me outgrowing Baby Claire. It was indicative of what was happening to our family but bothered him more so because I was the baby. I felt sorry for my daddy having to contend with it all." Just then, Claire's ride showed up and we reluctantly had to call it a day. Where had the time gone? It was for the best though because while her spirit was more than willing it was evident that Claire's tired, old body was not so cooperative. We all cheerily agreed to meet next week, same time, same place.

The week couldn't pass quickly enough for Ike. I

was getting antsy too but mostly because the gals had not been able to turn up any leads yet on Tim and Stash. I was becoming really frustrated on that front; if Cagney and Lacy couldn't find Tim and Stash, no one could. True to her word, Claire was waiting for us when we made our way to Senior Towne the next week. "Now, where did we leave off?" she feigned memory loss to test Ike.

Rough and ready Ike flipped open his little notebook, "We were talking about your dad having problems after The Palace changed to movies." All righty then, let's get down to business.

Claire picked up right where she left off, "It was a tough way to raise a family. We were always on the road and couldn't put any roots down. We couldn't join a regular congregation. For us, church was mainly daddy reading to us occasionally from the Good Book. Sometimes mother and we kids wondered, are we family or employees? Some aspects of our life I wouldn't trade for anything. Living and working together the way we did made us closer than most families. As a consequence, it was awfully hard for daddy to shelter us from the worries of a declining business since we were all in it together."

A dreamy look came over Claire's face and Ike could tell she was very fond of her father. "Daddy was resourceful and he was a scrapper. He was never one to

200

give up easily. The Great Depression really took a toll on vaudeville. As the economy worsened, more and more theaters moved completely to motion pictures. The Orpheum Circuit was bought out becoming the O in RKO pictures. We scrimped and saved to make ends meet and daddy had to let our booking agent go to cut expenses. He became what he liked to call a triple threat; that is, in addition to raising a family and performing, he also had to spend a lot of extra hours chasing down bookings. For a while in the '30s, we were able to keep all the balls in the air. We played smaller venues and followed the work to places like the Borscht Belt in the Catskills where live entertainment remained a staple for a while."

Claire's sweet smile was eclipsed by a forlorn countenance. "Eventually, it was just too hard. Daddy aged so much in just a few short years. We weren't bringing in enough money to keep us going and my brothers and sisters were starting families of their own. Like many folks in the business, they just started peeling off to join the workaday world in regular jobs. And trust me; beggars couldn't be choosers back then. If you were fortunate enough to find a job, any job, you took it." Claire sighed, "Daddy had always said the family that works and plays together, stays together. He must have been some kind of a prophet because once the act came apart we were scattered to the four winds. I was the last to go being the youngest but I left the nest pretty early. I was only eighteen in 1936 when I found my prince charming. Daddy abhorred the thought of me getting married so young, especially to a man seven years older than me. But he was a brick layer making $1.30 per hour which was much better than most back then and daddy swallowed his pride knowing it was for the best; that a good provider was a rare find for his daughter. I didn't mind that he had big strong arms, handsome features and thick, wavy black hair."

Claire shook her head in mild disgust. "If daddy had only known, he would never have consented. That bum took to drinking and lost his job. I think he had an eye for the ladies too. He up and left me after two years. The best thing I can say about him is that, at least, he didn't leave me saddled with kids. Daddy would have hunted him down if he were in better health. It would have been pointless though since I didn't want him back. It wasn't long after that that daddy died, God rest his soul. On top of everything else, I think our break-up was the final straw; I think daddy died of a broken heart."

Claire paused and then snapped to attention realizing that this was getting way too heavy for Ike. "You know what they say, all things work together for good. And the show must go on. Being all alone as I was and without anything to tie me down, I threw caution to the wind. Having nothing to lose, I resurrected my career. I used my looks, talent and experience in
202

vaudeville to break into movies and television; it was no tidal wave but I made a small splash in the pond here and there. It put bread on the table and I had some fun. I may have been small potatoes but I was able to rub elbows with some of the folks in the tall cotton."

Claire had purposefully done a U-turn from her melancholy past and tried to dredge up the good times for Ike's sake. "Yes, I met a lot of the old timers who were able to make the jump from vaudeville to movies and television in a big way; some of the real giants."

Ike lunged, "Ooh, tell me who Miss Claire, tell me please!"

She proceeded to reel off names that wowed me but left Ike underwhelmed, "Jack Benny, Bob Hope, Jimmy Durante, Groucho & Harpo and Red Skelton. I once sang back up for Kate Smith and even had a bit part in one of Uncle Miltie's skits. There was another time I got to dance in the chorus behind Sammy Davis, Jr. I was at the end of the line and barely visible on screen but so what? I can say I knew George Burns before he became god." Claire had no way of knowing that her Oh God reference caused me to have a flashback. But Claire could tell that Ike was unimpressed since he hadn't been exposed to our golden age heroes. She took another stab at it, "Ike, have you ever heard of Judy Garland, the lady that played Dorothy in the Wizard of Oz?"

"Of course, Miss Claire, that's one of my all-time favorites. Did you know Dorothy?"

"Yes, I did Ike. But I also got to know her long before that too. Her family was in vaudeville just like mine. In fact, her father, Frank Gumm, was pals with my daddy for a while."

Puzzled, Ike asked "How come he had a different name?"

"Actually, Judy's given name was Frances Gumm. She was just like me; they called her Baby because she got started in show business so early. We used to play dolls together when we weren't performing. She started dancing and singing about the same time I did even though I was more than 3 years older than her. She was something special." Ike was so enchanted by this personal connection to Dorothy that Claire wisely decided not to bemoan her own shortcomings by drawing comparisons to Judy Garland's enormous success. She also side stepped the issue of booze, pills and other failings that later caused her star to burn out prematurely. No, she saved the best for last and, in the spirit of a true entertainer, closed with a big finale. "You'll never guess who else I worked with back then."

Again, Ike took the bait vociferously, "Ooh, tell me please, who, who?"

"Believe it or not, Ike, I actually worked with Moe, Larry and Curly, the Three Stooges."

"Wow, really; what were they like in person?" Claire had no curtain call to top the Stooges so she closed on a high note. She was not about to get into a discourse on how tough the business was back then or how even the Stooges had their serious side, their demons.

"Ike, they were just as crazy in person. I never laughed so hard in my life. Curly was an absolute riot." She surprised me and Ike both when she did a pretty good woo-woo-woo-woo and nyuk, nyuk while plunking her fingers against her throat. She brought down the house.

As we closed out another session, Claire motioned for me to accompany her while she made her way to the shuttle. I asked Ike to stay back and go over his notes for a minute. As soon as we were out of ear shot, Claire visibly changed as though she had just removed her stage makeup. She looked gaunt and drawn and much more fragile than ever before. She took my elbow as we shuffled along and whispered, "I need to tell you something that I don't want Ike to know. He's such a precious little boy; I don't want to do anything to hurt him. So this will be our little secret, okay?"

"Of course Claire; what is it?"

"Mr. Paulson, I have pancreatic cancer. I'm dying."

Chapter 26

Garden Party

I knew enough about pancreatic cancer to realize that our time with Claire was limited. People half her age would be given six months to live, a year at the outside. It was a nasty, merciless enemy that took no prisoners. This presented a real dilemma in that Ike's assignment would be finished in about a month, so there was little worry that anything serious would transpire before then. But the longer this went on, the closer they would become. Ike was already adopting her like a member of the family. I wanted Ike to be able to enjoy as much time with Claire as possible but ease him out well before the grim reaper could pull the rug out from under him. Was it right to try to shield him from this harsh reality, the truth? Perhaps not but it was out of my hands anyway since I had committed to Claire.

Claire put up a brave front during our next visit. I wouldn't have known anything was different if she hadn't brought me into her confidence; that is, with one exception. She dialed back her sensibility toward Ike's youth and stripped a bit of the varnish. Claire didn't say anything but I sensed she wanted to share her legacy with more of the raw truth showing through. I suspect she made a conscious judgment that it would help Ike deal with reality better in the coming years. "Ike, I hope you never go into show business; at least not until you're old enough to handle it if it's what you want to do. It can be really tough on youngsters. I've known plenty of them and heard enough stories about others to know better."

"But isn't it fun, Miss Claire?" She recalled a lot of famous names, at least famous to me, to attest the difficulties of adjusting to an ordinary adult life after experiencing fame at an early age. Ike had heard of Lassie but couldn't place Tommy Rettig as Jeff Miller. Claire talked about the serious problems he encountered, including drug addiction, before he finally turned things around and gained notoriety as a software developer only to pass away at fifty four. Then she wheeled out Jeff Stone played by Paul Peterson on The Donna Reed Show. He had a rocky road after stardom but eventually experienced good success as an author after going back to school. Before Donna Reed, he was a Mouseketeer on the Mickey Mouse Club but was fired for misbehaving. In a famous quote that spoke volumes about the tribulations of child actors that would befall him, Peterson commented at the time, "I didn't know a kid actor shouldn't act like a kid." It turns out that God used this broken tool too. In 1990, following the suicide of fellow former child star Rusty Hamer who played Danny Thomas' son on Make Room for Daddy, Peterson became an activist and formed a support group for children in show business called A Minor Consideration. Ike was getting the picture but the names weren't registering so Claire tried to turn the clock ahead to make things more relevant but still wasn't able to connect with the Coreys (Haim and Feldman) or Gary Coleman. She finally hit pay dirt with Saved by the Bell's Screech and Lindsay Lohan since Ike had seen The Parent Trap a dozen times.

As Claire unraveled these difficult lives, it made me think of my own tormented childhood and the difficulties I had transitioning to early adulthood. My affliction was epilepsy rather than fame but I felt I had walked a mile in their shoes. Looking back, I felt thankful that I had at least suffered in obscurity. It was hard to imagine how much worse it would have been to go through that kind of pain in the glare of the public eye. Thankfully, I had come out of it okay as did many of them eventually. It's not how you start but how you finish, eh?

Ike, who was catching on as a journalist, politely challenged Claire a bit, "Aren't there any child stars without problems?"

"Everyone has problems, Ike, but I know what you mean. There are some that are able to make the transition better than others. Beaver Cleaver comes to mind. So does Drew Barrymore. She was so cute in E. T. Probably the best is little Opie Taylor. Ron Howard somehow survived even though his whole life has been in front or behind the camera; Andy Griffith, American

Graffiti, Happy Days and so many good movies he's directed. I think what helped him avoid the pitfalls was family. His parents were always close by and the Andy Griffith cast was like a big family too. He's a good family man in real life. There's something about baby bottles and dirty diapers that helps you keep your feet on the ground." Opie was very relevant to Ike thanks to the wonders of TV Land and syndicated reruns.

"Ricky Nelson was another phenomenon who started early and enjoyed success for most of his life. His radio, TV and real families were one in the same. I'm sure that had its plusses and minuses. The show was named after his parents, Ozzie & Harriet and included his brother, David. They were a lot like the Cleaver family. Ricky, the baby, wound up being the most famous one of them all. You see, he could sing like a bird with a lilting voice that carried you along on a warm breeze; and what looks! Pretty may not be the right word for a male but when it came to Ricky, he was the prettiest man I ever saw. He had big blue eyes surrounded by beautiful, long lashes, dark, luxurious hair, plump red lips and perfect features."

Ike giggled, "Did you like him?"

"My heart is beating faster just thinking about him. If I had been at least twenty years younger, look our Ricky! He was a teen heart throb, a top recording artist and movie star to boot."

210

Normally, I kept my distance and remained completely silent during these sessions but couldn't help blurting out, "Ricky played the coolest, good guy gun-slinger, Colorado, in my favorite Western of all time, Rio Bravo." I sheepishly regained my composure and put my enthusiasm back on the shelf, returning center stage to Claire.

"With all his success, there was still something missing for Ricky. I think it can be best summed up in his song, Garden Party. In the early '70s he tried to make a comeback at Madison Square Garden with all new material. The songs were great but the crowd booed him because they only wanted to hear their old favorites. While we all enjoy our memories, they can imprison us sometimes. For someone like Ricky, he couldn't stand to be trapped in the past when he had so many new things he wanted to do. He got it out of his system by writing Garden Party. His frustrations were summed up in the line 'If memories are all I sang, I'd rather drive a truck.' There was a happy ending to the song in that he found peace as captured in the refrain: 'But it's all right now; I learned my lesson well; you see you can't please everyone so; you got to please yourself.'" Claire lowered her chin reverently, "Unfortunately, there wasn't a happy ending for all of his fans like me. He died in a plane crash in 1985. He was only forty-five years old; much too young. We still miss you Ricky."

Chapter 27

Betty Davis Eyes

"I didn't mean anything disparaging by talking about child actors like that. They're only human like you and me. I guess it was my way of greasing the skids to explain my own problems." Claire leaned forward and looked at Ike remorsefully as she prepared to lay bare her own transgressions. "Although I wasn't what you might call a star in today's sense of the word, I had my own problems coping with the real world. Growing up in show biz is like living in fantasy land where normal rules don't apply. It lures you into a false sense of security and sets you up for a rude awakening. Mine came in the form of loneliness and insecurity as my marriage fell apart and then work started drying up." Claire was at the confessional now, taking pains to be honest while keeping in mind Ike's age and impressionability. "When you grow up in a big, tight knit family like mine, there's always someone around to catch you when you fall. My safety net was gone now and I only had two things to fall back on; my talent which was no longer in demand and my good looks. Driven by the need to feel safe and secure, I took the easy road. It didn't take me long to hook a man."

Claire continued to wade through the muck,

trying her best to help Ike understand without making excuses. "God was not part of my life back then. It wasn't so much that I made a conscious effort to push him away but just neglected him something terrible. When your role models are all show biz types, you lose touch with reality; especially when it comes to things like marriage." Claire's face took on a disgusted look as though a bad stench had wafted into the room. "Hollywood wedding vows are a sham; until death do us part, hah! I think the average life of a marriage there is two, maybe three years. Just look at Richard Burton and Elizabeth Taylor. He was married five times but that paled in comparison to her eight. The only thing that kept her from having the all-time record was the fact that she married Burton twice. No, you have to give the nod to Mickey Rooney who got hitched to eight separate women."

Claire noticed the astonished look on Ike's face. "I know, it sounds absolutely crazy, Ike. But who am I to talk. I fell into the same trap. Why, I was married three more times in the '40s alone."

Dumbfounded, Ike exclaimed, "You Miss Claire?"

"I'm not proud of it but it's sadly true. The problem was that I never married for love. It was always about financial security and companionship, never love ... at least not the kind of love that involves God. The

213

further I moved away from God the worse things got for me. Oh, I had nice clothes and a fine roof over my head and all. But I was so empty inside. That's why the marriages were so short lived. I had no one to blame but myself. There was never any real sense of commitment. I was completely selfish. If daddy had been alive, perhaps I could have avoided this sad chapter of my life. I wouldn't have wanted to make him ashamed of me."

Claire switched gears, "There's something about a change of decades that seems to offer a new lease on life. That was surely the case for me in the '50s. You see, I met this producer fellow in Cincinnati, Cliff. Yes, before you ask, I got married again. But this was a little different. He was quite a bit older than me and, I think in a way, he was a father figure to me. He brought a certain stability that I was lacking and we loved each other or at least needed each other in a sense that was better than my first four marriages if not ideal. With him being in the business, it helped me connect to my past, at first emotionally and then professionally. He was developing a daytime variety show and eventually came to the conclusion that I might be the perfect host. This wasn't about nepotism, Ike, you know, family looking out for family. He was familiar with my background and knew how many vaudevillians had migrated to TV variety shows; some making it really big like Ed Sullivan. But this was local TV and he needed someone down home who could relate to people in a very personal way but enliven things with some of the old shtick. He searched high and low before it dawned on him that I was right under his nose."

"This was what I'd call the golden age of local television. In their markets, local celebrities were larger than life; even local news anchors since this was before the age of 24/7 cable coverage. Although the networks had carved out space for national figures, there was plenty of pie left for the locals in just about every category; variety, news, music, cartoons."

I couldn't help myself, "St. Louis was no different. In spite of Dick Clark's American Bandstand, we had our own St. Louis Hop with Russ Carter. As for cartoons and Three Stooges shorts, we had Cookie and the Captain hosting while supposedly steaming down the Muddy Mississippi in an old paddle wheeler. And I'll never forget Charlotte Peters."

Claire beamed, "I knew Charlotte. She was a character, a real spitfire and one of the nicest people I ever met. My show was a lot like hers; live, unpredictable, zany and just plain fun. Her show lasted a lot longer than mine. For my money, she was one of the very best. Charlotte was one of the few that could have been regional, maybe even national if such a thing were conceivable back then. No, we didn't see Oprah coming."

"We had a great run; the show and me and Cliff. In many ways it was my favorite decade. I enjoyed the celebrity and was happy to keep things on the local level. The people were good hearted, genuine Midwesterners and we were able to put down some roots. It's funny how we blame God when things are going bad but drift so far away when everything is smooth sailing. That was the one thing that was missing from my '50s utopia. I drifted so far away without a care in the world. But all good things come to an end, don't they? In 1958, my cotton candy world disintegrated. Cliff died and so did the show shortly thereafter. He had been the glue that held everything together, not just the show but me too. It was a hard blow that laid me to waste. The terrible loss aside, what bothered me most is that I never really had a chance to talk to Cliff to see if he had made peace with God. Medical technology being what it was back then, we didn't see it coming. Heart attacks are sneaky culprits that pounce without warning. If only we had known. But, in our bliss, we had lived footloose and fancy free; carefree in thinking time was limitless."

Claire's tone became very somber. "The fact that we had gone nearly eight years without ever having a meaningful conversation about spiritual things or the after-life, ate away at me. At the time, we had given no thought to church or such matters. Now I could not escape those thoughts and burning questions. Cliff had left me financially secure with our affairs in good order but I had no foundation beyond that. I should have turned to God at that point but, being the fool that I was, I ran further away. I also made the mistake of shutting out the few friends we had made. As for the fans, they moved on as time passed and dust gathered on my career again. Being absorbed with self-pity and blaming God for it all, I really let myself go. The bottle became my best friend and I began living solely in the past. After a while, I couldn't recognize myself. By the time 1962 rolled around, I was a complete and utter mess. It's a miracle that I survived, thanks to Baby Jane."

"Don't you mean Baby Claire?" Ike inquired.

"No, sweetheart, this was another 'Baby' but it could have been me."

"How ironic it was that Whatever Happened to Baby Jane hit the silver screen in 1962. Talk about life imitating art. Baby Jane Hudson was played by Betty Davis, probably the biggest, most glamorous female movie star of the '30s and '40s. The mesmerizing impact of her big, beautiful, soulful eyes was immortalized by Kim Carnes in her 1981 hit: Betty Davis Eyes. She had it all; looks plus enormous talent and attitude. By the time the '60s rolled around, she still possessed two of the three with looks giving way to age. To keep her career going, she had to embrace the horror genre and trade in heroine status for villainess. Being ever the consummate professional, she did so with aplomb and frightening reality. I'll never forget the impact it had on me when the former beauty queen showed up on that screen as a demented hag in garish make-up and that oh so inappropriate chiffon and lace dress with girlish ribbons, singing the song that had made Jane famous as a little child: I'm Writing a Letter to Daddy." I remembered that movie well and got the creeps just thinking about how the ghoulish Jane tortured her poor, crippled sister, Blanche, in their isolated, decaying mansion. I had literally jumped out of my seat when she served her that dead rat on a silver platter. Speaking of irony, I couldn't help but think of Joan Crawford who played Blanche and how, later in life, she was accused of being a monster of sorts in her daughter's memoir, Mommy Dearest.

"Anyway, that's enough about Baby Jane, Ike. You can watch it for yourself sometime if you want a good scare. The point is, when I saw that movie, it shook me up something fierce ... thankfully. While I wasn't really that old or scary, when I looked in the mirror, I had Betty Davis eyes; not the glamour gal of the '30s but spooky, old Jane Hudson. I was cutting off my nose to spite my face and turning myself into something very unpleasant. I wasn't sure of exactly what I needed to do but knew I needed a change of pace. Seeing that frightful image in my head, startled me enough to stop boozing and get myself back in shape. I pulled up stakes and moved, needing a complete change of scenery."

Chapter 28

The Bad Samaritan

"That's what brought me to St. Louis, Ike, and I've been here ever since."

Ike was following the timeline carefully, "Did you get to see Stan the Man play?"

Claire shrugged, "Not only play but I met him too."

Ike was blown away, "Whoa!"

Claire stopped Ike in his tracks, "Let's not get off the subject, young man. I have a few more things I need to unload from my conscience."

Ike dutifully put pencil to paper, "Oh yeah, okay."

Claire continued, "It wasn't too long before I got the show biz bug again. I wasn't looking for the big time; I just wanted to keep busy, get back to familiar surroundings and use the gifts God had given me. Have you ever been to the Muny, Ike?"

Ike smiled eagerly, "Yes, just last year Granby took me to see Meet Me in St. Louis. We watched the movie too since it starred Dorothy, I mean, Judy Garland."

Claire chortled, "That's where I wound up in the summer of 1963. I felt right at home there, comfortable being in the background. I can still remember my small parts and all the wonderful shows from that year; dancing in The Unsinkable Molly Brown and singing in I Dream of Jeannie. No, it wasn't the one about the astronaut and the genie in the bottle. This Jeannie was about the old South and songwriter Stephen Foster. You never hear of it anymore because, unbeknownst to us at the time, it was racist and soon fell out of favor in the later '60s. I didn't know anything about all that; I just enjoyed singing those Stephen Foster songs like O Susanna. It was marvelous being part of a troupe of players again and made me think back to the good old days with daddy and the rest of the family on the circuit. I made some new friends that summer, one in particular that was special."

This vexed Ike, "Miss Claire, not again?"

Claire shook her head, "No, it was worse this time. I met a man friend but we just took up with one another as if we were married and never officially tied the knot. I was following my own plan again instead of God's. I knew it was wrong. But I put up a good front even though it tore me up inside sometimes. After hitting such a low point in Cincinnati, it helped my ego, or maybe I should say self-esteem in today's lingo, to know that at forty two, I was still able to attract someone as young and handsome as Trevor. They say you can't fight city hall and I should have known this would lead to no good but I refused to let my troubled conscience get the better of me." I was gripped by Claire's account and knew better than to interrupt but, as you've probably noticed, I have this tendency to find metaphors in familiar songs and couldn't help thinking about the Bobby Fuller Four's I Fought the Law or Mellenkamp's more contemporary Authority Song; I fight authority, authority always wins. Always the optimist, I was anticipating, hoping for some twist of fate in this tale that would redeem Claire. My mind jumped to the Ozark Mountain Daredevils; if you want to get to heaven, you have to raise a little hell. I knew this was really bad theology going all the way back to the misguided people of Corinth. Sinning is never good for us and we don't get to heaven by our own deeds but in spite of them, thanks to Jesus. But you get the idea. I was anxious for the other shoe to drop; for Claire to get to the revelation, experience a turnaround, the happy ending.

"St. Louis was a very provincial town back then and I guess still is. This wasn't Hollywood, Soho or Greenwich Village where these things would be so easily dismissed. I suffered constant paranoia that my libertine lifestyle and loose morals would be exposed. Trevor and I kept our relationship under wraps except with our fellow performers whom I supposed would be more understanding than regular folks. One day, I received an anonymous note that curdled my blood. It was brief and offered no explanation, simply pointing me to a particular Bible passage, John 4:4-42. I was reluctant to crack open a Bible, fearing God like Adam and Eve when they hid themselves in the garden after the fall. But curiosity, fear and anger lured me to find out what message my unknown malefactor intended. You're probably familiar with the story of the woman at the well, Ike." Ike did know the story but kept silent since he didn't want to interrupt Claire's train of thought.

"She was a Samaritan woman, one of those heathen people despised by the Jews. It's funny when we hear that term now, we almost automatically think of the good Samaritan." The phrase, you can't judge a book by its cover, immediately came to my mind. As the Jew who had been robbed and beaten lay in the ditch, near death, the upright, proper and stiff necked fellow Jews passed by without offering any help. But it was the unlikely, hated Samaritan who showed the type of compassion for his enemy that Jesus preached. "This was a bad Samaritan, a terrible, shameful sinner. When she encountered Jesus at the well, she tried to avoid his entreaties. But, being God in the flesh, he knew everything about her. The parallels were inescapable as I read how Christ enumerated her sins ... she had jumped from husband to husband five times and was at that very moment living in sin with a sixth man who was not even her husband." Claire looked so sad thinking back to this dark day. "How cruel, I thought at the time, that someone would viciously hurl this stone of reprisal at me. What had I done to deserve this? Who would do this, one of Trevor's jilted lovers? What did they want? Was this intended for some form of blackmail? Was it just recrimination from a sanctimonious sadist? I was so fraught with panic that I stopped reading at verse 22 and cast my Bible aside as though it were a serpent." *No, no, I thought, don't stop Claire please read on. There's more to the story, much more. My mind raced thinking this can't be the end. Please, not another unhappy ending, not another story without a moral.* Claire went on in spite of my silent protestations, "I have never felt so lonely in my entire life and could not contain my guilt and shame. I collapsed under the weight of the law; I was simply and utterly crushed by it." Claire was still so deeply affected by this agonizing memory that she began to weep.

The room was emotionally charged to the point where I felt the hairs on my neck tingle. I was powerless in that situation, paralyzed. Ike tried to comfort her with a gentle hug and Claire welcomed it with as tight an embrace as she could muster. *Atta boy*, I thought. That's when I noticed something was wrong, terribly wrong. This had happened once before and there was no mistaking the telltale signs. All talking ceased and nary a sound emanated from Ike or Claire. They almost

224

appeared frozen together except for a slight vibration as though they shared a pulsing current between them. Ike's hair almost stood on end and the air seemed charged with static. It was hard to tell if Claire was experiencing the same thing with her blue hair so tightly coiffed. I may have seemed composed like a scientist carefully observing an experiment but I was anything but calm. It was more a case of shock, having been caught so off guard. The gravity of the situation finally hit me full force and shook me from my lethargy. My first thought was to keep Ike from collapsing to the floor but I quickly had to reach out my other arm to Claire to keep her upright and in place. I held this position faithfully like the little Dutch boy with his finger in the dike and called for assistance from the staff. They sprang into action exhibiting the poise of someone well trained and prepared.

I thought back to the first episode with Tim and Ike to find some solace. It had taken Ike about thirty minutes to come to so I kept a close eye on Ike and my watch at the same time. Ike was similarly peaceful this time but perhaps too peaceful if that's possible. Something else was different too. Unlike Tim, Claire had not maintained consciousness.

Chapter 29

Sequel

I still couldn't believe this was happening all over again. This was one remake I had hoped would never be released. But at least I had learned some lessons from the first go-around and was quick to put them to good use. We didn't wait to contact the paramedics and they arrived within ten minutes. I also contacted TB and Sara immediately so they could meet us at the hospital. I asked TB to contact Doctor Bhatia to see if he could meet us there. Of all the specialists we had encountered in the past year or so, he seemed the most open minded and disposed toward my personal theories. It helped that he was a man of faith and had converted from Eastern Mysticism, which was an incongruence of sorts for a medical man, to Christianity some years before. We were able to share a much deeper, meaningful dialogue than mere medical jargon. It only took about ten minutes to reach the hospital so I wasn't alarmed over Ike's repose but quite anxious. My jaw and shoulder muscles became taut as I tried to use will power to jar him from his slumber. It helped break the tension when TB and Sara arrived and I was relieved to already see Doctor Bhatia, who happened to be making his neurosurgical rounds at the hospital. As we headed upstairs, I caught Claire's gurney out of the corner of my eye and was unsettled to see that she too remained unconscious.

To my untrained eye, Ike's dream state appeared different this time. He seemed to be in a deeper sleep without any of the expression he had exhibited before and, as far as I could see, no rapid eye movement. Doctor Bhatia seized the moment knowing that this might be a golden opportunity but a fleeting one to gather critical data about Ike's condition. He snapped into battle station mode and, like a general readying his troops, began ordering tests and procedures with abrupt, concise precision. The equipment in the room was made ready and additional paraphernalia was wheeled in and hooked up with mercurial speed. We were thoroughly impressed and kept track of this intricate potboiler as it unfolded. This kept our minds from going to the dark side, from simple worry to anguish. The cool composure of the staff rubbed off on us as they went about the business of checking all the apparatus and recording data.

With everything in place, the placid field commander, Doctor Bhatia, took the opportunity to quiz me on exactly what had transpired. I recounted the nature of the contact, the last second warning signs and everything I had observed while highlighting what I thought were the differences from the previous occurrence. Doctor Bhatia nodded thoughtfully while clasping his chin. He looked so peaceful but I could just see the wheels turning in his head. So much activity had occurred that I momentarily lost track of time but panic began to set in when I realized almost two hours had passed and Ike was still unconscious. I turned to the doctor and he assured us that Ike was in no danger but noted that something different was happening. TB, Sara and I tried to soothe one another but we soon exhausted all the small talk we could muster. Thankfully, Sally arrived in the nick of time with some fresh muffins and rhetoric. The muffins were gone in a flash and the dialogue dried up shortly thereafter. We then tried to occupy our minds by peering at the various monitors and read-outs as if they might reveal some good news. Although I had no idea what I was seeing, I could tell something had changed on the main monitor. My suspicion was confirmed when it piqued Doctor Bhatia's interest. I tried to breathe while awaiting his diagnosis. He huddled with other members of the staff for what seemed like an eternity and tried to affect a nothing to worry about look as he approached me, Sally, Sara and TB. "Please don't be alarmed" he opened. Alarm bells immediately began to sound. "Ike is in no danger but he has entered into an altered state of consciousness."

"What do you mean by that; what kind of altered state?" we almost said in unison.

"Please come across the hall where we can sit and relax." More alarms rang as we hurried across the hallway.

We were too jumpy to get comfortable but sat down to appease Doctor Bhatia. "Give it to us straight, Doctor, what's going on?"

"The best way I can explain it is," he paused trying to choose his words carefully "it appears he has slipped," another pause "Ike is comatose." Our gasps were clearly audible but we were all momentarily speechless. "I didn't want to use that term since it has such serious connotations but you really shouldn't be alarmed. Ike has not suffered any injury or trauma of any sort and, thus, there is no reason to think this condition will be long lasting, certainly nothing of permanence." He could tell by our ashen faces and stunned looks that his reasoned approach was not helping. "Please, look at me and listen carefully to what I am saying." He actually snapped his fingers to get our attention. "To put this in laymen's terms, Ike is in what you might call a trance, a very deep sleep. Right now he is in no more danger than someone under hypnosis." This helped a bit. At least we were able to follow his train of thought. "Ike is under the best possible care and we will watch him ever so carefully until this passes." We were breathing somewhat normally again.

It was a long night. TB, Sara, Sally and I were not about to leave Ike's side. Eventually, we formulated a watch schedule so we could each apprehend elusive sleep in small clusters. Morning came around and nothing had changed. Fatigue was a blessing in that

229

panic required more energy than we possessed. Doctor Bhatia was truly devoted to his work and, it seemed, very sympathetic to our predicament as well. After going home late to get some much needed sleep, he was up early pouring over the data gathered the night before. He took a few minutes to join us for breakfast in the hospital cafeteria but did not offer any insights. We gathered that he just wanted to provide us with some assurance before returning to the data. It was very thoughtful of him and gave us the comfort of knowing that he really cared. After eating, we returned to Ike's room determined to run this marathon as long as it might take. Having already gauged our resolve, Doctor Bhatia gave up any notion of trying to convince us to go home and recuperate for a while. As the day wore on, our determination waned. We used coffee and prayer to marshal resoluteness. Someone had slowed down the clocks. As dinner time came and went, we girded ourselves for another long night with none of us willing to abandon the fight. Then, just as we were settling in to a routine, Ike's eyes began to flutter, the monitors shifted gears and Ike came to, groggy but apparently none the worse for wear.

Ike couldn't quite comprehend our euphoric mood but it didn't take him long to get back to something near normal. He looked a little drained for someone who had just rested for almost thirty hours but still they almost had to tie him down to keep him from breaking loose from all the wires and tubes. He wanted to get out of there and go home and he wanted it to be fast. Doctor Bhatia explained that it was very important for them to continue monitoring Ike and gathering data to help them try to draw some conclusion about what had happened. That was probably the longest two hours of the whole ordeal but well worth it. Doctor Bhatia said he would call us when he was ready with a diagnosis. Our great burden lifted, we thanked the doctor and staff and prepared to leave. Doctor Bhatia called me aside and asked me to step across the hall for a moment. He had a grave look on what was normally an inscrutable poker face. "What is it doctor, is it something about Ike?"

"Oh no, it has nothing to do with Ike." My tension abated. "It is about your friend, Claire. She died last night just before six o'clock." I was speechless but he was able to read my emotions. "I'm sorry for waiting but I thought it would only make matters worse for you and your family if I informed you before Ike recovered."

"Yes, you're right; I understand. Thank you Doctor Bhatia." I let him leave first so I could gather myself before joining Sally, TB, Sara and Ike. I had to disguise my feelings and keep this to myself until I could find the right way to break the sad news to Ike.

I'm not normally one to procrastinate but I couldn't bring myself to carry out this dreadful task. I rationalized, and rightfully so, that it would be too risky to say something now with Ike's situation being so tenuous. I wouldn't dare tell Ike about Claire until he was clearly out of the woods and everything was firmly back to normal. There was just one problem. Ike was intent upon visiting Miss Claire again and completing his assignment. I stalled by saying Claire was not feeling well. If need be, I'd dodge further by telling Ike that she was away visiting one of her long lost brothers or sisters. Thankfully, it didn't come to that because Ike already had the material he needed to complete his journal. He had another dream to share. I diverted his preoccupation with Claire for the time being by encouraging him to write everything down as though he were recording it in a journal. It was just like another school assignment. That bought me some much needed time so I could turn my attention to Doctor Bhatia. It was time to meet with him and see if he had been able to draw any conclusions.

When we met, I didn't bring Sally, TB and Sara along. Their schedules and Doctor Bhatia's made it difficult to get on the same page. I eagerly volunteered to talk to the Doc and relay the information to them. It made sense to them from the standpoint of convenience and I felt it would provide for a much better, open dialogue with Doctor Bhatia in a small, more private setting. I was right. There was nothing to constrain me from asking difficult questions and tossing out my crazy theories. Doctor Bhatia responded in kind. He spoke openly with the caveat that the data was not conclusive. He stressed that theories are just that and should not be taken too far.

With that understanding behind us, he speculated a bit, cautioning me repeatedly to avoid drawing conclusions until more data was available. He delivered what I would call a good news/bad news story. The best news was that they had every indication to confirm that Ike's epilepsy was completely dormant, likely gone for good. Whatever condition had plagued him was fully ameliorated, non-existent. Doctor Bhatia even conceded that, somehow beyond his understanding, Ike's cure for epilepsy was likely a side effect of this new condition. As much as that relieved me, it was more important to me when he pronounced Ike out of danger with no permanent ill effects from the second trance. But then the bad news rocked me like a swift kick to my nether region. Doctor Bhatia was not sure what was happening during the trances but had hard data to indicate that some kind of degenerative trend was in play. "I thought you just gave Ike a clean bill of health, doctor? Is there something wrong with him that is getting worse?"

"No, there's nothing wrong with Ike right now, Mr. Paulson."

Enough of the formalities, "Please, Doc, call me

Baker."

"Okay Baker, let me try to explain. It's not that Ike has had any permanent side effect or change to his normal health or physiological functioning. He's the same today as he was a week ago or a year ago for that matter, except that, thankfully, his epileptic condition has vanished. My concern is related specifically to his condition during the actual trance. That's where the degradation has occurred."

I tried to grasp what he was telling me, "How can you tell, Doc. Is this a theory or something more?"

"Baker, it's more than just a theory. We have enough data now to establish a trend of sorts. More data would be helpful but I think there's enough to say that these episodes or trances are increasing in strength and duration."

I tried to stay focused, "What do you think is behind the trend?"

"It's very hard to say. If we were in a laboratory, I'd control the variables and isolate the cause and effect. For example, I would try to repeat the first occurrence with the same subjects, in the same setting with all the circumstances being identical. But, of course, that's not possible. We can't even control the most important variable, the outside stimulus provided by the second party. Even if we wanted to repeat the *experiment* with the first subject, we couldn't do so for fear of the harm that might come to Ike through repetition."

I pondered, "So where do we go from here?"

Doctor Bhatia raised his shoulders and palms, "I wish I knew Baker. But the only way to test our theories and draw valid conclusions is to gather more hard data. Unfortunately, the only way that can ethically be done is during an occurrence."

I thought I knew the answer but asked the question anyway, "Is there a way to safely initiate another trance without putting Ike in danger?" He took me to his desk and laid out a chart. I'm not claiming to have fully understood it but there was no mistaking the line on the graph. It was headed down and was steep.

"Baker, this is what we know for sure. This graph depicts the actual data we've been able to capture." He explained the correlation to bodily functions charted along the other axis. It was Greek to me but I knew this much; Ike's heart, brain and lungs, among other vital organs, were affected during the trances. I nodded so that the doctor could proceed. "With all the other possible variables aside, one thing is clear; the more events that Ike experiences, the greater will be the impact on his vital organs and critical functions."

I looked heavenward and then straight in his eyes, "So it sounds like what you're telling me is, given enough of these events, Ike could be in real danger." He was not going to pull any punches at this point.

Doctor Bhatia traced his finger along the trend line, "We're up here, Baker, but if this line ever crosses this point." He paused to raise my eyes from the chart to his, "We can't let those lines cross. It's just that simple."

Chapter 30

Tracts of My Tears

It was good to do something perfectly ordinary as a family. It was a relief to do something as mundane as grabbing a bite to eat together. There were no frills, it was not a special occasion; just an excuse to get out of the house and unwind a little. There's something therapeutic in a perfectly poured Budweiser draught in a tall, chilled glass; the clear golden nectar topped by a frothy foam collar, spilling just over the edge and slowly escaping down the side. TB and I saluted each other, "Prost" and took a long, thirst quenching draw. Ike was quick to tip glasses too using his lemonade, not wanting to be left out. Sally, a tea toddler, and Sara, a winebibber, joined in the fun.

The PC crowd might have blown a gasket over the inclusion of a seven year old in this ritual but TB believed it set a good example by letting young people see how alcohol can be enjoyed in moderation rather than recklessness. I taught TB well. After comparing notes on the menu, we placed our orders and settled in to relax and chat aimlessly, blathering about nothing in particular. When the salads and hot rolls arrived, we bowed our heads and prayed as we always did. We didn't try to hide anything or make a show of it either. It was just a simple table prayer, either "Come Lord Jesus, be our guest, let thy gifts to us be blessed" or sometimes "God is great, God is good, let us thank him for our food." We did this so regularly that no one was self-conscious; this was just normal for us.

I think I created a monster with cub reporter, Ikestein. Ever since I gave him the journalism assignment, he had been even more observant and inquisitive than normal. He said, "Granby, why are we the only ones who pray in restaurants?"

Initially, I tried to brush aside any meaningful discourse by explaining it away, "Ike, we're not the only ones who pray in public."

He would have none of it, "Granby, I've never seen anyone else pray like we do. And there are some times we don't pray when we're with other people at the table." He had me dead to rights with that last point. With ever curious Ike, school was always in session. I could see that resistance was pointless so I straightened up and took a good, long swig to gird myself. I looked at TB with a raised eyebrow to see if he wanted to tackle this one but he waved me on with a theatrical sweep of his hand as might Ed Norton to Ralph Kramden.

"First of all, Ike, the reason why we don't pray sometimes when other people are with us at a restaurant is no disrespect to God. If we're not sure where they stand or know they are of a different faith, it would be wrong to impose upon them." Ike nodded as if to say, okay, go on. "I'm only guessing but I think most people, even people of faith, avoid praying in public places like restaurants because they're uncomfortable; they've been taught that it's impolite or somehow wrong-headed. It seems like everyone is trying to stamp out any trace of God in our society. It all started with that intentional, diabolical misinterpretation of Thomas Jefferson's remarks regarding the separation of church and state. It's gotten so far out of hand that at your daddy's alma mater the football players can't even pray before and after the games anymore. There are some kooks that want to ban God from the Pledge of Allegiance and take In God We Trust off our money."

I had to pause for another cold gulp since I realized I was getting too worked up. "The important thing to remember Ike is why we pray before every meal, whenever possible. It's not to come across as holier than thou although it hopefully sets a good example for some people. No, there are two simple reasons we should always keep in mind. First, it's a helpful reminder to be thankful for everything God does for us on a daily basis to care for our material needs. You know, give us this day our daily bread, right? Also, and perhaps more importantly, it should remind us every time we eat that we need to be fed spiritually too. What happens to your body if you stop eating?"

Ike didn't skip a beat, "You'd die, Granby."

"That's right, Ike. Likewise, you'd die spiritually; your faith would falter without spiritual food. You know where to find that kind of food, right?"

"Sure Granby, we learned that in Sunday school. It's in the Bible and Holy Communion."

"Right you are my man! Now, let's chow down on some daily bread, eh?"

This little lesson and Ike's enthusiastic participation reminded me of how much I enjoyed home schooling with him. But right now I was dreading our next day's session. I was still a little worried about how to keep Claire's death from Ike for now but was much more concerned about what the second dream would reveal. More to the point, I was apprehensive about another letdown. Claire was such a wonderful, caring, thoughtful person that I couldn't believe she had remained as distant from God as she had portrayed up to that point. But she gave no indication otherwise. Would this be a bitter ending even worse than the Faces' saga, with no uplifting ah ha moment, no fatted calf? Why did she stop at verse 22? She was so close! When I thought of Claire it made me sad not only because of how Ike would take the news but I missed her too. She had the same impact on me; I felt like we had lost a member of the family. I had come to relish listening to her repartee with Ike. I'm not sure if Ike picked up on my mood or, like any good journalist, was just throwing out a teaser but he piqued my interest and changed my outlook on tomorrow's session when he said, "I can't wait until tomorrow Granby because you're in the dream this time."

That one kept me up for a while that night because I was fairly convinced that these were not really dreams and Doctor Bhatia concurred with that sentiment. This was based not only on the content of the first dream but now also on observable behavior during the second trance. If only we could track down Tim and Stash, I might be able to close the book on this open question once and for all. That was another sore spot for me and wasn't getting any better based on the last update from Cagney and Lacy. In any event, I still had no idea what these were if not dreams or what they were meant to convey to Ike and me. And how were these images being transmitted if not in dreams; what was the physiology behind this phenomenon?

I was certain it involved electrical energy of some sort but that didn't explain the images themselves. Was it purely God's hand at work? This made me think of the Apostle John, exiled to the tiny Greek island of Patmos in the Aegean Sea. How exactly did John receive God's great revelation of the close of the New Testament age and the apocalypse? Was there something like a giant IMAX screen unfurled in front of

241

John in the cave? Was Ike some kind of revelator? Anything is possible with God but I kept reminding myself that God has chosen to work through his means of word and sacrament in New Testament times since the death of John. And if this was an inspired revelation, why was it so literal whereas John's was captured in such figurative language. Besides, God's stories always have a happy ending, something that was lacking so far with Ike's.

The first thing the next morning Ike wanted to launch right into his journal. Instead, I told him I'd like to review it on my own while he did other school work. He reluctantly agreed and I appeased him by promising to have a Q&A session when I finished. Ike never ceased to amaze me so I shouldn't have been surprised but I was really impressed with his journal. His writing style was concise, expressive and descriptive and he commanded an expansive vocabulary for someone so young. His thoughts were well organized too as if he had done several edits before penning this draft. Conveniently, as if purposefully or perhaps just coincidentally; the journal picked up right about where Claire's personal account had left off. At first, I was just eager to find my part in the dream but soon was able to park that thought in the back of my mind. Ike's retelling sounded so Claire-like it transported me to another world and I was soon deep in thought. It would not be until later that I would get a first-hand peek at this second vision but Ike had painted a very life-like portrait anyway. Between Ike's journal, our Q&A session and my own viewing, I hope I can share a vivid picture of Claire's remaining years.

My first impression was disappointing to say the least. Claire had received no revelation or change of heart. The only difference was that her heart grew colder and she more distant. Her relationship with Trevor met its inevitable end more quickly than I would have expected. Rather than him walking out, it was more accurate to say she pushed him out. She didn't literally show him the door but let her guilt drive a wedge between them. For all her bluster, Claire cared what other people thought about her and what God had to say too. She knuckled under to God's law but there was no delight. Claire did so strictly out of obligation. The law remained a crushing weight upon her chest. Her reluctant compliance led to bitterness and resentment toward God. There was no love in their relationship, as Claire saw it. To her, God was just a stern, angry, vengeful deity. He was to be feared and avoided at all costs. She was Pharaoh and God was just there to visit the plagues upon her if she so much as stepped out of line. But God did not need to harden her heart as he had done with Pharaoh. Claire was doing a fine job of polishing that frigid granite orb all by herself.

Claire felt that God was unfair and exclusionary; he played favorites. The parallels between her and the woman at the well were seared into her mind. She was the Samaritan, hated by the Jews, despised by the King of the Jews, Jesus, she supposed. She also identified with the Canaanite woman whose daughter was possessed. But in her jaded mind's eye, Jesus had rebuffed the Canaanite woman and gave the crumbs to the dogs rather than help a heathen gentile. Claire had fitted herself with a thick set of blinders. She couldn't see God's grace and certainly didn't equate him with love. To her God seemed more like the gods of Greek mythology; fraught with human character flaws, those conniving, scheming, mischievous titans cavalierly wreaked havoc upon mankind for their own sadistic amusement. I squirmed in my seat, fearing the worst. It didn't seem humanly possible that Claire's icy cold heart could ever be thawed.

It only got worse as I proceeded. I likened Claire to a grape vine cut off from essential nourishment; the master of the vineyard unable to graft her into the strong, life giving vine that was so close nearby. Any fine wine she had yielded was turning to vinegar and her remaining grapes were shriveling and dropping into the dust. She never married again, never had another relationship like the one she shared with Trevor. This was an indentured servitude to her, not a joyful, willing commitment or labor of love. As a result of the anonymous note comparing her to the woman at the well, she became irrationally suspicious of others and eventually withdrew from or drove away her friends. As her talents and good looks succumbed to the attrition of time, she abandoned any thoughts of returning to show business. Since she didn't need the money; thanks to Cliff, she was content to slip into self-imposed exile. It was hard to see her beauty and vivaciousness erode as the years passed. This unforgiving process was expedited by the tremendous stress and corrosive bitterness she heaped upon herself. It was even more difficult to witness the spiritual deterioration she suffered as her tormented soul descended deeper and deeper into the abyss.

Claire was near rock bottom. Age had overtaken her. She was completely forsaken with no family nearby or close friends, devoid of normal daily contact. Jesus promises to never leave us or forsake us but Claire had locked and bolted the door against the Good Shepherd and was deaf to his knockings. This made me think of the time Ike had inquired of our pastor in Sunday school, "Why do some people go to hell if Jesus died to save everyone?" Rather than trying to explain something so complex that it confused many theologians, he drew a simple picture of a sad, angry, hunched-over man with a big umbrella that was keeping the rain, God's grace, from touching him. Claire was carrying a big, black umbrella. She had even been robbed of her memories. Every time she tried to find solace in the good old days of vaudeville with her family and dear daddy, Baby Jane came back to haunt her. Claire knew she was close to the edge and feared that she could become addicted to her recollections like Baby Jane, lose contact with reality and be committed to a padded cell called the past.

But there was one soothing memory that still came to her periodically in the quiet times. A warm peace would always wash over her when she thought about those little *church services* with daddy when he would call the family together and read a short lesson from the Good Book. Over time, this gradually drew Claire back to her old, neglected Bible. But her search for guidance, edification and the truth was feeble, what our pastor called lucky dipping. That's when you throw open the Bible to any given page and read a few verses expecting God to speak directly through happenstance. What she really needed was help from a shepherd or kindly brother or sister in Christ to search the scriptures in an organized, purposeful way to find the scarlet thread of the gospel that runs throughout it. But that was anathema to Claire; she would no more seek that kind of fellowship than she would entrust herself to a rattle snake, or worse, the type of person who would use the Bible as a weapon of scorn like that anonymous detractor who had laid her open with John 4:4-22.

This was another bad movie. Even the enticement of seeing my own part in this drama was not enough to pull me forward. I felt like ejecting the

DVD, snapping it in half and tossing it into the can. If only I could hear a bugle blowing to announce that the cavalry was on the way, I could go on. Then, at the point of despair, as if on cue, a plot twist occurred. It was oh so subtle but just enough to avert disaster. This is where I made my entrance. It was so surreal to view myself inside someone else's dream that probably wasn't a dream at all. Then, I came and went so fast that I had to hit rewind several times to capture the meaning. My only part in this movie was a scene where a younger Baker was out on evangelism calls knocking on doors and leaving tracts behind when people were not at home or refused to come to the door. As I pondered, two possibilities came to mind. Perhaps this was intended as personal reassurance to remind me of the purpose God had given to me, like so many others, in his great commission. Or maybe, my personal experience in witnessing was meant to be an archetype for the blessings that can flow from any such evangelistic endeavor. In any case, I was a little deflated by my miniscule role. But it left enough intrigue that it nudged me forward to see the conclusion.

Claire was the type who would never open her door to a stranger, no matter how harmless and friendly they might appear, especially if they wanted to talk about religion. So the efforts by faithful evangelists in her neighborhood were all for naught. Even when they left tracts on her doorstep she would throw them away without a glance. My goodness she was stubborn! Those tracts were just what the doctor ordered for someone frustrated by the dry wells turned up by lucky dipping. Each one would focus on a particular topic like, "Why is God Angry with Me", "Why Do Bad Things Happen to Good People", "Dealing with Death" or "Are You Burdened with Sin?" and organize pertinent Bible passages into a compact treatise to arrive at the answer. There were hundreds of tracts available on every subject imaginable but you know what they say. You can lead a Christian to communion but you can't make them drink.

This was getting depressing again. But one day, an anonymous benefactor left another tract on Claire's porch. This one was different. I recognized it right away as the little red tract used by so many Christians to spread the gospel. There had to be thousands, no, millions of these in circulation everywhere. It stood out because it was shaped like a Bible but was a miniature version at just 2" x 2 ½"with thirty one tiny, little pages. On the red cover it read, "Personal Bible Verses: Comfort, Assurance & Salvation." On the inside of the back cover, it had a small space to stamp the name of your church so as to provide an invitation to worship. Our church, like so many others, used these little red bibles all the time because they were so effective and inexpensive. They only cost pennies to purchase but were chock full of pure gospel passages like John 11:25-

248

26, John 5:24, Romans 5:8, Acts 16:31 and, of course, John 3:16-17. Maybe it was just because it looked so cute but, for some reason, Claire did not dispose of that little red bible. Ah, at last, a ray of hope.

There's really no need to carry on with all the rest. Please allow me to fast forward because this was the beginning of the end; for Claire a happy ending. By the simple act of some unknown, faceless servant, Claire's life was completely transformed. Of course, it was not that person who transformed Claire. They were only the messenger, privileged to do God's bidding. The Holy Spirit did the heavy lifting by working through God's chosen means, his word of life and truth. Claire was moved to pick up the little red bible and read. This small snapshot was completely different from her conception of God and his book of wrath and judgment. The words truly did bring comfort, assurance and salvation as advertised. You see, this book had just what she needed, what Claire longed for. She had no need for the law. It had already ground her into the dust. She needed some hope, restoration, forgiveness and a new foundation. She needed to be reborn, brought back to life from her exile in suspended animation. She longed for a true and trustworthy friend. Claire longed for true love and salvation. She found it all in the precious words of that little red tract and was ripe for the harvest. Under normal conditions she might have procrastinated, thinking it would take time to overcome sins so great as hers, but the breakthrough that turned her stony heart into one of flesh came when she read the words of II Corinthians, "Behold, now is the accepted time; behold, now is the day of salvation." She finally received the Good News.

Claire's transformation was so complete, inside and out, that you could not only see the change in her attitude and outlook but some of the crippling effects of age that were so etched in her exterior vanished as though washed away by a spring shower. She had discarded that big, black, ugly umbrella so the rain could drench her with its cleansing power. However, her makeover was not quite complete. There was still something that haunted her, a boogey man lurking in a dark closet. She had to vanquish him to truly be set free from the shackles of her past. One day, she mustered the courage to open her Bible to the Gospel of John and turned to chapter four. As she read the first twenty two verses, the feelings of guilt and shame returned. But now she had the strength to read on, to the end of the story of the woman at the well, through verse forty two. Claire could now see that she had stopped one verse too soon. She thought of every terrible thing that had happened in her life since then, needlessly, thoughtlessly, solely because of her own ignorance and recalcitrance. The sheer magnitude of her folly would have mired her in total despondency before, but not now. She was just grateful for her release from that prison and only wanted to look forward.

Claire had drawn such a perfect parallel to the woman at the well before when her sins had been laid bare by Jesus. Now the parallel was even closer for her as she pondered the end of the story. Jesus did not condemn the sinful woman or turn her away because she was a Samaritan. Instead he comforted her and revealed himself as the Christ, the long awaited Messiah bringing redemption and eternal life. She believed and was saved. Like with Claire, the transformation of the woman at the well was all encompassing and astonishingly swift. She didn't hesitate but went immediately to tell her fellow Samaritans about Jesus. Her sinful past did not matter. She was doing her Lord's work and it bore fruit right away. At her urging, they came and heard Jesus' words from the Lord, himself, and many believed and were saved. Jesus did not care that they were of the hated race of Samaritans. He loved them and gave of himself willingly to save them too.

Now the parallels with the woman at the well were no longer a source of pain, shame and sorrow to Claire. She found new life and purpose. Unlike me with my thick skull, Claire was quick to discover her purpose. She received her great commission through that Samaritan woman. It brought tears to her eyes. In our Q&A session, I couldn't help but drop a pun on Ike calling the little red bible the tracts of her tears, hearing

251

Smokey Robinson & The Miracles in my head. Joy is such a short, simple word but one that is perfect in capturing an otherwise indescribable emotion. I thought of sweet Claire finally finding true love, purpose and salvation. Then I thought of what would be a glorious reunion in heaven with her someday and my eyes melted into tears of joy.

"Why are you crying, Granby?" asked Ike, looking very concerned. I was embarrassed and tried to brush away the tears without Ike noticing but it was too late.

In this flood of emotion, I knew it was time, "Ike, there's something I need to tell you." He just stared, waiting, "I don't know how to tell you this but our dear friend, Claire, died." Ike remained silent, stunned and saddened and his lip quivered a bit as tears welled up in his eyes. I continued abruptly now wanting to get this over with as quickly as possible, "Ike, Claire was very sick with cancer. She's much better off now. She's no longer in pain. Claire's waiting to see us in heaven again someday." It was all true but I intentionally left out that one little detail about how the trance brought the end sooner than expected. There would be no good purpose in that for Ike or anyone else. Still embarrassed by my show of emotion, I tried to change the subject. Ike loved trivia and was quite good at it thanks to my incessant trips in the way back machine. I threw down the gauntlet, "Hey, speaking of tears, do you know who recorded 96 Tears?" I successfully stumped him. Then I set the bait, "Okay, I'll give you a hint, it was the first Latino garage rock band."

Still stumped, Ike pleaded, "Give me another clue, Granby."

I consented and continued to lay the snare, "Okay, last clue, it's the same group that recorded Can't Get Enough of You Baby."

Ike tilted his head and answered with a question, "Smash Mouth is Latino?"

I gleefully sprung the trap, "No, silly, it's Question Mark & The Mysterians." Ike just shook his head. He would have to consult You Tube to figure this one out. There's nothing new under the sun.

BOOK SIX

Riches to Rags

Chapter 31

Lost and Found

It took a while for things to get back to normal. Funerals are for the living and not the dead. It helps us to bring some closure to a part of our grief. Claire's body, in her last act of altruism, was donated for medical research at one of our local university hospitals. She had spared her family, wherever they were, from that unpleasant duty and everything was handled quickly and easily. However, the memorial service was delayed for several weeks thereafter as her pastor searched for surviving family members, basically one brother and a few nieces and nephews. In the meantime, Ike and I tried to settle back into our routine although I avoided our normal *field trips* to NWP. One day, Ike asked, "Granby, aren't we going to walk at the mall anymore?"

I really wanted to but countered, "Wouldn't that make you sad seeing Senior Towne?"

Ike, little Ikestein, offered, "Yes, but in a way it would make me feel better too." Off to the mall we went.

We hadn't been away all that long but NWP had changed. It was really going downhill fast now. Visual reminders were being dropped on a daily basis leaving only memories, memories which were becoming harder to recall. There was little evidence of any remaining retail commerce. Telltale signs of disrepair began cropping up here and there. Pot holes were left unfilled creating a mine field in the parking lots. Outdoor mall signage was no longer updated, misleading unwary visitors to seek out shops that were already closed. Water leaks damaged ceilings and archways. Burned out light bulbs were left unattended. Although it was still kept clean by the faithful janitors and safe by the trusty security guard here or there, it really began to resemble a ghost town. As we roamed the hallways, I felt like Gary Cooper as High Noon approached. My hand was at the ready of my imaginary holster as I anticipated when the villains might jump out from behind a dark nook or cranny.

I was thoroughly dejected by each store closing. The real blow came earlier when Macy's shut its doors. As we passed by there each time, I looked up to see the once proud rotunda and wondered again and again if it had been inspired by the arched design that had adorned old Busch Stadium. Looking into the bare space, I recalled how impatient the kids were when I wandered into the old Famous Barr store to shop for some new ties. Ah, another lost art obliterated by year-round casual days in the workplace. Sears had not posted an official date but the rumors were rampant and there were constant sales with heavy discounts. Even though I was lacking empirical data, I thought for sure that merchandise replenishment had ceased and inventories were dropping. With so few stores open, it took a keen eye to notice the changes, the signs of the end. While imperceptible to most, they were very clear to me. The coin operated kid's rides were finally removed; the gyrating motorcycle with its flashing headlight and push-button, tooting horn, the submarine with its captain's hat, eyes, nose and moustache; and the old fashioned bi-plane were all carted away. Why were the ATMs still there? Did they even work? I knew where the last stand would take place. The candy dispensers were still there. When they were gone it would be all over but the crying. I was tempted to bring a felt tip to NWP and mark the levels on the glass globes to see if any candy was actually being consumed. When Ike and I walked past Senior Towne, our conversations always ceased briefly in an unspoken but mutually understood show of reverence for Claire.

It was our conversations that took our minds off NWP's deterioration and inevitable end. As you might expect, they were laced with memories. I had Ike convinced that the frothy concoctions offered at the NWP Orange Julius were somehow far superior to anything at the newer OJ's at surviving malls. With the mall's structure showing signs of age, I often turned back to the days when it was an open air mall, especially when we passed what used to be the grand fountain in the center court. The trouble was my memory was already failing. I could picture the fountain in all its glory but could no longer place the stores on the corner locations surrounding it. One shop, I thought, might have been Union Jack, where I had purchased so many hip articles of fashion back in the '70s. Or was it the Chess King, where the styles were even more avant-garde? Thankfully, enough memories remained that I was able to give Ike a resplendent depiction of what used to be. The contrast was so distinct from the dead husk surrounding us that I commented to him on several occasions, "Ike, you can't judge a book by its cover, even when it comes to malls. Who would guess what we once had here, who would guess?" One time I mentioned this just past the old Macy's location as we headed down toward Senior Towne.

As we approached, Ike broke the code of silence and said, "That sure was true for Claire, Granby." I just nodded as I squeezed his hand.

My memory lapses became more bothersome. I didn't like letting go of my cherished NWP memories. There were some things I could recall through web crawling but even there much of the history of NWP had been lost. One day I commented to Ike as we passed by a now defunct mall directory, "How can I pass the memories on to you if I can't remember them myself? I wonder how much more I'll forget once they've torn this place down to the ground." Then off the cuff without thinking about my audience I foolishly muttered, "Maybe I should just steal the poster from inside that old directory before I forget anything else."

Ike admonished me, "Granby!" Then after an appropriate silence he proposed, "Maybe you should just write it all down in a journal like mine before you forget." Smart kid, I thought.

The day came and we attended Claire's memorial service at her old church. I sometimes dreaded funerals and even weddings held at unfamiliar churches. It seemed there was no longer any real unity of faith among Christian denominations. For that matter, true fellowship was even lacking inside individual denominations, ours included. Truth was just a relative thing and everyone was entitled to their own opinion or private interpretation. As far as I was concerned, the whole mess hearkened back to Pilate when he washed his hands and said, "What is truth?"

The root cause of all this confusion within the church was that people didn't put much stock in the authority of the Bible anymore. Even those that believed it was the true word of God thought it was subject to their own private interpretation. We no longer could point to an absolute standard of truth, if you believed the *sages* in most churches. I could feel my blood pressure rising and thought, *"Come on people, haven't you ever read II Peter 1:20?"* It peeved me when wedding vows were rendered meaningless. No wonder there are so many divorces. Funerals were different though. When the truth was adulterated or thoroughly lacking at the passing of a loved one, it left me truly grieved. I couldn't help but wonder if the dearly departed had been saved amidst such heterodoxy. It made me cringe when Christian pastors focused on the kindness, generosity and good works of the deceased rather than Christ's righteousness and atoning sacrifice as if we might be able to earn our way into heaven apart from Jesus' merit alone.

Thankfully, my apprehension was unfounded on this day. Claire had been a member of a Lutheran church that still clung to the founding principle of sola scriptura, that is to say they trusted in the Bible as the inerrant, inspired word of God, the only standard of absolute truth. They were what I would call an old fashioned Missouri Synod congregation. As I became more comfortable with these surroundings, I was glad that TB, Sara and Sally had joined Ike and me even though they had never met Claire personally. Still they felt they knew her based on the stories that Ike and I had shared. The hymns were beautiful. What they may have lacked in melodiousness was more than made up for by the sound, comforting meaning of the lyrics and the rich tones that bellowed from the old organ. There were many fond remembrances from the people whose lives Claire had touched that brought tears to our eyes. Although Ike and I needed no further evidence of

Claire's repentant and purposeful life, it warmed our hearts to hear so many confirmations of her faithful service in spreading the gospel. Although there were many testimonials, I was very pleased to see that the pastor's sermon was the centerpiece of the service. He preached on Ephesians 2: 8-9, "For by grace are ye saved through faith; and that not of yourselves; it is the gift of God: not of works, lest any man should boast." As the sweet truth boomed from the pulpit, he left no doubt about Claire's final destination and how she got there, by the all availing sacrifice of Jesus Christ.

In closing, the pastor asked if anyone cared to offer another testimonial before the service concluded. I think most everyone thought this was done more out of politeness than anything else, so we were surprised to see a hand raised at the pastor's invitation. Two fellows several pews in front of us stood up and began to make their way to the lectern. I thought nothing of it at first since I had not met any of Claire's friends or relatives and wasn't familiar with anyone in the crowd as far as I could tell. Then, as these two gentlemen turned to face us, I was thunderstruck. I had to adjust my glasses to make sure I wasn't seeing things. I was not hallucinating. Sally and Martha had done their best to turn the town upside down only to come up completely empty handed but here before me stood Tim and Stash as plain as day. You could have knocked me over with a feather.

They offered a brief but beautiful testimonial explaining how Claire had reached out to them with the gospel. It was straight from the heart, very moving. At that moment, I began to doubt part of my theory about the dreams being reality. The authenticity, compassion and faith exhibited by Tim and Stash would have been completely foreign to Ace and Nature Boy, oil and water. It just didn't click anymore. My mind drifted back to Dorothy's dream and how she had morphed Hunk, Zeke and Hickory into the Scarecrow, Lion and Tin Man. This mental setback made me all the more anxious to talk to Tim and Stash to hopefully get to the bottom of this mystery.

As we exited the pew, I hung back to talk to them. I wasn't prepared and didn't know what to say but I realized as I waited to catch their attention that this was not the right time or place to get too deeply into what promised to be a very involved conversation. I extended my hand, "Hi, I don't know if you remember me, I'm Baker Paulson."

Before I could say another word, Tim assured me, "Of course, Baker, how could we forget you and your grandson after that encounter at the mall. I hope he's fully recovered and doing okay."

I stretched the truth a bit, "Oh yes, he's fine. But there's something I've been meaning to ask of you. Is there a time we could get together and talk?" We

262

chatted as we made our way to the exit and exchanged a few tidbits about Claire. I complimented them on their testimonial. There were some travel plans and other obligations standing in the way but we were able to agree on a date and time about two weeks out. On the way home, I excitedly informed Sally about this big break in our case, what had dropped into my lap at the lost and found. She was relieved and anxious to see what they might reveal. Sally passed the news along to Martha that she could stand down. Martha was elated that we had located Tim and Stash but, in a way, was disappointed to no longer be assigned to the case.

Chapter 32

Detour Ahead

Although we had finally located Tim and Stash, I was not about to rest on our laurels while awaiting the upcoming meeting. In addition to Ike's schooling and our mall adventures, I remained hot on the trail of a medical explanation by staying in close contact with Doctor Bhatia. While we had not been able to establish a definite cause and effect, Doctor Bhatia had agreed, in principle, with my crossed wire theory. He also agreed that, even though we didn't know exactly what it was that made the stimuli, Tim and Claire, cause such a reaction in Ike, it was apparent that physical contact was required. Call it energy, electricity or bad wiring, whatever was inducing the trances had occurred only during contact, through that actual body-to-body connection.

Doctor Bhatia warned me not to reach a final conclusion from what was no more than a coincidence at this point. I mentioned to Doctor Bhatia that Tim had once been subjected to shock therapy and Claire had been resuscitated via defibrillation, at least according to what we gathered from the dreams or trances. The wheels in his mind were turning again. He was slow to draw conclusions but speculated that such traumatic events involving electrical shock could possibly have affected them in a way that primed them for our trance events with Ike. In my simple mind, I took that to mean the shock treatments had scrambled their wires somehow. He cautioned me from jumping to conclusions again and noted that there are thousands, maybe millions of people who have undergone similar treatments. Doctor Bhatia was not willing to venture further down this path on such thin evidence but I could tell he had tucked this thought away for future study.

Noting the downward trend on Ike's chart again, Doctor Bhatia cautioned that probably the best way to try to avoid another episode was to limit Ike's physical contact with unknown subjects; at least until we had enough information to develop other potential cause and effect relationships. That made sense because we hadn't been able to pinpoint what was different about Claire or Tim outside of my WAGs and thus had no way of screening out potential candidates. It would be impossible to restrict Ike from all physical contact but we didn't need to be concerned about familiar folks with whom Ike already had regular contact. So, my mission was to keep Ike away from anyone new, untested. It really didn't seem all that difficult since we ventured outside our normal sphere so infrequently. The main source of potential outside contact was at the mall during our walks but that was easily manageable since there were so few people there. I took to the task seriously and watched Ike like a hawk, especially when we were at the mall or elsewhere out in public.

In spite of everything, NWP still had a pulse left. The life was not in its commerce or any hope of a white knight's rescue. No, it was found in a most unlikely source, parasites you might say. There were still a few hearty souls like Ike and me that were determined to walk the mall until the day they pad locked the entrances. Whenever we approached other walkers, my antennae went up but there was really nothing to worry about. The only contact that usually occurred between mall walkers was verbal; a simple greeting or inane comments on the weather and such. People were preoccupied with their exercise regimens and didn't want to halt their momentum to engage in idle chit chat. Nevertheless, I went through my mental checklist like a seasoned FBI profiler every time someone approached. Were they brand new, had we seen them before, had there been any prior contact with Ike, did they look like the friendly types that might initiate contact? So on and so forth, I repeated the procedure again and again. If it were in my power, I would have required each person to fill out a survey before beginning their walk. Have you ever undergone shock therapy, defibrillation or had an exotic brain scan or been involved in an electrical emergency or accident? I knew I was taking things too far but I couldn't get the image of that trend chart out of my mind.

One day, I noticed an odd fellow as we made

266

our way around the mall. He was dressed too heavily for the weather and looked quite disheveled. His face had not made the acquaintance of a razor for at least a week and his hair looked like it had been combed with a pork chop. He wasn't pushing a shopping cart or carrying a duffle bag but there was no telling what he could have been amassing under his droopy overcoat. Everything pointed to him being homeless. Since skies were clear and it was not that cold outside, I didn't think he was in NWP seeking shelter. I was at the ready but he passed by us without as much as a word or glance. As we approached him off in the distance on our second lap, I noticed that he had stopped to talk to another mall walker. Perhaps he was seeking a handout but we didn't see anything change hands. I was especially wary as we passed by going opposite directions but he ignored us again. I turned my head to follow his progress behind us and he approached another person in the same fashion as before. Again, there appeared to be some dialogue but no exchange of money. It struck me as odd that he would avoid us while seeking charity. The two other people he had stopped were very old men who didn't give the appearance of having two nickels to rub together, whereas Ike and I probably looked like more worthy targets. If he was a panhandler as I suspected, he wasn't very good at it.

I hadn't harped at Ike about avoiding physical contact with strangers. He knew better and I didn't want to alarm him by being overly protective. As long as I kept him close to me, I could see to it that nothing of the sort happened. I began to feel sorry for the old fellow, down on his luck with so few prospects and poor solicitation skills. Jesus' words regarding strangers came to mind, how we should deal with them compassionately, as Christ would deal with us or them. And here I was, thinking the worst of this poor man and doing my best to avoid him. Shame on me, I thought. I made up my mind to try to lend him a hand at our next, last pass but it was apparent that he would pay us no mind again. So I gave Ike a heads up, "Ike, do you see that man coming this way, the one we passed by earlier?" Ike nodded. "He looks to me like someone who could use some help. I want to see if we can offer him some money for a good, hot meal, okay?"

"Sure Granby" Ike beamed. The prospect of helping someone in need cheered him. He had no qualms whatsoever about his appearance. Ike had a special affinity for older folks, even before we got to know Claire.

"One thing, Ike, don't say anything unless I ask you. Some people shy away from charity. It can be embarrassing to them so we have to be careful what we say and do."

Ike was almost vibrating with eagerness, "Got it, Granby."

268

Ike and I veered off course to intercept him and finally captured his attention. Ike was just to my right as we closed in. The stranger surprised me a bit when his mouth curled into a warm smile, his eyes touched mine in an open, caring way. I expected him to be standoffish, tinged with guilt over his apparent begging. He extended his right hand to Ike first and I quickly reached out to receive his hearty handshake. "Hi, I'm Baker and this is my grandson Ike," I said as I continued to shake his hand to ensure no exchange with Ike.

He didn't offer a name, "It's a pleasure to meet you both." He didn't attempt to shake Ike's hand again. Perhaps he assumed from my protective behavior that I didn't want Ike exposed to any germs and he certainly realized he fit the part of a possible carrier. His easy, forthcoming nature pulled me off course. I was hesitant to offer a handout feeling it would appear crass and paternalistic. Giving him the third degree seemed out of place too as it might be interpreted as territorial. What brings you here could come off as what in the world is someone filthy like you doing in our tidy little mall. To break the silence before awkwardness set in, "Ike and I are regulars here. You seem to be new here so we just want to take a moment and welcome you."

"Well thank you, it's very kind of you." I was ready to move on.

The kindly old gentleman smiled again as we

turned to leave. Ike didn't understand. We were leaving with our mission unaccomplished. He still had two dollars left from his allowance in his pocket and was determined to see this good deed done so he reached in for the money. Before I knew what was happening, Ike twirled and hurried back toward the stranger, thrust the two dollars into his hand and said, "Here mister, this is for you." I felt a paralyzing jolt and then utter horrification as I watched them immediately seize up as though flash frozen and then collapse to the ground together in a heap. The money remained trapped inside the tight clasp of their hands. I was so stunned I just stood there aghast, not having any strength left to go through this again.

On the verge of fainting, a ridiculously inappropriate image popped into my head; Tooter Turtle was spinning out of control and calling out, "Help Mr. Wizard!" Like Tooter, I needed some magic to escape this terrible mess; I needed to hear Mr. Wizard declare, "Drizzle, drazzle, drozzle, drome, time for this one to come home." Was this the delirium that preceded unconsciousness? I had never felt so helpless before, even with my own childhood epileptic seizures. With my last gasp of lucid thought, I prayed *"Help me Lord."* As though touched by God's hand, perhaps to squeeze my adrenal glands, the fog dissipated and I regained my faculties. Guilt and shame stepped in to replace my wooziness. I had let everyone down. How could I break this news to TB and Sara? Thankfully, my sense of duty took over and I sprang into action.

Not that you could call such a thing routine but this event had much in common with the past two … only it was much worse. I hated going through this again but at least was getting good at it. Like they say, whoever *they* are, what doesn't kill you makes you stronger. We were becoming much too familiar with ambulance rides, gurneys, emergency rooms, hospital beds, monitors, tubes and wires. If I never saw any of these things again it would be too soon. The only familiar thing that was welcome was Doctor Bhatia and his staff. I referred to him as the Data-meister because of his rock solid commitment to empiricism and scientific principles. Sometimes when I offered one of my theories which were merely speculation he would say, "Baker, in God we trust; everyone else bring data."

Unfortunately, he had been right about Ike's downward trend and now had another point of data to prove it. This hospital stay was twice as long as Ike's last one. This time he had a roommate of sorts. Two doors down, the stranger from the mall was also hospitalized, unconscious but stable. Having Doctor Bhatia there with his strong convictions, solid track record with Ike, self-assured commitment to excellence and caring bedside manner was a comfort and calming influence to us. It also helped that we had been through this before so we were not so unsettled by Ike's comatose condition. But a palpable panic gripped us when Ike's condition took a sudden turn for the worse and he was put on life support. All we could do was turn to God in faith and pray. We committed Ike to the Lord's loving care and hoped for the best. I pulled out a book mark with the words of II Chronicles 1:11-12 printed on it, "And God said to Solomon, Because this was in your heart, and thou hast not asked riches, wealth, or honor, nor the life of your enemies, neither yet hast asked long life; but hast asked wisdom and knowledge for thyself, that thou may judge my people, over whom I have made you king: Wisdom and knowledge is granted unto thee; and I will give you riches, and wealth, and honor, such as none of the kings have had that have been before thee, neither shall there any after thee have the like." This was a great example of how we should pray.

Doctor Bhatia must have been God's emissary. There's no other way to explain his composure. If there was any internal stress, we could not detect it in his cool, calm exterior. He methodically went about the business of gathering and analyzing the latest data and then used it to reassure us that Ike would be okay. As he had projected, Ike snapped out of it almost right on schedule and returned to normal. Just like the last time, he asked me to step in for a quick briefing before we left. Before he could start, I asked about the stranger. He was very weak but stable. Doctor Bhatia could not offer a prognosis on when he might come to but promised to keep me informed. The Doc was apparently reading my mind and knew I was interested in more than just his well-being, "This time, after you've gone over the dream with Ike, we can check the facts with the subject when he regains consciousness."

The Data-meister then brought out his chart which had been updated to reflect this episode. His look was serious, akin to the grim reaper, "Look at this Baker, the trend line has remained almost identical but look at the location of the third data point." It was more than halfway down the slope from the prior entry and the point of no return. No emphasis was necessary as he added, "Now that we have three solid data points we've calculated the standard deviation and established that our trend line is statistically significant." Before I could ask, "Baker, I have a high degree of confidence that Ike's condition will worsen if another trance occurs. I can't say with absolute certainty but I believe there's enough evidence to indicate that we could be in the danger zone within two more events." My heart sank into the pit of my stomach as he pointed to the chart and the intersection where vital functions would be jeopardized.

Chapter 33

Vanity's Child

With a sense of urgency, I jumped right into dream-review mode with Ike the next day even though I probably should have eased into it a bit more. Ike was more than willing and I was desperate to fill in some of the missing puzzle pieces which I hoped would fall into place as soon as we could compare notes with our hospitalized friend, God willing. It was hard to recognize the stranger at first. Let's call him John for now. I'll explain later.

As a young man, he cut quite a dashing figure. Unlike later in life, he appeared to have all the trappings of extravagant wealth; from stately mansion to private plane to exotic automobiles to finely tailored suits all the way down to his perfect hairstyle and manicure. However, he was not a child of affluence. As John Houseman used to say in the Smith Barney commercials, he made his money the old fashioned way, he earned it. He wasn't dirt poor as a child but it would be hyperbole to call his a middle class upbringing. He was able to go to college through the sweat of his parents' brows and secured a decent paying job upon graduation. Although he was industrious and bright, John's future seemed limited by his less than advantageous circumstances. In the corporate rat race, he seemed destined to top out at the middle management rung, if he was lucky. John seemed to sense the same and it weighed his spirit down as he moved from carefree twenty-something to the more serious thirties. Seemingly trapped in this lifestyle with a cubicle serving as his cell, John became disenchanted and then down-right depressed. To make a long story short, his life spiraled downward until, as he liked to say in deference to his enthusiasm for sports, his stats were really bad: divorced, lost his home, directionless and stuck in a dead end job with no future. Oh, and as you might guess, he let this affect his spiritual life too. Even though he was raised in a Christian home and attended parochial schools, he rarely darkened the doorway of his church.

John's turnabout came early though, at least his first one. He was not only interested in sports but had played them as well from early on. Perhaps those experiences shaped his character. John had been an exceptional athlete who had pro potential until the injury bug bit him. Even though he was robbed of his athletic ability, he never lost the desire to win. It was that competitive fire burning inside him that kept him going and convinced him that he didn't have to settle for such a mediocre existence. With absolutely nothing to tie him down or hold him back, he picked up stakes and left town on a lark. He moved to Dallas with not much more than the clothes on his back and desire in his gut. With his *bad stats*, he couldn't get a line of credit back in the late '70s so he had to convince one of his relatives to lend him ten thousand dollars. What some would consider paltry was an incredible sum to him back then. It was enough to rent a small apartment, install a phone line and purchase one of those newfangled personal computers; everything a budding industrial magnate needs, right? Yes, all he needed now was a brainstorm.

John's idea was not very complicated. Since he didn't have the money to invest in capital, he decided he would have to offer a service. That service would be freight forwarding. I'm not sure how he reached that conclusion since he had no background whatsoever in logistics but he hit a gusher anyway. At first, all he had to offer was a promise, over the phone no less. If you pay me, I'll make sure your package gets from point A to point B in this amount of time. It really came down to salesmanship and, of course, performance once you had closed the deal. Your customers didn't care how you got it there as long as it arrived on time in one piece. Let them think you owned a big fleet of planes and trucks if it made them feel better. Did it make a difference if you used someone else's assets as long as you could pull down a profit after paying their fees? His trick was this; if people were willing to pay the price for second day air but you could get the job done with a freight carrier, they'd be happy and you'd be able to pocket a nice profit. That was the model; it was just that simple at first. Federal Express was not shaking in their boots though.

Through inspiration, elbow grease, charm and wits, John turned these humble beginnings into a formidable empire by the mid-nineties. Through organic growth and several key acquisitions, his company went international and employed thousands of people generating billions of dollars in annual revenue. He was on top of the world, a captain of industry, master of his own destiny and amassed personal wealth in the hundreds of millions of dollars. Only one thing was missing. He had the same problem as little old me way back when; he lacked a sense of purpose. That must sound odd for someone with so much power and responsibility but it was true. Oh, he enjoyed his business, the competition of it all and the trappings that went with it. John was also a good corporate citizen supporting the arts, education and various foundations. But these things didn't fulfill him. He always questioned his own motives. Was he doing these things to benefit the welfare of others or more so to build up good will for the corporation to help the bottom line? He had topped every goal he ever set regarding the size of the business in terms of employees, offices, revenues and profit. John was humming that same tune that I had recalled so long ago, Peggy Lee's: Is That All There Is? What goal would he set, what would be the next mountain to climb? When could you say enough is enough and call it a job well done?

John attended a local church but that left him feeling hollow too. It was a large, very wealthy congregation where the social gospel seemed to trump the real thing. They were world beaters when it came to charity, no doubt. But again, were they doing so out of compassion for the needy? Or was it more a case of putting on a good show or doing so out of a sense of obligation? Or worse yet, was it a good tax write-off for the members? John's situation was the exact opposite of Claire's. She had been crushed by the law but could not find relief from the gospel anywhere. With John, the law was nowhere to be found. Everything was love and kindness and good works. There was no room for talk of sin. And where there's no sin, there's no need for a redeemer, is there? John was doing everything the world expected. He was an upright pillar of the community who by all appearances was quite generous. Did it matter about motivation, whether he was a cheerful giver? No, what mattered was that he was wildly successful. Being so blessed with material wealth and all the worldly things most people craved, God must have been pleased with him. You would certainly think so but, for John, something was still missing, something was just not right.

Maybe John's past was haunting him. He thought of the passage that he had heard often in the humble, old fashioned church where he grew up. Most people misquoted it as, "Money is the root of all evil." John knew better, that money is not evil in and of itself. No the proper quote is, "The <u>love</u> of money is the root of all evil." He wondered whether he loved the money too much. He asked the pastor at his mega-church for some advice and guidance regarding this passage. The pastor assured John that there was no cause for concern, his generosity toward the church was proof positive. With all his responsibility of running an empire, John was always extremely busy but this was nagging at him so much that he took the time one day to call an old buddy in St. Louis, Jack, who had become a pastor at a small church there. He laid out his concern and asked for some guidance. Jack gave him four passages to review and told John to call him when he was done if he wanted to talk about it. John didn't realize it but he was about to get something he hadn't had for many years, a big dose of the law.

The first passage, II Timothy 4:10; referred him to Demas of whom Paul said he had been forsaken due to Demas' love for this present world. There's not a lot known about Demas but from what we can gather, he was under Paul's tutelage for the ministry but opted out to chase material wealth and temporal pleasures. This grabbed John's attention as he turned to Luke 18:18-23 and read about the rich young ruler who asked Christ what he must do to inherit eternal life. Jesus, being God, knew exactly what was going through his mind and told him he would have to follow all the commandments perfectly, an impossible task. Jesus knew that this man would foolishly claim righteousness saying that he had followed all the commandments faithfully. Jesus did not challenge him on this point even though he knew that no man could ever keep God's law perfectly. Instead, with the stage set, he presented him with what he knew was the true stumbling block in his heart. Jesus said okay there's only one more thing you need to do then; go sell all your possessions, give the money to the poor and follow me. It did not matter that Christ pointed out he would receive something far more valuable in return, treasure in heaven. The rich young ruler left dejected because he knew he couldn't part with all the wealth he had amassed. John paused and thought; the love of money is the root of all evil. Would I be able to give up everything to gain heaven?

The next two passages had no story built around them. This was mainlining, a straight injection of law, perhaps a fatal one. John blanched as he read first Proverbs 13:11 and then 10:2. "Wealth gotten by vanity shall be diminished: but he that gathers by labor shall increase. Treasures of wickedness profit nothing: but righteousness delivers from death." At first, he was offended and even angry that his old friend would recommend these passages with their harsh, accusatory implications. But, after a while, in a calmer, contemplative mood, he was able to let it sink in. No one could argue that he hadn't worked hard for everything he had and it was obvious that his earthly increase was great. But he thought, was there vanity involved; were his accomplishments really driven by his desire to magnify his own glory? As for wickedness, look at all the good he had done. Then he thought about his true motives and wondered if they were really as pure as they seemed on the surface. That last line was the kicker. Would any of this make a difference in the end? Although his trendy mega-church preached something wholly different, he knew down deep in his soul that he couldn't earn his way into heaven. These passages stuck with him in spite of the flurry of activity that always surrounded him. He found himself drifting off frequently and coming back to these words over and over. In time, they took root and he began to identify with the rich young ruler, much to his dismay. The truth hurts.

As the narrative unfolded, Granby knew John was approaching a cross roads. The law was finally having its effect on John and preparing him for the gospel, the genuine article that had eluded him in the midst of the misguided social gospel he had been steeped in for so long. The only thing Granby couldn't anticipate is how God would deliver the Good News. Perhaps he should have guessed that the little red bible would come into play again. Yes, there it was; that tiny package filled with the giant, explosive charge. Two

281

passages seemed to speak directly to John, "A man's life consists not in the abundance of the things he possesses" (Luke 12:15) and (Mark 8:36) "For what shall it profit a man, if he shall gain the whole world, and lose his own soul?" That second one really struck a chord and seemed to hit the bull's eye; the question that had been plaguing his subconscious for so long. He read through the rest of the tract and all the answers he needed were right there. Real treasure was only found in heaven. Eternal life was the true goal to be prized above all else. And it was a free gift, purchased at an infinite cost through the perfect life, suffering and death of Jesus Christ. It was all free, right there for the taking.

John was used to people fawning over him. Whether employees, solicitors or just about anyone else, people went to great lengths to please him and especially to avoid anything that might draw his ire. He now realized that this was not so much a sign of respect for him as it was motivated by the almighty dollar of which he had plenty. That's why John had been so offended by his old friend, Jack. But now he saw that his intentions were not to judge or accuse. Instead he wanted to open John's eyes and lead him to the richest treasure possible. John was so moved that he dropped everything and flew to St. Louis to meet with Pastor Jack. On the plane, John likened himself to an old miser who denies himself while hoarding his wealth. John had surrounded himself with the best things that money could buy but he had denied himself true satisfaction. In a way, he felt he was the poorest rich man in the world. It was good to see Jack and it brought back fond memories of whom and what he used to be. It didn't matter to John that Jack's church was, at best, a tenth the size of his own or that jack labored in relative obscurity for wages that were about half short of a pittance to John. No, John considered Jack to be the richest man in the world. Their conversation went marvelously and helped to complete John's transformation and allow his new life to take root. Pastor Jack helped John to see where good intentions, rightly motivated actions originated. He showed him the agape love of God in Christ. Jack shared an acrostic that John would never forget: GRACE, God's Riches at Christ's Expense.

John's transformation was radical, a complete about-face. He shocked everyone when he immediately went to work on finding a buyer for his business. He cashed in his entire mountain of chips and moved back home to St. Louis. John devoted himself to helping others, not for self-aggrandizement but for all the right reasons; true love and charity and thankfulness toward God. John had become a cheerful giver. Finally, we had a dream with a happy ending! This rich young ruler heard the voice of Christ and responded affirmatively by trading earthly wealth for the real, lasting treasure of the gospel. However, the dream ended a bit short to suit me. A few questions remained. Why was such a wealthy man dressed like such a bum? And why had he been soliciting those down trodden denizens of our dead mall?

Chapter 34

Connecting the Dots

I chuckled at the thought of Ike trying to foist his last two dollars upon a multi-millionaire. Only two days had passed when Doctor Bhatia informed me that John had regained consciousness and was able to take visitors. I wasted no time in making my way to the hospital. I was motivated by more than curiosity. Sure, John's story, like Claire's, was chock full of real moral fiber. We had been enlivened and inspired by these heartening renditions. But something was still missing, something more than a few minor puzzle pieces. Yes, there was undoubtedly a powerful lesson in seeing how God used these broken tools to accomplish such marvelous things in the building of his heavenly kingdom. Still, they were just fresh reminders of truths I had already known but lost track of somewhere along the way. The puzzle did not present a full image yet. There seemed to be an entire section missing that carried another meaning altogether. This feeling reminded me of when I discovered my purpose, my great commission but had lingering thoughts that something more specific was in store for me too. There was only one way for me to find out.

It struck me how John's and Claire's trances occurred in reverse order. Claire had recounted her life personally, to the low point, and we had to wait for the dream to see the happy ending. Now with John, we saw the happy ending up front and were about to get the postscript personally. I hoped that we wouldn't see a reversal with his happy ending somehow turning south on him. But I must admit I was concerned in thinking back to his ragged image at NWP. When I stepped into his room, I was pleasantly surprised by his clean shaven, well-scrubbed, wholesome appearance. He still was as warm and affable as he seemed during that brief encounter at the mall. John was very forthcoming, an open book willing to answer any question without reservation. Thus, I dove right in to get the scoop on his destitute appearance.

John was not his real name. As promised, I can fill you in on that little secret now. After hearing his explanation, I dubbed him John as in John Beresford Tipton of television fame in the late 1950s drama, The Millionaire. You see, when John decided to put his money to good use in helping others, he didn't want to take the easy way out. In the past, his charitable efforts consisted mainly of something quite easy for a person of great wealth; simply writing checks. Actually identifying a good cause and then getting the aid dispensed properly was somebody else's problem. This time around John wanted to take a hands-on approach. He remembered the old TV show and how the fabulously rich industrialist John Tipton went about the business of helping others. Fictional John would mingle with the dregs, incognito, to study them and find the right subject and then bless them with an anonymous gift of one million dollars, an incredible sum back then. What our John liked most about the old story lines was how the millionaire took the time to find someone who had the need but also the proper heart and disposition to do something meaningful with their windfall.

Now it all made sense to me. That's why someone so affluent was adorned like a homeless vagrant. It also explained why the stranger seemed to purposefully ignore two worthy marks like me and Ike to instead seek out the more destitute types. He wasn't panhandling; he was looking for his next beneficiary. Ike and I had heard of Secret Santa's who brightened up Christmas with anonymous gifts to unsuspecting strangers but never anything like this. We were so enthralled by John's new life that we insisted he share some of his true life experiences with us. He agreed to do so on the condition that we protect his anonymity for his work was not nearly done. He left out certain details to protect the identities of the recipients of his generosity but these stories were exhilarating nonetheless, much more powerful than anything in the fictional realm. The most interesting and uplifting part was seeing how he went about choosing just the right beneficiaries and what they did afterwards. It was like a true to life version of Pay It Forward. John truly was a cheerful giver, delighting in making memories rather than money; resurrecting lives gone awry. The more money he gave away, the more blessed he felt. He had every intention of dying without a penny in the bank.

We were able to put one mystery to rest. Talking with John settled the question about dreams. Ike's trances were definitely not dreams in the normal sense. Everything he had witnessed from John's life turned out to be historically accurate and completely factual, down to the gnat's eyelash. Knowing that, I probed further trying to seek some connection beyond the ubiquitous little red bible tract. John had never heard of or come in contact with Claire to the best of his recollection. I searched every side street and alley way with John but could find no missing link. I had hesitated to delve into the Faces with him since I was on shaky ground there anyway. What did I know about them, really? But there was no other possible connection now that we had ruled out Claire so I took a chance. John found my truncated version of the Faces' saga to be amusing in parts and disturbing in others but it didn't spark any memories. During their heyday, John was busy chasing his dreams in Dallas. As enlightening as it had been, my conversation with John appeared headed for another dead end. I did my best to hide my disappointment and frustration as I prepared to wrap up and take my leave.

John wanted to finish one last story so I waited. He had been trying to explain how he took the leap from a large, successful U. S. firm to a global juggernaut. He recounted his basic strategy of providing air service at road freight costs. Then he shared his organizational strategy; he frequently sought people with some kind of athletic background, even if it was just little league ball or JFL football. He wasn't looking for coordinated motor skills. What he wanted were highly motivated people with competitive fire in their bellies. This simple strategy had served him oh so well. But his big breakthrough came when he expanded his service offering. That's when he added logistics consulting to the mix and really took off. This was all very nice but I was losing interest at that point having happily escaped the corporate world myself. But then, just as I was about to get out of my chair and offer my farewell, I caught something that cemented me in my seat.

John was getting into too much detail to suit me about how he developed his own custom software in-house. He felt this was the key; that it had given him a competitive advantage that was hard to duplicate. But with programmers being so expensive to retain as full-time staffers, he had minimized some of the cost by purchasing several tertiary applications off the shelf. He would have never bothered to mention such a mundane detail like the name of the software salesman except for one thing. My ears perked up when he mentioned he was visited by a software sales executive named Stan who went by the nickname Stash. The only reason he had met with such a low level individual personally was that he was from his home town of St. Louis. I thought, no way, could it be our Stash? Then he released the real zinger, "I wouldn't have brought this up but this Stash fellow was the one who gave me the little red bible tract in passing." My mind raced. Finally, just maybe, I had found the missing link that would allow me to connect the dots. It wouldn't be long now. My meeting with Tim and Stash was only two days away.

BOOK SEVEN

Redemption

Chapter 35

Two Wild and Crazy Guys

What better place to meet Tim and Stash than at a bar, right? Actually, it was more of a bar/restaurant called the Train Wreck Saloon. During the day, you could find a quiet table and enjoy a long, easy lunch with a few cold ones. I picked this spot specifically because I anticipated a rather long discussion ... or perhaps a very short one if it didn't set well with them. As anxious as I was, I couldn't just jump in with both feet and say; come clean, you're the Faces, aren't you? No, after exchanging greetings, thanking them for agreeing to meet and ordering some lunch and a round of beers, I eased into it with the background.

I explained what had happened at the hospital after we parted ways with them and then the subsequent occurrences. For the sake of time and not wanting to tip my hand too early, I told them about the odd nature of the dreams without sharing any particulars. I cast the conversation in the context of my underlying cause which truly was to ensure Ike's well-being more than anything else. Thus, I spent the most time laying the groundwork for the medical issues and the incomplete but intriguing hypotheses Doctor Bhatia was pursuing. I could tell from their expressions that I had successfully conveyed an appropriate sense of urgency. Tim inquired, "What can we do to help you?"

I proceeded cautiously, "Well, first we need to pinpoint the nature of these dreams. You see, we don't think they are normal dreams at all because they are so true to life and heaped with very specific minutia that seems well beyond Ike's imagination. For example, have you ever heard of a couple of guys known as the Faces?"

They looked at each other and then back at me with slack jaws and Tim replied, "Unless you're talking about Rod Stewart or John Travolta, you're looking at them." I sat there in stunned silence. Okay, there it was, right out on the table. Now where do I go from here?

I thought for a minute and said, "Don't say anything more, right now, okay?" They nodded, still incredulous. I explained, "You may be thinking, so what, perhaps there's a reasonable explanation for me knowing you as the Faces. Thus, before you reveal anything else, I'm going to share Ike's dream with you in every detail down to the brass tacks. Then, you tell me if it's real or Memorex, okay?" Again they silently urged me on.

They sat patiently while I played back the whole reel. They followed my instructions and didn't utter a peep. But I had my answer before they spoke from the looks on their faces. They were mesmerized. I could tell they couldn't believe what they were hearing. I shared the whole thing, not sparing one sordid detail other than, I must confess, I did some heavy editing on the fish story to save us all from some embarrassment. When I had finished, Tim just shook his head in disbelief but Stash still clung to a faint hope that this must be a sham and challenged me, "Tell me one thing, what was the name of our pet piranha?"

I snuffed out any last bit of doubt, "I believe that would be Mr. P."

Tim looked up and conceded softly as if he had been caught with his hand in the cookie jar, "That was no dream. I'm sorry to say that it's the truth; everything happened just as Ike saw it."

I told them how surprised I had been to see them at Claire's funeral, "I don't mean to offend you but seeing The Faces in a church threw me for a loop. It didn't seem possible. I've got to tell you, when I heard your beautiful testimonial, I tossed out my theory about the dreams as a bunch of hooey. The contrast was just too stark."

"We're not offended at all," Stash offered; "sometimes we find it hard to believe ourselves. Looking back to those days seems like a dream to us too; a bad dream."

I don't mean to pry but something amazing happened to you. I'm curious to know if you don't mind sharing. Besides, it might help us in cracking the code on Ike's condition by knowing more about you. Tim, one of the things we need to figure out is what do you, Claire and John have in common that made you good subjects to induce these trances in Ike?"

Although he was clearly hesitant, Tim put valor ahead of discretion and said, "Okay, if you have the time to listen. First, let's order another round of Buds."

Tim was ready to tell the rest of the story, as Paul Harvey used to say, and take us through the '80s to today. But Stash interrupted him, needing to get something off his chest, "Before we go on, there's something I need to add. I don't mean to make excuses but I think it's important that you know we weren't really such bad guys. We did a lot of careless, stupid, foolish things and needlessly wasted a good chunk of our lives. However, the thing you've got to understand is that it wasn't some kind of premeditated strategy on our parts. There was never a master plan. I can't exonerate us by saying we were clueless; it was more a case of us just being impulsive, living for the moment. In a way we were just like Dan Akroyd and Steve Martin, those two wild and crazy guys. Yortuk and Georg Festrunk didn't have an evil bone in their bodies. They weren't deep thinkers. There really was only one motivation behind all their misguided, goofy antics; a

295

single driving force, a solitary animal instinct that kept them going: the quest for hot American chicks. We were that uncomplicated. Ace and Nature Boy were just two characters we created to get a few laughs. But then we found out the Faces were a lot funnier than plain, old Tim and Stash and people seemed to like them better. For a while there, our alter egos just took over." Tim and I just nodded repeatedly as if to say we understand. Stash had made his confession.

I felt like I had to say something, "Stash, somehow I don't think those years were wasted. As painful as they were, they helped to shape you and bring you around to who you are today. And don't forget, God delights in using broken tools."

Chapter 36

Bust Out the Fatted Calf

Tim and Stash were ready to tie up the loose ends. I had all the time in the world and wouldn't miss this for anything. This would be like stumbling upon a one hundred ten year old Jesse James in 1957, somehow a miraculously reformed man, and having the chance to chronicle his transformation from outlaw to good guy. Okay, so I was letting my imagination run a little wild but you get the idea. Stash kicked things off, "Things started catching up to us finally. You just can't go at that pace of abuse well into your thirties without something giving way. It was nothing major but cumulatively the boozing and late nights took a toll on our health. Times were changing and our little brushes with the law were not so easily excused. We knew it was only a matter of time before we were hit with a serious infraction. How would that look on our records? We were smart enough to realize that something like that could derail our careers which had progressed reasonably well for such irresponsible party boys. But old habits die hard and we stumbled frequently as common sense gave way to old urges."

Tim grabbed the baton, "Stash is right. I really don't think we would have ever made it over the hump of our own accord. But things finally took a turn for the better for us and then we met our wives. Yes, we both remarried. With our disrespect for women, the acrimony we held toward our first wives and the type of bimbos we usually associated with, you'd never guess who we married the second time around. Would you believe a couple of Sunday school teachers? It's true."

I asked, "Where did you meet them?"

Tim smiled, "We ran into them at the ball park. Can you imagine that? We were there on a Sunday afternoon when a bunch of Lutherans happened to have their annual Cardinal Day outing. Lucky for us we ran into them at the concession stand in the first inning before we could consume too many brews. I think they liked our singing. We used to do a take-off on Joe Frazier's song from the Miller Lite commercial only we substituted Bud Light being loyal St. Louis boys. Then we'd entertain the other customers waiting in line by singing our own original composition: Cold Beer Baby." They actually sang a few bars for me and gave me a hint of the old Faces' showmanship as if to say, we've still got it.

Stash jumped in continuing the tag team routine, "I think they liked us in spite of our singing. I don't know if we scared them or intrigued them more. They probably had never encountered two goofs like us before. The girls wouldn't give us their phone numbers but were brave enough to give us their first names and told us where they went to church. They may not have been our normal cup of tea but were very pretty in a muted way; at least it seemed muted in comparison to the flash dancers we normally encountered at the bars. There was something different and refreshing about those two that attracted us to them. It took a strong attraction to convince us to look them up at their church the next Sunday. We had just started attending another church at the invitation of a friend but were still uncomfortable with the whole routine. I remember how Tim kept looking up as if to see whether a lightning bolt would crash down to zap us. We were as skittish as two, well, the two Faces in church. But it was worth it seeing Karen and Shawn. And they gave us their last names and phone numbers."

Tim carried on, "That really heralded a new beginning for us. It changed a lot of things. Getting to know Karen and Shawn helped us let go of our bitterness and anger. We had a whole new lease on life and outlook toward the female persuasion. And gradually, very gradually, we began feeling more comfortable in church and around normal folks again. As these changes occurred, the under pinning of our old, foolish lifestyle began to slowly crumble. But there was always that fear of discovery since we were in no man's land, somewhere between the Faces and our new lives. What if these good, church going folks ever got a load of what we had been; what if they caught the Faces' real act? I'll never forget the night Pastor Martin dropped in on us unannounced. He had a huge heart but was a no nonsense evangelist. He basically laid it on the line saying we had been visiting for months and needed to make a decision whether to become members or not. Looking back, I thank God that Pastor Martin didn't allow us a lot of wiggle room. What could we do? We signed on the dotted line. It was one of the best decisions we've ever been coerced into."

I listened excitedly as Tim and Stash went on about their gradual but amazing transfigurations. It filled one of the voids I had been carrying with me. Ike's first trance had left me completely in the lurch. It troubled me to no end to think about these lost souls, the Faces, stumbling along to an inevitable end filled with dread and doom. I couldn't bear to think of the loss, an eternity of regret. But now, the story that had finally unfolded was so different. Tim and Stash married Karen and Shawn and started families. They enjoyed successful, fruitful careers. At Pastor M's prodding and coaching, they became involved in the work of the church in their free time. They were happy, productive, caring, generous individuals who wound up providing a good example for others. The time came when they could even learn from and laugh about their past instead of worrying that it would be dredged up. They were able to admit their sins and welcome Christ's forgiveness to release their guilt. Tim and Stash even brought their alter egos, the Faces, back to life from time to time in a sort of parody of their former selves. But they never let it get in the way of their true purpose in life now that their priorities were well in order. In their older age, Ace and Nature provided comic relief to relatives, co-workers and friends, especially the younger ones. To them, it was just a big joke, a stand-up routine filled with self-deprecating humor. The Faces were fictional characters in a far out sketch and Tim and Stash were just a couple of funny guys who livened up parties and family reunions with their mugging, shtick and silly, harmless gags.

Of course, Tim and Stash toned down and edited everything quite a bit when they rehashed some of the old tales from the glory days. Or should I say gory days? Today's version of the Faces reminded me more of Leo Gorcy and Huntz Hall than the Festrunk brothers. They were like the Bowery Boys, Slip and Sach, posing as gangsters in Bowery Bombshell: very funny but not believable. The young Turks loved to hear their stories but always assumed the Faces were exaggerating since no one would have dared to really pull such stunts. Whenever this happened, they simply smiled and thought ... if they only knew.

I was so thrilled to finally put this to rest with such a wonderful, fairy tale ending. It must have been like that for the woman who found the lost coin or the shepherd who located that one lost sheep. I was sure that at some point the angels in heaven had shouted with joy over Tim and Stash's homecoming. Another one of those quirky images popped involuntarily into my head. It was a famous Wendy's commercial from the '80s. There was old Clara Peller demanding to know, "Where's the beef?" Now we had the answer. It was time to bust out the fatted calf and celebrate. They were lost but now were found. I turned to Tim and Stash and said, "Do you guys remember the deli that used to be on the lower level at Northwest Plaza?"

Stash said, "Sure, it was the Fatted Calf." The Fatted Calf was long gone and a good thing too. We had celebrated enough already and had just the right amount of cold Budweiser and it was time to call it a day.

I had one more question though, "It's obvious that the word of God changed your lives. I could tell that from your testimonial at Claire's memorial service. But things usually don't happen so gradually according to God's plan. Do you recall any kind of ah ha moment that really made the difference?"

Tim answered first, "I like what Martin Luther once said about God's word, that it has little hands and feet that come after you and apprehend you."

Stash chimed in, "That seemed to be true for us. Thinking back, it all started with that little red bible tract."

Chapter 37

Through a Glass Darkly

I thought, bingo, we've scored a hat trick. Not only had all three dreams ended joyfully but in each case, that little red bible tract had played a small but pivotal role. Ike's first dream had given me a window into a hidden chamber. At first, the glass was nearly opaque, clouded with soot, grime and grease. Each new trance helped to remove a layer of film. Every discussion with Claire, John, Tim and Stash wiped away some of the obstructions. Doctor Bhatia provided a powerful cleaning agent too. My vision was no longer impaired and certain things came into focus sharply. Everyone had their imperfections. We were all broken tools in one way or another. But it did not deter God. Each and every one of us had found our purpose in him and his great commission. We also learned to use God's cosmic scale to compare the value of things, both material and spiritual. When you see things in the perspective of eternity, worldly treasures lose their luster. It's much easier to set priorities. Sometimes it takes a lot of hard knocks but we find out that God's way is infinitely better than ours. Peering inside that chamber had given me a sense of purpose and true peace.

There was at least one more loose end to tie up with Tim and Stash. We had run out of time and energy but they asked if they could stop by my house to see me again to give me something. They had planned on doing so anyway but were not prepared when we met at the Train Wreck since I had given them no hint about my intentions. As it turned out, they would have sought me out anyway even if I had not stumbled upon them at Claire's memorial. Claire had been doing a little detective work of her own and I was the subject of her investigation. She too had been trying to connect the dots. Through the course of our journal sessions with Ike, she had picked up a tidbit here and there that made her think we had crossed paths before. She had never said anything to me, wanting to have some concrete evidence before drawing conclusions. Even after she confirmed her suspicions, she waited in order to surprise me. Unfortunately, death came sooner than any of us expected.

When Tim and Stash came by, I noticed they had one of the familiar red tracts with them. We sat down and Sally offered everyone some coffee. I warned them about the instant crystals and they opted out. Stash started, "Do you remember how I told you one of these little tracts made a turning point in our lives?"

"Yes, I do Stash."

He continued, "Well, this is a special one, it's one that Claire wanted you to have."

My mind was flooded with a thousand

questions but all I could utter was, "Oh?"

Tim took the tract from Stash, "These things are all over the place, a dime a dozen. But this one is very special to me, Stash and Claire. It's the very same one she gave to us way back when, right when we were hitting rock bottom. I'll never forget that day as long as I live. We were at the Ball Park again with nothing better to do on a Sunday than to assault our livers once more. It was just weeks before our fateful meeting with Karen and Shawn. The Cardinals had their Senior Day promotion that afternoon and the place was crawling with geezers. We were past the point of being happy drunks and were making things unpleasant for the fans around us. Someone took exception to our unruly behavior and spicy language and we responded poorly, nearly causing a fracas. We really showed our rear ends, as the Old Pro used to say, and caused quite an ugly scene as we were escorted to the exit by a host of attendants. Most intelligent people gave us a wide berth but almost out of nowhere, this little old lady, older than my mother, walked right up to us and handed me this little red bible tract. She seemed oblivious to our obnoxious behavior and with a hint of motherly love, understanding, compassion and forgiveness, sweetly patted my hand and whispered to me, 'you read this honey when you get home and call me if you have questions.' Along with the tract, she had quickly scribbled her phone number on a Sport Service napkin. We were always looking for girls to give us their phone numbers but this was not quite what we had in mind. The way she reached out to us hit me like a bucket of ice cold water. We calmed down immediately as if shot with a tranquilizer dart."

Tim continued, "Normally, we would have tossed that tract in the can like so much garbage before we got past Musial's statute but we were so captivated by her gesture that we held onto it. Maybe it was because she was some kind of maternal figure to us. Don't forget our motto: you don't talk mean to your momma and you don't mess with the Faces. We didn't follow her instructions exactly but only a few days passed before we read through it, Stash first and then me. It had taken years of self-inflicted damage to quiet our stubborn, rebellious spirits but we were finally receptive to outside help. At that point in our lives, we were ready to be rescued; we desperately needed someone to throw us a life preserver. Did Claire somehow sense we were ripe for the picking? The soil of our souls was well plowed to accept the good seeds planted by this little red tract."

Stash explained, "We worked up the courage to call Claire to thank her and apologize for our rude behavior at the stadium. Nothing had changed on her end; she was still as sweet and kind as could be. Then, she gave us her name and address and insisted that we come over for a visit. We thought, *was this woman crazy*? How could she invite two strangers like us over to her home without so much as a care in the world? Wasn't she afraid of being mugged or robbed blind? She acted as if this was all perfectly normal. We had no choice but to pay her a visit. When we arrived she welcomed us with some warm, home baked Toll House cookies and milk. Can you imagine the Faces sharing cookies and milk with Grandma Moses? We had a wonderful talk with her. She wasn't preachy or judgmental. Claire even shared stories from her own checkered past to make us feel at ease. She was a really cool lady and we got a kick out of swapping war stories with her. There was no ulterior motive with her; she just wanted to help us. How could we resist someone like Claire? She won us over completely. As we were wrapping things up, we asked her what we should do next. Claire invited us to attend church with her. On our way out, she grabbed my arm and gave us some motherly advice, 'Go home and read Lamentations 5:21 and then pray on it.' Boy did she hit the mark. I'll never forget those words: Turn thou us unto thee, O LORD, and we shall be turned; renew our days as of old."

Tim closed the story, "God must have been conspiring with the women in our lives because soon after that we met Karen and Shawn. Everything was turning us away from our old ways and pointing us toward a new life. We didn't see Claire as much after that. We started going to the other church with our gals. Then we were married and wrapped up in raising our families. We tried to stay in touch occasionally but, over time, we drifted apart from Claire, at least physically. However, we never forgot her or what she did for us even though our contact was limited mainly to exchanging Christmas cards and such. She would always send along a nice note to keep us up to date. It made us happy to know that her time was spent mostly in doing the Lord's work; in coaxing other wandering sheep to get into the word and close to God."

"Much to our surprise, she called us a while back, just a short time before she passed away, and asked me if we still had the little red tract she had given us so long ago. When I assured her we would never dispose of such a cherished memento, she asked if we would bring it over and show it to her. It was so good seeing her again. When she took the little tract in her frail hands and leafed through the brittle pages, she seemed to be relieved as though someone had returned a lost treasure. Claire never explained her odd request but gave us very specific instructions. She made us promise to give the little red bible tract to you upon her death. Claire wouldn't entertain any questions. It was kind of mysterious. She was very insistent though and gave us your name and address. Neither Claire nor we had any idea we had already made your acquaintance at NWP. So, you see, we were just as surprised as you when you introduced yourself to us at her memorial.

Well, I hope that explains our visit today. Here you go, Baker."

I took the tract from Tim and held it as though it were a rare, priceless gem. It looked like every other little red bible tract I had ever seen, except that this one was old, worn and tattered. I thought about Claire as I perused it. Just as I was about to tuck it away and let Tim and Stash be on their way, I flipped to the back inside cover and received some shock therapy of my own. Even though the ink was badly faded, I could still read the stamp at the bottom of the page: Holy Trinity Church. And there, in small hand scribbled letters were the initials: BP. I literally felt light headed as my mind reeled and I thought for a moment I might fall out of my chair. Apparently, Claire was very good at keeping a secret because Tim and Stash had no idea about what just happened. They just stared at me with puzzled looks as though they were worried I might be having a stroke.

I had to stop and think for a minute to gather my thoughts. One of my mother's favorite passages came to mind: For now we see through a glass, darkly; but then face to face: now I know in part; but then shall I know even as also I am known (I Corinthians 13:12). This referred to the imperfections of our present world and our lack of understanding of God and his revelations, not because of any imperfection in God's word but in our limited ability to comprehend. In ancient times, their mirrors were made of polished metal giving a reflection but not a distinct image. This passage assures us that one day, when we've passed from this world to the next one, we will see and understand with perfect clarity as if viewing an image face to face. We'll be able to comprehend God in all his glory and fully understand his good and perfect will.

Looking back, my understanding of God and his will in my life had grown clearer with age and the edification of Holy Scripture. Yet still, I had so many questions. But this was truly a breakthrough for me. Holy Trinity was my church, you see, and those were my initials penned so long ago. That is why I appeared in Ike's second dream. It was me who had left the little red bible tract on Claire's porch all those years ago. I had found the missing link. That small act had such an impact on Claire and she in turn on Tim and Stash and, finally, on John through his chance meeting with Stash in Dallas. How many lives had God touched through them since then?

I was stunned. All of this was from one tiny, little red bible tract I had distributed while fulfilling my privileged purpose in God's great commission. Now the trances made sense. This is why God wanted Ike and me to see the Faces as the prodigals they once were. He led us to Senior Towne and Claire. He urged us to approach John Tipton. Somehow, Claire must have known the priceless value of the gift she had bequeathed to me. In

310

this little tract, I had validation; it was as if I had received God's stamp of approval on my life's purpose. I was not just a number, an inconsequential speck on this big blue ball called earth. Thank you God for allowing me to make a difference!

Chapter 38

Blue Brother

I was soaring like an eagle. The only thing that could have made things more perfect would have been for God to take me home right then and there and say, "Well done thou good and faithful servant." But that didn't happen and my euphoria was short lived as reality sank in. How could I be at peace with Ike's life hanging in the balance? I was so thankful that Ike's epilepsy was gone but this new ailment had advanced to where it was more dangerous, even life threatening, if we could not prevent the trances from happening again. The more I dwelled on this, the more my mood changed from amber to dark blue. I started to worry that I was manic depressive or something. How could I go from the top of Mount Everest all the way down to this low, dark valley so quickly? If I were the eighth dwarf, Snow White would have named me Mopey.

A few days later I received a much needed kick in the pants when Doctor Bhatia called. He had been gleaning new information from John Tipton and asked if I could help arrange a meeting with Tim. Good old Doc had not given up. To his credit he was still hot on the trail of a diagnosis and then, hopefully, a cure. In his consultation with Mr. Tipton, he found out that John, in his homeless get up, had once been shot with a Taser-gun by an over-zealous, young police officer who mistook him for another dangerous suspect. That, along with earlier revelations about Tim's shock therapy and Claire's defibrillation treatment provided a strong link between the three of them. John had allowed Doctor Bhatia to run a battery of tests on him and now the good Doc wanted me to see if Tim would consent to the same, if not purely to advance the cause of medical science then, hopefully, for Ike's sake. He also wanted to interview Tim about the dream and his past to see if he could glean any new clues.

Tim was not fond of doctors or hospitals. He had a phobia about needles and once had fainted while getting a simple blood test. This phobia apparently extended to electrodes, those conductive patches used to hook a subject up to a monitor. When I approached him with my request, his first reaction was to say he'd rather jump into a box full of snakes. He didn't give a hoot about advancing medical science but Tim was a trooper and eventually agreed to face these demons in order to help little Ike. His consent was given on the condition that Stash could be present during the tests. He figured that way he could cut up with the Nature Boy to keep his mind on something else. This was unusual but Doctor Bhatia agreed since the trance had occurred while the Faces were together. He wasn't sure it made any difference but thought it would be best to try to duplicate Tim's condition and frame of mind exactly as it was during that episode. Even stoic Doctor

Bhatia was not immune to the Faces and had trouble concentrating amidst the barrage of slings, barbs and one liners that Tim and Stash hurled at each other during this circus. Even at their age, boys will be boys.

Tim, Stash, John and Doctor Bhatia were an incredible blessing. Where would we have been without their time, commitment and willingness to extend a helping hand? The Doc had ulterior motives in advancing the cause of his profession and potentially finding a cure that might benefit others but he sincerely cared for Ike and me and we would have never been so blessed were it not for his generosity in using his research grants to aid us. The tests and interviews with John and Tim proved critical to Doctor Bhatia's work. In time, he called me with the good news that he wanted to meet and brief me on his findings. He struck me as different right off the bat. This time around he was not so preoccupied with cautioning me about drawing conclusions and so forth. Instead he seemed intent on laying out a theory, not a set of hypotheses but a firm, well tested theory. It only took him a minute to lose me in a maze of technical gobbledy-gook. He had coined a phrase to describe the phenomenon we had witnessed three times: neuro-electrical declarative memory transfer. That in itself was a mouthful but it was only the beginning. He left me dazed and confused with talk of catalysts, receptors, atomic particle structures, gateways, neutron alignments and such. Those were just some of the words I recognized. There were many others that didn't even register in my brain. I hated to do it because he was obviously very excited but finally I interrupted, "Whoa, Doc, Whoa. You've lost me here. Can you bring it down a few hundred notches and explain it in terms I might be able to understand? Just talk to me like you would a fifth grader. I won't be offended."

Doc laughed, "Okay Baker, you've got it."

He was still excited but slowed down and patiently explained it to me in a way that made sense to me. "Baker, you know that everyone is unique in certain ways, right? Just look at finger prints and retinal scanners. Those are just the physical manifestations that we can see. Think of all the unseen differences that aren't so evident. What attracted you to Sally; was it driven by pheromones or something deeper and more psychological? Why do we hit it off so well with some people and others turn us off right away? If we could figure that out, think of the money we could make with our 100% guaranteed dating service." I tried to laugh politely at his lame doctor humor. "Anyway, I've been looking into a particular area of differences, our wiring as you put it. What I've found is that we run on different currents so to speak." I started to get that perplexed look on my face again. "Sorry Baker, that's not a very good analogy. Let me put it this way. Each of us is electrically wired in ways that make us unique. Think of it as something like our blood type. Only certain blood types are compatible. Some are quite common and others are rare. What I was trying to tell you before was that I've found certain attributes or distinctive markings in Tim, John and Ike that make them very different from the norm. They're not only different but in some ways very rare. I think they were wired differently to begin with but somewhere along the line received what might be called an interrupted infarction."

I objected, "There you go again."

Doc looked a bit impatient with me but gathered himself, "Yes, I'm sorry Baker. This is where your loose wire comes into play."

I smiled, "Now you're talking."

He marched on, "Normally, infarctions are bad things. It can occur, for example in a stroke when there's a blood clot or blockage that cuts off oxygen and glucose causing vital circuits to be shut off. But when it comes to our electrical circuitry, there are certain blockades or what we might call non-conductive insulators that keep us from getting shorted out by contact with other people. Think of it this way. If you're working around live electricity, you'll wear something non-conductive like rubber gloves to prevent from getting shocked. That's why they put rubber handles on jumper cables. You know what happens when you

316

accidentally touch the copper clips together when the other end is hooked up to a battery."

I nodded, this I could follow but added, "Doc, I hear you but I'm not sure of why this is important or what it has to do with Ike."

This was a good reminder to the Doc to keep it relevant and get to the point. He repositioned himself, "Thank you Baker. Our natural insulation serves a purpose. I think it's intended to protect us or maybe a better way is to say it protects our privacy. People can observe and try to control our speech and behavior but our thoughts are our own. No one knows what's going on inside our heads, other than God, of course. Can you imagine what it would be like if they ever figured out a way to hook us up to a machine that could read our thoughts? There are people working on this, you know. So far, there's nothing that can break through this invisible barrier. Even polygraph tests can be beaten. That's why they are not admissible evidence. What if law enforcement could not only read our current thoughts but could tap into our memory banks? It would revolutionize criminal investigation techniques and courtroom procedures."

I didn't have to say anything. Doc caught himself and thought, *stay relevant, get back to the point.* "They were wired differently to begin with but when Ike, Claire, Tim and John experienced some form of shock experience it reversed one of these infarctions or insulators in a way that it left them with, well you said it before, a loose wire. When they touched, there was nothing to stop a circuit from closing between them. They were literally connected in a way that normally never happens between two people."

Doc was doing a good job of keeping it simple and I was following so far. He shifted gears, "Here's where it gets really interesting. These loose wires that formed the connection were along a particular pathway or circuit, namely the one that leads to memory storage. Even within this particular circuitry, there are many different paths that we are only beginning to understand. From what we do know, I can tell you that this connection was even more unusual than anything we might have imagined. Forgive me for getting a little technical but there's a reason I called this declarative. Tapping into someone's memory is strange enough but declarative memory is even more unlikely. While far-fetched, if I were going to try to invent a machine to tap into someone's memory it would be easier to seek the path of procedural memory. That's the part of our subconscious where we store learned skills like driving a car or operating a lawn mower. Declarative memory is where we store our history, all the facts and events in our lives. This can be broken down further into semantic memory where we keep general facts and knowledge that are independent of our personal experiences. For example, I've never been to Istanbul but I can locate it on a map. Finally, there is episodic memory where we store specific experiences and events like Tim and Stash attending a ball game. This is the mother lode of memory which is the most secure under normal conditions."

Doctor Bhatia paused and stared me in the eye with an excited look like a kid who was about to share something really special with his grade school classmates during show-and-tell. "I can't pinpoint it exactly but there is something truly unique about Ike, his wiring. He has some kind of receptor that makes him susceptible to these trances or memory transfer events. If Claire, Tim and John came into contact with each other, nothing would happen in spite of their own unique circuitry and loose wires. But with Ike, everything was just right for him to tap into that forbidden part of their psyches. "

Doc was ready to bring it all together and could tell from my face and attentiveness that I was tracking well. "Baker, we were thrown off by the notion of dreams, a totally different operation that runs on different circuitry that is completely internal. Oh, we've all had dreams that incorporated outside stimuli but these things are always placed into our memory banks first and are never dropped directly into our dreams."

I interjected, "Yes, like when Dorothy yanked

Hunk, Zeke and Hickory from her memory during her dream of Oz."

Doc was pleased, "That's exactly right, Baker. But therein lies the difference; with Ike his dreams seemed too real and accurate. They weren't dreams at all but instead he actually viewed past events as they were recorded and stored in Tim's, Claire's and John's memory banks. I don't claim to understand the mechanics of it yet, Baker, but think of it as you might your PC. Ike is sort of like a thumb drive. This whole strange convergence of events and circumstances set up ports in Tim, Claire and John that were just the perfect size and pin configuration to accept Ike's thumb drive. So he wasn't experiencing a dream or seeing a vision. It was just as if a copy of their memories was being downloaded to him."

As wild as all this sounded, in light of everything we had experienced, it made perfect sense. However, it raised a few questions, "But Doc, why did these events change and become longer and more dangerous?"

"I'm not really sure but here's my best guess. You know that it takes a lot of energy to run your PC, right?"

"Yeah, if there's any doubt, all I have to do is look at my electric bill."

"Well, I think it's the same way with these

320

memory transfers. I believe there's an incredible amount of human energy involved." That helped me to explain a lot of things. Tim had not passed out even though he told Doctor Bhatia during the recent interview that he had felt ill for a few days after Ike's first trance but just thought he was coming down with something. Tim was in good health at the time of the first event and the duration of the trance was shorter. With Claire and John the transferences were much longer with larger downloads. John's health was not as good as Tim's and poor Claire was in such a weakened condition that she could not survive the rigors.

Unfortunately, there was one question it didn't answer for me, "Doc, how come Ike is trending downward?"

Doctor Bhatia lamented, "I'm very sorry Baker but I just don't know. All I know is that his condition is changing with each occurrence. Something is happening that I can't explain yet."

"Doc, did you find out anything that would help us prevent this from happening again?"

"Unfortunately, the answer is no. It's certain now that physical contact is required but there's no way of knowing who else might have this same circuitry or even the odds of how many other threats might be out there."

I felt manic depressive again; I was overjoyed to finally get to the bottom of the trances but right back down in the dumps knowing the threat to Ike was as real as ever. I was blue again, brother. The Blues Brothers popped into my head. As I thought of Jake and Elwood Blues, I smiled sardonically. This was no time for comedy. But wait, I thought, maybe that's the ticket. I still had a mission to accomplish, perhaps like Jake and Elwood, a mission from God. I turned to Doctor Bhatia, "Doc, do you think whatever it is that made Ike so unique could be genetic? I mean, look at me, I was epileptic at that age too."

"Baker, it's entirely possible but even if there was a genetic component, there are so many other variables to consider, not the least of which is the shock trauma that seems to be some sort of catalyst."

I didn't even think of my *shock treatment* with the old record player until later but posed the question, "But would it help if there was something genetic we could spot?"

"I don't know Baker but it might give us another test subject, you. You know me; I'm always on the hunt for new sources of data."

"Well Doc, what could it hurt? If you think it might help and you're willing, I'd be glad to be your guinea pig."

Chapter 39

Maharba's Altar

I got to experience firsthand what Tim had gone through. It wasn't as bad for me but it wasn't a complete picnic either. Although I didn't have a phobia about needles or electrodes, the wires were very constraining like so much spaghetti forming a strait jacket so I got a little claustrophobic and restless as the time wore on. Finally it was over and I gave the Doc an expectant look as though he would immediately be able to reel off an answer for me. He explained that it might be a few days before his analysis was complete but assured me that he would get in touch with me at the first opportunity. What's a couple of days? It was enough to drive me stark, raving mad; that's what. Fortunately for me, things were back to normal with Ike and I was able to fall back into our daily routine to stay occupied.

It was good to be back in my familiar role as home school teacher. I had several thorough lesson plans in hand to ensure the coming days went by quickly.

It took Ike less than five minutes to get me off track when he asked a seemingly innocent question that had deeper theological implications, "Granby, what do you think Jesus would say about diversity?"

I couldn't resist so I set the lesson plan aside and waded in, "Ike, I guess it depends on what type of diversity you're talking about. You remember how we talked about two kinds; how diversity can be good or bad?" Ike didn't need to nod because I knew such a thing couldn't escape his steel trap mind. I laid the ground work for a while and then got to the meat of the matter, "So, unlike our politicians who are just a bunch of wind bags, Jesus is the real deal. All of these politicians claim to be uniters, not dividers, but only Jesus is the great uniter. He loves everyone the same regardless of sex, race, skin color, wealth, education, nationality; you name it. And he proved it by suffering all that pain and torment and sacrificing his own sinless life for each and every one of us. In the end, there are only two kinds of diversity that count. Jesus taught plainly that you're either with him or against him. None of these other things we call diversity will make any difference on that final day; you'll either be sheep or goat, wheat or chaff. No one knows for sure where others stand today except for God. That's why it's so important that we reach out to everyone with the gospel whether they are a lot like us or very different." Ike nodded and smiled in agreement which I took to be my signal to get on with our daily lesson plan.

Just as I was ready to move to math, Ike threw me another curve ball, "Granby, what's wrong with me? Why am I having these dreams and why do I keep ending up in the hospital?" I had to exhale on that one. I hadn't shared much with Ike about Doctor Bhatia's findings but I tried to do so now in a way that Ike could understand without causing any alarm. After laying out the cause and effect relationship as best I could in simple, straightforward terms, I had to plead ignorance on the rest. "Ike, I don't know how to explain electricity. I'm not sure anyone really knows. I mean, we can see what it does, we can feel it, we can even diagram it as part of a power grid or a house's wiring blue print. But what is it and where does it come from? Energy is a lot like the wind I guess or maybe gravity. We feel the effects of gravity every time we take a step or lift up a stone. We can even see what it's like without gravity on the moon or in space flight. There are some fancy theories to explain it but can anyone really tell you what it is or where it comes from?"

Ikestein shot back at me, "You told me once, Granby. Don't you remember you said Jesus is gravity?" He was right, the little scamp. He was referring to the passages we had studied in Colossians 1:16-17: For by him were all things created, that are in heaven, and that are in earth, visible and invisible, whether they be thrones, or dominions, or principalities, or powers: all things were created by him, and for him: And he is before all things, and by him all things consist.

"Right you are Ike and I'm sure Jesus could tell us all about electricity too. What I'm trying to tell you is that I'm not sure what's behind your trances. But I'm sure of one thing; it means you're a very special little boy with a great gift. Somehow, with Doctor Bhatia's help, we will figure this out and make you better so you

325

won't have to spend more time in the hospital."

At that point, I really wanted to move on and was bound and determined to get back on schedule with our lesson plan. But something, I guess the uncertainty of it all, was bothering Ike. He seemed to need some comfort and assurance right then and asked if I would go over one of his favorite Bible stories with him again, "Granby, can you read to me about Abraham and Isaac again?"

I ruffled the hair on top of his head playfully and said, "Sure buddy." I'm not sure why Ike enjoyed this story so much. Maybe it reminded him of us. Maybe he liked to identify with his namesake. Perhaps it was Abraham's and Ike's great show of faith or God's compassion and the surety of his promises being fulfilled. We had read this one so many times before, over and over. But as is so often the case with the Bible, you find something new every time you read it. This time was no different except that the new revelation came to me all at once in a single spark of inspiration. Just like that, I saw my purpose. It wasn't like the great commission or even the way my life's work had been summed up in connecting the dots between me, Claire, Tim, Stash and John. This was much more definitive. Everything came together in one very precise intersection like when a master diamond cutter takes aim to strike a raw gem and, somehow, I knew exactly what I was destined to do.

I pictured myself as Abraham to Ike's Isaac. Only I imagined a complete role reversal. What if God had not provided that ram? What if Abraham would have substituted himself as the sacrifice to save Isaac? Didn't Christ teach, "Greater love hath no man than this, that a man lay down his life for his friends (John 15:13)?" Weren't Isaac and the ram archetypes of the coming Christ who would lay down his life for all of us as the final substitute, suffering the punishment we deserved to pay the price for all our sins? It all seemed so clear. I was destined to be Maharba, Abraham in reverse sent to save rather than sacrifice Isaac. Ike wondered aloud, "Are you okay Granby?" My mind snapped back in place with that and we went on to finish our normal lessons.

I could barely contain myself waiting for Doctor Bhatia to call. When he did, I asked to meet at the very first opportunity. When the Doc shared his analysis with me, it did nothing to deter the scheme I had hatched. It only seemed to make things fit together all that much tighter. "Baker, the tests were very revealing. I'm inclined to think there may be a genetic component as you suggested. I can't say for sure but all the same markers seem to be there. But there are differences as well. First of all, we know that your receptors are not aligned quite like Ike's. I mean, you don't seem to be set up like a thumb drive like him. Also, your wiring is different in that you've never had a trance episode even though you've been exposed to physical contact with the same stimuli. My best guess is that the difference lies in the lack of a traumatic shock event or loose wire." I told the Doc about my experience with the old hi-fi when I was younger. "I don't know, Baker, perhaps such things wear off over time or you've had another experience you've forgotten that reversed the effect and put your insulation back in order. "

I was so convinced of my mission that I blurted out without any fear of the repercussions, "Doc, what if you gave me some kind of shock treatment to prime the pump?"

Taken aback Doctor Bhatia lashed out uncharacteristically, "What do you take me for Baker, some sort of modern day Doctor Frankenstein?"

With the obliviousness of a true believer, I was unfazed by his sharp remark, "Seriously Doc, think about it for a moment. If you could break down my barrier or infarction or whatever you want to call it, think about what that could mean for Ike?"

Nonplussed, he retorted, "What would you do then, use yourself to subject Ike to another trance episode? I thought you realized how dangerous it could be for him to experience even two or three more events."

"I do Doc. That's the whole point. Based on everything you've told me, we have maybe one more chance to get things straight through some kind of trance experience before Ike is in mortal danger."

Now the tables were turned, "I don't get you Baker, what are you trying to suggest?"

"Bear with me for a minute Doc. We know that physical contact with John or Tim would cause another trance, right? But what if we introduced a third variable?"

Doc remained confused, "I'm not following you

Baker."

"Doc, I know as much about electricity as I know about brain surgery. But it seems to me that the only way to carry the energy away from Ike is through him along to another circuit. Maybe I could be like a ground wire or lightening rod."

As this wild hair sunk in, Doc's face went from puzzled to contemplative as though it might actually make sense, "You mean we'd make a human chain with John or Tim on one end, Ike in the middle and you on the other?"

"Bingo, now you've got it!"

Maybe there was a bit of mad scientist in Doctor Bhatia. Or more likely he was feeling that desperate about Ike's situation. It seemed like it would be only a matter of time before a real tragedy occurred. We both knew there was no way to protect Ike from physical contact forever. That thought brought back memories of Travolta again. If Saturday Night Fever was his most significant and triumphant role, 1976's Boy in the Plastic Bubble had to be the low point. Although that was supposedly based on a true story it seemed ridiculous to envision Ike in that situation. The plan we were hatching was probably more outrageous than the plastic bubble but we rationalized together to make it seem almost reasonable. I was healthy and certainly would be in no danger from the shock therapy that would precede the human chain experiment. Another trance experience would be too risky for John but Tim, if willing, was hearty enough to weather a second event. And Ike, well, Ike didn't have a lot of options.

We referred back to the graph on Doc's trend chart and it seemed certain that Ike could only survive one more trance. After that, it would be entirely too risky. Doc's main concern was not his own well-being but mine. If we didn't have complete trust in one another he would have never considered such a far out, experimental stunt. He knew there was no need to fear recriminations or lawsuits from us. But he had no data; there was nothing concrete to indicate how the rigors of trilateral transference might affect me. "Doc, that part has to be my call. I'm willing to accept full responsibility and any consequences. If it comes down to me and Ike, I'd gladly sacrifice my own life for his."

"I just don't know Baker."

"Doc, do you have a better recommendation? If you have some other solution, I'm all ears. But you and I both know that we couldn't live with ourselves if we didn't at least give this a shot and then something happened to Ike."

He said in a very subdued tone, "Give me some time to think about it, Baker."

I knew Doctor Bhatia would come to the same conclusion. As soon as he came around, I wanted to move immediately before anything else could get in the way. We had a lot of work to do. Doc and I laid the whole situation out for TB and Sara to get their consent and they were like minded when confronted with the facts and the harsh reality facing Ike. We talked to Tim and Stash. That was probably the easiest part since Tim was the sort who would run through a brick wall to help a friend in need, especially someone as young and vulnerable as Ike. The toughest part would be preparing Ike. I wanted to hold off until the last minute. I figured there was no need to put him through that until I had been through my shock therapy and cleared for liftoff by Doctor Bhatia. There had been no qualms leading up to that point but the nerves set in as they prepared me for the treatment. My palms grew sweaty as I lay there thinking back to the jolt I had received from my folks' hi-fi player. It didn't help that I was once again hooked up with all kinds of wires and paraphernalia so that Doc could gather more data on my condition. When he turned up the dial and the procedure kicked in, all I could think about was R. P. McMurphy. There was no Chief to rescue me.

It really wasn't all that bad. To me, it paled in comparison to the frightening images that remained from my battle with the evil record player in my parents' basement so long ago. It definitely sobered me up. Doc was pleased with the results but cautioned me that there was no way of knowing for sure if he had exposed a loose wire in me. He spared me another lecture on the possible danger I might expose myself to in undergoing the trance. He didn't have multiple data points to develop a trend or draw any firm conclusions so what was the point anyway? I really wasn't afraid of any physical harm coming to me, not even death. The prospect of going through this experiment and then having no effect on Ike is what scared me the most. What if we played our last trump card and lost?

Everything was set now except for one thing.

We had to bring Ike up to speed. Since we were all in this together, we decided it would be best to break the news as a group. Even though I took the lead, it helped to have TB, Sara, Sally, Doctor Bhatia and Tim there with me to lend moral support. "Ike, do you remember when I told you that Doctor Bhatia and I would find a way to make you better so you wouldn't have to spend more time in the hospital?"

"Sure, I remember, Granby."

"Well, we think we've found a way to do just that and we're all here to help you together. We think there may be a way to make the trances go away for good. But we've got to be honest; we can't be 100% sure."

"Why can't you be sure, Granby?"

"Ike, like I told you before, you have a very special gift. Even Doctor Bhatia has never seen anything quite like it before. So this is an area of medicine where we don't have much experience. However, Doctor Bhatia is very smart and we have the best technology known to man."

"So, is it safe, Granby?"

I couldn't help but tell a little white lie, "Ike, there's absolutely nothing to worry about." I had to be completely honest about one thing though, "Ike there's just one thing you need to know. We'll have to put you into the hospital for this treatment and since you'll be going through another trance, you may have to stay in the hospital for a while afterwards. But the best part is

332

that we will be right there with you and if everything goes as planned you may not have to see the inside of a hospital again for a long, long time." Ike smiled at that prospect. He was on board.

The day finally came and we were all together in one room that had been specially prepared for the experimental treatment. I couldn't help but think of old Abraham building that stone alter in that barren spot up on Mount Moriah. This was quite a bit different. Maharba's alter was totally high tech in close confines surrounded by a huge hospital complex filled with hundreds of people and buzzing with activity. This did not change one thing though. God was surely here just as he had been present with Abraham and Isaac on Mount Moriah. There we were, Tim, Ike and I stretched out on tables next to each other with wires running to and fro from us to the battery of monitors that filled the room. On the one hand, this reminded me of Doctor Frankenstein's laboratory. I could just picture Doctor Bhatia throwing back his head in maniacal laughter and shouting, "It's alive!" I was glad that Ike didn't know we were also hooked up to life support systems, just in case. Other images flooded my mind as we lay there on the tables waiting. I could see the stone altar laden with wood for the burnt offering as Abraham prepared to sacrifice Isaac. Then my mind skipped to the final, all availing sacrifice of Christ, stretched out on the hard wood of the cross like us on these tables. How fitting, we were on three tables just like the three crosses of Jesus and the two thieves.

The moment we clasped hands, I could feel it; not pain so much as an oscillating pulse of energy

333

coursing through my body. As it grew stronger, it seemed as if centipedes were crawling along my veins. Although this repulsed me to the point of frantically wanting to withdraw, I was frozen in paralysis. Then the visions came in rapid fire covering many years in just minutes. This was my private viewing. Everything that had been transferred to Ike in the three trances was being downloaded to me. Then, all at once, it was finished. I thought of Christ's final victory cry from the cross. The experiment was over. I couldn't open my eyes but I could hear Ike ask, "Are you okay, Granby?" That was all I needed to know. Ike had survived the trance and had not slipped into a coma as he had before. Normally, I would be in a panic being conscious but unable to open my eyes, like someone sleeping but tormented with night terrors. My natural inclination toward claustrophobia never materialized. Instead, a warm, peaceful feeling flowed over me and I concentrated on what I could hear. The last thing I remember was being able to separate one sound from all of the other noises in the room, the isolated sound of my life support system.

EPILOGUE

Even though his eyes were closed, Granby heard the beep, beep, beeping of the monitor turn to a high pitched monotone and knew he had flat lined. As the sound faded and darkness descended, his fleeting thoughts were peaceful. He was not concerned with his legacy or who might capture his memories; Dirk's, Pop's wrench, the past glory of the dead mall, his purposes fulfilled or the lessons to be learned from their strange encounters with memory transference . He was completely free of his addiction to the type of nostalgia that had gripped him with such yearning every time he walked through the emptiness of Northwest Plaza. The Valley of the Shadow of Death was a peaceful place after all. He could smell the green grass of the pasture and sense the quietness of the still waters. What a fitting end, indeed ... if that were the end.

It was me, Granby, who penned this prose for posterity's sake. My passing was postponed. It was not the Lord's appointed time for me, not yet. He hadn't brought me to this point without a reason; he was not done with me. Acts 2:28 came to mind, "Thou hast made known to me the ways of life; thou shall make me full of joy with thy countenance." I guess he wanted me to share the wealth, the treasure of hard knocks and experience with which he had blessed me. Yes, God was smiling down on me that day. Like old Abraham with my faith secured, he didn't need a sacrifice from me. He provided me with a sacrificial ram of sorts when he resuscitated me. It not only brought me back to the living but, I think, the defibrillation straightened out my old crossed wires too. What had been sacrificed was that part of me that had been clinging to the past, to the things of this world.

Before I forget, I want to apologize for opening this postlude in the third person. I didn't mean to mislead you; well, maybe surprise you a bit. But there comes a time when nicknames just aren't appropriate anymore. They can trap you in the fourth dimension. I felt apart from Granby, that temporal identity. It was not quite what you'd call an out of body experience. I'm not sure how to say it but I, the soul of Baker Paulson, was no longer constrained by time. If you don't know how to express it in words, like the late Jim Croce, sometimes you have to say it with a song. The one that came to mind for me was, "I'm but a stranger here, heaven is my home." Oh, I'd still be Granby to Ike, Sally, TB, Sara and the rest but my head was on straight now; I'd never again forget my final destination, my real home while sojourning here. Like the disciples on the Mount of Transfiguration learned, I knew better than to try to make my permanent tabernacle here. "Let not then your good have evil spoken of it: for the kingdom of God is not meat and drink; but righteousness, and peace, and joy in the Holy Ghost" (Romans 14:16-17).

My dear NWP, our dead mall, was facing possible demolition but I was able to accept this with peaceful resignation. Perhaps it was partly because the memories would live on through Ike and in this book that God allowed me to share with you. But mostly, it was because God had taught me how to put my priorities in order. Oh, I wouldn't hesitate to try to live life to the fullest but I'd do so, God willing, according to God's plan. It always brings the deepest satisfaction in the end. I would also, hopefully, go about the business of creating new memories to add to our already abundant treasure store. But I would never again cling to those memories as an end in themselves, giving them undue prominence in life's search for meaning and purpose. I had learned that if we live for memories alone, we're just in a trance, stuck in time, as dead as Northwest Plaza, facing the same, inevitable end. That was not for me. As Ricky Nelson put it so well, if all I had were memories, I'd rather drive a truck.

I felt like King David when he penned Psalm 28:7: "The Lord is my strength and my shield: my heart trusted in him, and I am helped: therefore my heart greatly rejoices: and with my song will I praise him." Whatever time I had left would be filled with peace and purpose. There's a real tranquility that comes over you when you hand the reins over to God, really giving him full control; trusting in his love and promises to care for all your material needs. The biggest trick though is in looking beyond the temporal, to the spiritual; realizing that final victory is already assured in the cleansing blood of the perfect sacrificial lamb, Jesus Christ. Our hope in new life, life eternal was sealed forever by God in Christ's glorious resurrection. That's the proof of the pudding. This train was leaving the station, locked onto the right track. God had helped me put my priorities in order ... "But seek ye first the kingdom of God, and his righteousness; and all these things shall be added unto you" (Matthew 6:33). I had never been so thrilled about the prospects of life before. I couldn't wait to see what he had in store for me next. Lead on, Lord, lead on.

A Resurrection of Sorts ...

A couple of years have passed since I completed Tracts in Time. Sears did close. Then Senior Towne and the shoe repair shop folded up their tents. The doors to the mall entrances were pad locked in January 2011. A few stores remained open but only through exterior doors. There was no access from inside the shuttered mall. Now everything but the office tower is closed. The 24 hour fitness center ceased operating in September 2012 and a few days later the *last man standing*, the plus sized women's apparel store said goodbye. You can say sayonara to all two hundred plus stores and nearly fifty years of memories.

Yet there is good news for our old friend, Northwest Plaza. A white knight on a trusty steed has materialized in the form of Raven Development. They've purchased NWP and, according to reports in the local paper, plan to demolish most of the deteriorating, old structure and rebuild with some retail outlets and restaurants. As rumor has it, the office tower will be spared along with the buildings that once housed Macy's and Burlington Coat Factory. We shall see. Perhaps Baker, Sally and Ike will roam this hallowed ground yet again.

Steve Stranghoener

Other books by Steve Stranghoener ...

- The Last Prophet: Doomsday Diary
- Murder by Chance: Blood Moon Lunacy of Lew Carew
- Asunder: The Tale of the Renaissance Killer
- The Last Prophet: Imminent End

These books are available at www.amazon.com.